The Rooming House Gallery
Connecting the Dots

A companion book to
The Rooming House Diaries
Life, Love & Secrets

Bill Mathis

Published by Rogue Phoenix Press
Copyright © 2020

ISBN: 978-1-62420-503-3

Credits
Cover Design by Ms G
Editor: Sherry Derr-Wille

Dedication

To Rick Dexter

Chapter One

Josh Sawicki, Age 29
Andres Rodriguez, Age 28

4822 South Justine, Chicago, IL – Back of the Yards Neighborhood

Monday, June 8, 2009

The old house smelled. To Josh, it was a musty mix of dust and age, but the closer he and Andres moved toward the kitchen, the stronger the odor became of urine and Pine Sol overlain with coarse cigarette smoke.

Manny Rodriguez, Andres' old uncle, rested on top of a grungy, threadbare sheet in an ancient recliner, his feet up, his back almost straight. An oxygen tube ran across the floor from the large container of liquid oxygen and over the top of the recliner, its nosepiece rested close to Manny's left ear. Josh wondered why he wasn't wearing the oxygen mask. Was it turned on? Why was a recliner in the kitchen? He glanced around and noticed the chair's proximity to a bedroom and the bathroom. Guess it made sense.

Manny wore a stained tank-style undershirt with burn-holes and clean blue pajama bottoms. A dented plastic juice bottle, half-full, sat on a stool, tucked against the right side of the chair. A cordless phone rested in his lap, next to the twisted fingers of his left hand, his left shoulder bent at an odd and awkward angle, as if out of joint. The tobacco-stained fingers of his right hand held a hand-rolled cigarette upright, carefully balancing a tall pile of ash. Josh stared at the cigarette, then the oxygen nose piece. He took a half step closer.

Noticing Josh's concerned looks at the oxygen piece, Manny rasped in a Spanish accent, "Only use it at night. It's turned off when I smoke." He grimaced and looked from one to the other as he growled, "About time you two got here. Andres, I'm still pissed your dad waited two months to send you over." He broke into a hoarse, deep cough and hacked up a honker, leaned over and without spilling the ash, lifted the bottle with his right hand and spat into it.

"Hi, Uncle Manny," said Andres. "You don't look good."

"I'm dying. Soon, too. If I wasn't, I'd be looking better. I told your dad in April, I needed to see you two before I croaked." He started coughing again.

Josh looked around and filled a glass with water from the sink faucet and held it for him to sip.

He wheezed a thank you. "So, you two are still lovers, huh? Been together about ten years. Right?" He tried to smile.

"*Si, Tio*. You can't go wrong with a gay Polack."

"*Bueno, bueno*. You know I'm gay too." Both nodded as the old man wrinkled his forehead into a deep furrowed frown. "Did Art-the-fart tell you I have AIDS? He's such a *dupek*." He spat the words out, then coughed again. Josh snickered at the Polish word for asshole. Manny managed a weak wink at him. "I swear good in Polish, too."

Andres replied, "Dad tried to tell me that years ago, but I didn't believe him. You'd be dead by now if you had AIDS. I think it's these cigarettes killing you." He bent over and gave the old man a hug.

Uncle Manny put his head back. Just before his eyes closed, he lowered his right arm and dropped his cigarette into the juice bottle. It sizzled as the acrid smell of stale urine and ashes wafted up. Without opening his eyes, he muttered, "You two go look this place over, it's going to be yours, both of you. Don't take long. I want you to see the papers while I'm still around."

Josh froze, staring at Andres, both in shock. He started to speak. Andres put his fingers to his lip and motioned toward the door, which, they discovered, led to a back apartment, along with stairs to the outside door and the basement.

In the back apartment; a kitchen-living room with a cramped

bathroom and small bedroom, the double bed still covered in an old flowered quilt, Josh let out his breath. "What does he mean, this place is going to be ours?"

Andres shook his head, looking perplexed.

"Andres, Andres. What does he mean? Do you know something else?"

"No, Josh. I don't know anything else. Dad left me several voicemails yesterday morning. We connected last night. He said he didn't realize it was so urgent, just to get out here today, pronto." He paused.

"What else did he say?"

"Give me a minute, Josh. Just slow down and let me finish. He said *Tio* Manny had been wanting to see me and you together and for us to get our butts our here ASAP. He said Uncle Manny was dying. He didn't know when. He sure didn't say he should have told us two months ago." He paused. "He should be here, too. They're half-brothers. That's the way things are between them. And between him and me. You know how Dad is." His voice trailed off.

Josh shook his head again, touched the mole on his left cheek, a habit when he was concerned or trying to concentrate. "I understand how he might want you to have this place, but why me too?"

They spent less than thirty minutes exploring the outside and the upper floors. It was a weathered gray, three-story rooming house with nearly thirty rooms between the second and third floors, plus the two apartments on the first.

Somehow, a faint recollection of a rooming house drifted through Josh's mind. *Where did that come from? Why wouldn't Andres inherit it in just his name? It would be a great place for Andres to make art in. What would we do with the bedrooms? We don't even have kids. Besides, Uncle Manny probably was senile and the place wasn't truly theirs.*

After poking around, they ran down the two flights of stairs and into the living room. They slowed as they passed through the hallway between the living and dining room and heard Uncle Manny groaning and cursing from the kitchen, cursing in English, Spanish and Polish. He was attempting to stand up, but he was so weak he kept falling back into the recliner. "Help me, you two, I gotta piss." Andres slid his hands under his armpits and carefully pulled the frail man to his feet and waited for him to move toward the bathroom. "In the bottle," he rasped through the cigarette dangling from his mouth.

Josh grabbed the bottle, pulled the shrunken man's pajamas down and aimed the bottle roiling with urine, ash and cigarette butts at Manny's penis. "Ahh, *amigos*, you are just in time." Manny stumbled as a coughing fit engulfed him. Josh followed the flopping penis, trying to keep the trickle of dark yellow urine from hitting the floor, or either of them.

"*Bueno. Bueno.* Put me back now. I have much to tell you."

Josh ran the bottle to the bathroom, emptied it and rinsed it out. When he returned, he straightened out the sheet under the old man as much as possible, saw an afghan and covered him.

Exhausted, Uncle Manny leaned his head back and closed his eyes, his cigarette still fuming, ash floating down onto the afghan. Andres looked at Josh and shrugged.

"See that dresser? In the dining room. There's the papers I want to show you." Manny's voice was weak, barely audible. "There's lots to talk about, especially with Josh, there's secrets in those ledgers." His raised his right hand from the wrist and pointed his index finger toward the dining room.

Josh looked at him in surprise, but the old man's eyes were closed. He seemed too worn out to open them.

Or breathe.

Josh and Andres stared at him. Josh noticed Manny's breath become lighter, raspy and slow down. He glanced at Andres, ready to ask if he noticed the same thing. Before he could speak, the kitchen door opened. Two men entered. One was older, gray-haired, the other of slight build with jet black hair; both wore black short-sleeve shirts with clerical collars. They stepped close to Manny and all four men watched him suck in a large ragged breath, before slowly letting it out in irregular gasps. Each man leaned in closer, waiting for the next breath. There wasn't one. The cigarette dropped from Manny's lips onto the afghan. Josh pulled it away and tossed it into the sink where it sizzled out.

Andres pulled out his phone. "I'll call 911. Josh, start CPR."

The smaller of the two men placed his hand on Andres' arm.

"Manny's gone. He didn't want any resuscitation efforts made." He pulled the afghan up and covered the dead man's face, tucking the faded yarn gently around his body. "Father Frank will call the funeral home. All the arrangements are made." He stuck his hand out. "Hi, I'm Padre An, that's spelled with just an A and a N." He next shook Josh's hand, then placed his hand on Andres' shoulder, patting him. "We're surprised he made it this long. We think he's been hanging on, waiting for you two."

Andres put his arms around Manny's covered shoulders. "*Tio* Manny, *Tio* Manny. *Por que? Por que?* Why?"

Father An said, "That's a good question. I think we can help with some answers. At least the basic ones." He paused, then pointed to the other priest. "This is Father Frank, we're both from St. Bobola's Church, just west of here. We've known Manny for a few years, but got better acquainted the past few months as his health deteriorated. We've been checking on him several times a day. Two days ago, we managed to give him a shower. This morning, he only allowed us to give him a sponge bath and put on clean pajama bottoms. When we went to remove his t-shirt to put on his clean pajama top, he told us he had to save his energy for you two coming. Said he didn't want to die before. Looks like he timed it as close as possible. Surprisingly though, he allowed us to give him last rites this morning."

Father Frank shook Josh's and Andres' hands. "Manny managed to phone us while you were looking around, said to get over here, that he hoped he could hold on. He was either going to piss himself or die. He hoped to see you guys before either happened."

Andres wiped his eyes and grasped the priest's hand. "I'm Andres Rodriguez and this is my partner, Josh Sawicki. We don't know what to do, we had so many questions. This is such a surprise. Now he's gone." He scratched his head. "It took both of us to help him pee. Then he told us to go check the dining room buffet. Something about paperwork. Then…"

"Was…was he of sound mind? We haven't seen him in over five years and he just said this place belonged to both of us. I'm confused…" Josh quit talking. Did he just sound rude? Asking about the place being theirs before the guy was cold or in the grave? "I-I didn't mean to sound selfish. This is such a shock and I don't know what to think."

"He was of sound mind," Father Frank replied. "A physician examined him, along with a lawyer. He knew exactly what he was saying to you. Let's have Padre An take you two into the living room while I call the funeral home." Noticing their reluctance to leave, he added, "It's okay. There's nothing else that can be done for him. He's at peace. We will feel the pain of his passing for many years. Though, knowing him, I'm sure he would want you to get on with your lives, which is the reason we're all here."

Josh and Andres followed Padre An through the dining room, down the short hallway lined with aged photos of family members, and into the living room. He motioned for them to sit down on the old, overstuffed couch, the dust rising as they lowered themselves. "I am the one who helped get all the financial papers in order…"

"Is this for real?" Josh interrupted. "He told us this place was ours. Both of us. He said to look at the papers, something about secrets…Well, then you came in and he…"

Padre An smiled. "Yes, that's true. I'll try to quickly bring you up to date. I know you haven't seen Manny in years and this is a shock." He motioned for the two men to slide back on the couch. "About two years ago, Manny learned he suffered from advanced lung cancer, stage four. He refused invasive medical treatment. This spring, he asked me, I'm also a notary public with extensive experience in financial matters, to prepare his will, get a lawyer and finalize his desire to transfer the property to you two." Padre An paused when Josh started to interrupt. "Josh, let me finish, then I can answer your questions."

Josh nodded, still confused and surprised.

"At first, the house was going to just Andres, but when he realized how you two seem to have a solid, long-term relationship, he became so excited. He kept saying, 'I can keep it in both families. Both families.' He was as happy as I've ever seen him."

Josh couldn't contain his anxiety. He shifted forward on the couch, dust motes flying in the early evening light. "I don't understand. It's wonderful. I just don't get it! And what's he mean, both families? Is that what he wanted to tell me? Is that the secret?"

Padre An motioned toward Josh and Andres to remain seated. He

6

stood, walked into the dining room and returned with a ledger. He slid between the two of them on the couch and opened it to the middle pages, where everything was written in Polish. "Josh, do you recognize that name?"

"Um, it looks like it could be Sa-wic-ki. A Josef Sawicki?" His eyebrows started to rise.

Padre An turned more pages. He pointed to a name written in English. "And that name?"

"Hank Sawicki. Oh my God! Hank Sawicki was my great-grandfather's name, his wife's name was Mae. They owned a rooming house my Grandpa Joey was raised in. You mean this is the same place?" He looked at Padre An in amazement at the significance that his blood ran deep in this old place.

Padre An smiled. He waited for Josh to calm down and Andres to wipe his eyes. "Men, this is happening in real time. Now, when you're ready, follow me to the dining room. I want you to see the materials Manny was referring to."

At the oak arts and crafts style bureau in the dining room, near the hallway to the living room, they waited as Padre An slipped the ledger he carried onto a stack of three others and rearranged some papers across the top. He motioned for Andres to pick up the top paper. It was a Cook County receipt for property taxes paid, followed by receipts for the gas, electricity and water bills. He gently moved Josh's hand to pick up a bank savings book showing a balance of twelve thousand dollars.

The two men carefully surveyed each piece spread across the top of the buffet. Still not sure why the old man did this, still wondering if this was for real. Josh glanced at the stack of ledger books again, each numbered. He wondered why there would be secrets in them.

Padre An picked up two papers and showed them to the men. One was a title with their names alongside Manny's. It was clipped to a quit claim deed removing his name and signing over the rooming house to the two of them. In wonderment, Josh glanced at Andres who looked equally as shocked. He picked up the other paper, another bank statement with two cards clipped to it, awaiting their signatures. A drawer was partially open. Josh noticed scads of photographs and albums stuffed inside.

Andres pulled Josh into a hug. "Is this a freaking dream?"

Father Frank walked up to them. "The funeral home is on their way. Here's a copy of his funeral plans, already paid for. He's to be cremated. We will inter him Wednesday morning, unless you have major conflicts with the date." He looked at Andres who shook his head as if the suddenness of a funeral was too much. "Manny never liked waiting around or wasting time. He said the quicker we get this over, the quicker you two can move on with your lives." He shook their hands. "I need to leave for the hospital to visit an elderly parishioner. Padre will stay with you and help with any details needed today." He smiled. "My sincere condolences. Manny was the type of guy I wished I knew all my life. Oh, by the way, Manny insisted we leave you some refreshments. It's homebrew beer. The bottles look old, but the last brew was made several months ago, still safe, and good. I hope eight are enough. Doesn't matter, that's the last of them. Just be careful, they can knock you on your butt if you're not used to them." He stepped toward the front door, then turned back. "Men, why don't you ride with us to Oakwood on Wednesday? It's simpler than you trying to find us there. We'll pick you up here at the house, around nine-twenty." He walked briskly away.

"Good idea," Padre An said. Looking at the two men, he asked, "Would you like to spend a few moments alone with Manny? The funeral folks will be here momentarily."

Andres looked at Josh. "Briefly for me. I haven't seen many dead people. I think I'd like to remember him from when he was healthy, not the way he looked today."

They followed Padre An into the kitchen where he started to remove the afghan.

"Wait." Andres said, "I don't need to see him uncovered. Leave him covered." He pulled a kitchen chair closer to the covered body and sat. He pulled a pencil and small pad from his bib overalls pocket and began sketching.

~ * ~

Andres forced his mind to focus on sketching; something that

8

normally came easy for him. He'd developed the discipline to tune out the world around him when he sketched. This was harder, though. He had few relatives and had never seen one dead. While his visits with Uncle Manny were scarce, they did have a bond. Both gay, both not accepted by Art Junior, Andres' father; Manny's half-brother. Both barely knew Art Senior who treated Manny horribly and was a vague, demanding presence to Andres as he was growing up.

He sensed Josh's hand on his shoulder and felt the warmth, the support. His sketched lines quickly suggested the shape of an old man: head slouched to one side, sitting in a recliner. He added some texture to show the afghan. He left the face blank. *I'll fill that in later,* he thought. *Right now, I just want to capture the essence and sadness of death. Later, I'll decide where to take this.* His hand flew as the lines expanded to include a sense of the kitchen, the cabinets, old refrigerator… old, old, old. Death, death, death. His eye caught tulips. Wooden, once bright, hand-made, red, blue green and white: tulips marching over the cabinets.

He glanced up at Josh. "Look, Josh, look. The tulips; I noticed some plants by the front porch." He put the sketch book and pencil back into his pocket.

What a loss, he thought, glancing at the covered form of Uncle Manny. *I barely knew him. I could kill Dad. Two damn months, we could have been getting to know each other, now we're burying him Wednesday and all I know is he left us an old rooming house. As excited as I am, I think I'd rather have had time with Manny while he was alive than inherit his house.* Andres stood up as the people from the funeral home entered the room, trundling a gurney with a white sheet.

~ * ~

Josh stood with his hand on Andres' shoulder and watched the fingers fly. As usual, he was amazed at the emotion and sense of reality Andres produced in the few lines, curves and shaded areas. He squeezed Andres. His partner could tune out the world in almost any situation. Yet when one saw his art, you grasped all the thought, emotion and imagination that flowed through the man. Over time, he realized viewing Andres' art made the lack of connection with him when he was making it, bearable. Usually.

Josh and Andres stepped back. They watched as two men in coveralls and a tall, business-looking woman with short gray hair, dressed in dark slacks and a blue jacket bearing the name of the funeral home, gently handle Uncle Manny's body.

"Do you wish to view the cremation?" the woman asked. Josh and Andres shook their heads. "That's fine. He already provided us with a pottery urn with sunflowers on it made by a Mexican artist friend of his. It's beautiful. I will be present at Oakwood Cemetery for the interment of the urn in one of the Sawicki plots. I understand those arrangements were made nearly fifty years ago." She looked puzzled. "Our funeral home goes back to the late 1800's and I discovered we have buried many Sawickis." She looked like she wanted to ask why they were burying the ashes of an old Mexican alongside them, but she didn't.

Josh shivered at the thought his relatives helped make arrangements for Manny's place of rest all those many years ago. Just how deep did their connections go in this place? Unconsciously, he slipped his hand into Andres' and squeezed. Andres squeezed back, then put his arm around Josh, hugged him and gave him a quick kiss on the cheek. Josh tried not to snicker at the fleeting expression of shock on the woman's face or the surprised looks of the assistants. He purposely snuggled closer into Andres' embrace. *Deal with it,* he thought. *It's 2009 and you act surprised at a Mexican being buried in old Polacks graves and young men in love with each other.* He winked at the woman and watched her face turn pink. It was his turn to look surprised when she winked back and gave him a thumbs up from behind her back as she turned to follow the gurney.

Chapter Two

The Funeral Service

Josh and Andres rode with Father Frank and Padre An in a faded blue Volvo sedan stick shift that looked over twenty years old, with the windows rolled down on a bright warm Chicago Southside day. "Sorry, the air conditioner is shot," Father Frank said as they took off with a lurch. "Volvos last forever, but my ability to pay for non-essentials doesn't."

At the entrance to Oakwood Cemetery, they pulled in behind the black funeral home van and followed it through the vast complex of meandering drives. At last, they came to a stop near several gigantic, weathered oak trees. A small mound of fresh dirt waited next to a low double headstone that read, Henrik (Hank) Josef Sawicki, Sept. 10, 1885 – Jan. 17, 1967 & Mae Abigail (Wojcik) Sawicki, Jan. 3, 1900 – April 1, 1980.

"This is amazing," said Andres. "My uncle is being buried with your great-grandparents. Did you ever think we were connected like this?" He carried a bouquet of tulips.

Josh shook his head, surprised himself at the sudden news in their lives.

"I'm Meg Nowak." The same woman from the funeral home who winked at him stuck her hand out. "I'm so sorry for your loss. I did some research, Josh, and your great-great-grandparents are buried right over there. Close by are several other Sawicki relatives. I'll walk you around when we're finished." She reached to shake Andres' hand. "I also googled your uncle. There's not much about him. He lived at that address since 1958, then apparently inherited the rooming house in 1980. Do you know what he did with it since then?"

Andres shook her hand. "We have no idea. I never visited him at his home, didn't even know it was a rooming house. The relationship between him and my father has been distant at best. As you can tell, Dad isn't even here. Neither is my mom, she doesn't drive." Andres turned away and blew his nose.

"Well, it looks like there was other family who loved him, maybe not blood folk, that's the way it is for some of us." She put her arms around Josh and Andres, gently steered them toward the gravesite where a bright yellow urn sat next to the dirt pile and the two priests waited.

"This will be very informal and unofficial," said Father Frank. "Still, we want it to be meaningful. Sometimes we Catholics go overboard on the ritual and circus of religion, especially at funerals." He smiled and glanced down at the urn. "Manny allowed us to give him last rites on Monday. I think he did it to please us, not because he was worried about his future. He didn't even know if he was baptized a Catholic or not, yet figured being Mexican and from Tijuana, he probably was. So, this won't be an official Catholic funeral. Please don't report us to Archbishop Francis George. Padre An and I are already known as ecclesiastical renegades at times."

"Let's hold hands, if you're comfortable with that." Padre An motioned for Meg to join them. "If you know the 23rd Psalm, please repeat it with me. If not, listen closely. It was written during a time of stress, loss and grief and has brought comfort to many in sorrow for several millennia."

Josh recognized the words, just not enough to repeat any. He felt his shoulders relax and his breathing slow as he listened to the calming words of peace and hope. Andres squeezed his hand. Josh realized Andres was quietly repeating the verses with ease. *This man never ceases to amaze me,* he thought.

Meg's voice was soft, but solid and confident. She also firmly squeezed his hand.

There was silence when Padre An finished reciting the passage. He waited, then wrestled an early model CD player out of his suit coat pocket. "We met Manny two years ago when we needed some minor repairs made around the rectory and a parishioner mentioned his name as someone who might be able to help. Said he'd been around a long time and had a reputation for good work. We went to visit him and asked if he could help us out. He invited us in, served us some pozole, all the time coughing, hacking and swearing in several languages." He paused as everyone chuckled. "He told us we should pray harder for the repairs. He wasn't sure he could do them as he'd just been diagnosed with stage four lung cancer and might not have the breath to do the work."

Father Frank picked up the story. "Anyway, he ended up coming over the next week, we drove him, and he made the repairs. Slowly. Afterward, he invited us over, said he had some refreshments for us. Say, Josh and Andres, did you sample the refreshments I mentioned?"

"No. We didn't. Maybe when we get back. We both had to work yesterday. We're planning to look through the place this afternoon," Andres replied.

"Well," Father Frank continued, "apparently, the recipe has been around since the original owner of the rooming house. Hopefully, you'll find it and invite us over for more once you get settled."

"I think we need to get back to the service," Padre An joked. Holding up the CD player, he said, "So, when we were planning today, I asked Manny what music he wanted played at his service. 'No hymns. No choirs. No organ.' He pulled this out and threw it at me. 'Play some of this,' he said. 'It's Latin Jazz and as close to heaven as anyone will ever get. Bet you don't know these guys, they're *The Buena Vista Social Club* and are playing at Carnegie Hall." He squeezed a button and the bouncy Cuban Jazz blasted forth.

Josh and Andres couldn't help wiggling to the beat. Father Frank started snapping his fingers, it was evident he had no sense of rhythm. Padre An was the least inhibited. He held the player high as he jived and stomped in circles. Meg stood in place and moved well to the music. When the song ended, she said, "Padre, I've been to a lot of unusual funerals with you, but I think this one takes the cake."

Padre An stuffed the player back into his pocket. He took out his handkerchief and wiped his face. "You know, I'm half Vietnamese as well as half Mexican and the first time I heard that music from Manny, I knew I truly had Mexican/Latino blood running through me. Now, who wants to say something about Manny."

There was silence. Finally, Andres said, "My first remembrances of Uncle Manny are vague. We only saw him at holiday get-togethers when my grandmother Maria and Mom insisted that he be invited. The first time I brought Josh home was the time I remember the most. That was about ten years ago. We were just getting used to occasionally drinking beer and Uncle Manny started giving us mixed drinks with vodka. We got pretty sloshed, so did Manny. In fact, Grandma Maria drove him home and Mom made us spend the night. However, the thing I remember most from that time was him telling me the world always needs art and creativity. He said we need engineers and doctors, dentists and lawyers, assembly lines and technology, but none of that counts if we can't enjoy beauty and words and imagination." Andres paused, cleared his throat. "He also said 'I meant art, not people like Art.' Art is my dad and grandfather's name, both dentists. They weren't nice to him."

Everyone moved closer into a group hug. Padre An said a simple prayer. The entire service lasted nineteen minutes.

As they broke away, Josh asked, "Can we throw the dirt on top of the urn? I think that's a Jewish thing. Somehow, I would like to do that."

Meg placed the urn in the plastic vault. She motioned for Josh and Andres to help her put it into the hole. Andres placed all but three tulips on top, then they each began dropping handfuls of dirt on top. Andres dropped to his knees and began pushing large handfuls of dirt into the hole. Josh did the same till the hole was level. They tamped it down with their shoes, added more, and Andres noticed the waiting sod square. He ran over, picked it up and gently covered the fresh dirt with it, patting down the edges like he was tucking a blanket around a baby. He rested the remaining three tulips on top.

Meg and the two priests watched with tears in their eyes.

On their way toward the car, Padre An took a phone call. After disconnecting, he looked at Meg. "Could you get these two men home? Jorge's mother-in-law from the grocery store collapsed and I want to go straight to the hospital to be with them."

"Of course. It's not out of the way at all."

Andres jumped in the front passenger seat of the van and Josh

14

climbed into the bench seat, sitting in the middle. "It sounds like you've worked with Padre An and Father Frank before," said Andres.

"Yes. We're part of the community and have been for years, the same as the church. We've all seen a lot of changes over the years and I think we've been a part of maintaining some stability in the midst of those changes." She checked her side mirrors, then glanced in the rearview at Josh. "Josh, I gave you a funny look yesterday in the house when Andres kissed you on the cheek."

Josh nodded.

She smiled. "I apologize. I was surprised to realize you two were gay. Mostly though, I was surprised to realize Manny owned the place and had such a strong connection to the Sawickis. My parents knew some of them and spoke highly of them, I don't know which ones. After my parents died, I lost track of the name, and with all the changes in the community, I forgot about the old rooming house or what became of it." She sighed. "You'd think being in a mixed-race marriage I wouldn't be surprised when I encounter a mixed relationship or find a Mexican ended up with an old Polish couple's rooming house."

Josh smiled into the mirror at her, glad she was so honest. "What does your husband do? How many children to you have?"

"Now it's my turn to surprise you," she replied. "Roxie and I are lesbians. We got married in 2005 in Toronto, shortly after they legalized it there. Roxie's a Chicago policewoman, we have four children now, aged twenty to twenty-four. We each had two. To blow your minds even more, their father's sperm came from a mixed-race gay couple who are good friends and have stayed very active in their lives. We live in Beverly and they're close by, kinda like our own little village."

Andres shook his head as Josh muttered, "Wow." They were quiet for a few minutes. *Kids,* Josh thought. *Why do I suddenly seem interested in them? Is it because we might have space for them? Is it something like a biological time clock? Cripes, I'm only twenty-nine, I've got plenty of time. Besides, I have no idea how interested Andres is in the subject. We've never discussed it, at least not seriously.*

Meg glanced at Andres as she waited at a stop light. "How long you two been together?"

"Ten years, but who's counting." Andres snickered.

"Well, I never thought I wanted children, then after several years with Roxie, we decided to pursue the idea. I'm so glad we did. They're a lot of work, especially four in four years, but once we got them all in school, things settled down. Of course, having four teenagers at the same time wasn't always smooth either. We're so proud of them now."

She turned the van from Garfield onto South Laflin and began pointing out different two flats and homes. "You can tell there've been some efforts in improving the housing stock around here," she said. "There's a growing need for solid, decent apartments and homes. I'm not talking about gentrifying. More and more young people are looking for something they can move into that's fixed up. Not luxury, just livable and respectable."

She turned onto 48th and then south onto Justine and stopped at the curb in front of the rooming house. "It would take some work and investment, but I bet those upper two stories could easily be renovated into two apartments on each floor. That could be enough income to more than pay off your investment in a few years and more than pay your mortgage and taxes. Plus, you'd be doing something needed in the community."

Andres smiled at Josh. "Thank you, Meg. To be honest, this all happened so fast, we're not sure which way to think. We haven't even given the place a detailed look-over."

"You two do have a lot on your minds. I hope you keep the place and move in. We need more young stable families around here."

Josh noted Andres tense at the word families. Meg must not have noticed. "Guys, I'm not pushing you into anything. Please excuse me, I grew up near here, much of our business is from the greater area and I so much want to see the neighborhood stabilize more and families are what will help that. By the way, if you're interested in considering children as a gay couple, Roxie and I would be happy to explore those options with you. We network in the LGBTQ community and have a lot of contacts. Everything from real estate, to good schools, to foster care, to adoption and surrogacy. Of course, if you die, I can even bury you." She laughed and waved as they closed the doors.

"What the hell!" Andres fumed as the van pulled away. "I thought

I liked her, but my God, talk about having a captive audience. Jesus. We just buried my uncle, have barely looked at the house, haven't made a decision whether we even want the place, and she's lining us up with surrogate women to carry our babies." He stomped his foot, and hit one fist into his other hand. "What the hell made her think we want kids? I sure as hell don't."

He fumbled with the keys at the front door, dropped them, then kicked them toward Josh. He picked them up and calmly unlocked the front door of their new, one hundred and twenty-two-year old, three-story rooming house that still smelled of Pine Sol and urine.

Josh didn't know how to respond. He was excited over the prospect of their own home and was quite certain Andres was as well. Why Meg set them off on the idea of a family and becoming landlords, he wasn't sure. He figured she meant well and was certainly invested in the area, which was good. What truly surprised him was Andres' reaction to having a family. Why the sudden intensity? What was bugging him? He loved kids, good grief, he worked with them, taught art part-time at Benito Juarez High School, ran an afterschool art club, plus gave individual lessons. He turned and held out his arms. "Umm, Andres. How about a hug? Then let's try a refreshment from the fridge, order a pizza and slowly walk through this place. Okay?"

Andres slipped into the hug. "I'm sorry. That woman really set me off, that doesn't happen often. I agree. Hey, I've never had a homebrewed beer. Have you?"

Josh led Andres to the kitchen, opened the turquoise Frigidaire refrigerator and pulled two brown bottles out. Ancient amber bottles with old fashioned wire swing caps and seals. "Guess we don't need an opener for these. Aren't these cool?" He released the wire and pulled the top aside, sniffed it and made a face. "Wow, this smells potent!" He took a sip as Andres opened his and took a sip.

"Oh, my God. This is different. I could get used to this."

He took a big glug and sat down on a kitchen chair. "This stuff is strong. I can already feel it. Quick, order a pizza, I need something to help absorb this stuff. This sure ain't Budweiser or Corona."

While Andres exclaimed over the beer and appeared to be back to his normal self, Josh ordered a pizza, almost giving their Pilsen address. He pulled out his ever-present notebook and began making notes about the steps needed to ascertain how much it would cost to rehab the building. He noted contacts he knew from his job as Office Manager at Guiseman Whitley & Chan, a medium-sized law firm in the Loop that focused on international business and construction. "Title, deed, liens, mortgage, back taxes, utilities," he wrote.

Andres slugged the rest of his bottle and dashed outside where he ran around the yard, counting the windows, forming his hands into a square to frame the flowers growing wild and unattended as if taking a picture to paint later.

Josh followed and paced off the exterior dimensions. The building was approximately twenty feet wide by eighty feet long. His eye for detail took in the patched roof, paint-bare wood siding, rusted-out gutters, single pane windows. The garage next to the alley looked like cement block walls had been added to steady it.

The pizza arrived and they gulped it down at the kitchen table, along with another beer. Andres took off, yelling for Josh to hurry. Josh was surprised to see how sturdy the rooming house was, how few leaks or little rain damage they found, how tightly constructed it appeared; no broken windows, the lack of mice or bird droppings. He was beginning to feel buzzed. He thought Andres was as well. God, this stuff was potent.

The first floor held the narrow, yet large-feeling four-bedroom apartment where Uncle Manny lived. A thought niggled at Josh about this being an ideal, permanent home for him and Andres. Behind the apartment was the small one-bedroom unit.

The second floor held fifteen bedrooms and two closet-sized spaces, one with two showers and a sink, the other with a toilet, urinal and tiny sink.

The third floor held thirteen rooms. Each contained its own sink. A closet, similar to the second floor, held showers and another held two toilet stalls, both were tucked along the north wall. At the back was also an efficiency apartment the size of two rooms combined. It contained a narrow range, ancient refrigerator and cold-water sink. It shared the bathrooms as well. It was obvious to Josh no one had lived in the rooms for years. He wondered how many.

His excitement grew by the second, especially about a lasting home for them. He forced himself to stay calm while Andres skipped around, chattering about skylights and large windows and a gallery on the second floor with studio spaces on the third.

As Andres swung around in a circle, excitedly pointing out the walls he wanted to tear out, Josh recorded, "Determine load-bearing walls."

He thought again, can this be real? This was exciting, but what was stirring inside him? The idea of their own place to call home? For Andres to make art?

He wondered a bit about asking Denny James to look at the place. An architect specializing in historical rehab projects who the law firm frequently consulted, Denny was obnoxious. He was also one of the best historical preservationists in Chicago. Josh knew they could get a straight answer from him about whether this place was worth fixing up or not.

~ * ~

What a place, thought Andres. Both floors have north and south side light exposure. I could have my own gallery and studio. Hell, I could have a gallery for some of my emerging artist friends. Maybe a co-op where we could share the expenses and make more money than paying galleries half the sale price. What would folks think of coming to Back-of-the-Yards to see an art gallery? Location, location, location, but still, this place is easy to find and, with quality art, people will go to marginal areas in the city. Look at what's happening in Detroit. It's always the artists that help bring a community back.

"Josh, I want to tear out these walls and put some skylights in from the roof. Can't you see some of my art here?" He giggled, realizing he was feeling the home brew.

"Let's make sure the foundation is good and the walls are solid before you start, okay? I'm making notes."

"You're always making notes and being so dammed practical."

Andres pulled Josh into a sloppy hug and kiss. "I'm feeling the beer, let's go down and finish the pizza."

"We already did."

Andres sat down, pulled out his pad and pencil and began sketching ideas for a long narrow gallery. Eventually, he put his pencil down and stared down the narrow hallway. Who lived here? What were they like? Why would men move into a rooming house?

He heard Josh going down the stairs, slowly, as if he was checking for each step. He stretched out on the dusty floor. Uncle Manny, Uncle Manny, there's so much I want to learn about you. Mostly, why me? Why us?

Can we really fix this place up? Josh will love the idea of a house, a home. So will I, I guess. That seems so permanent, so tied down, so traditional, almost like a family. I love being a couple. We're a good couple, most of the time. But a family? Why did that pop up? Damn that Meg, why did she bring that up? A family of our own. What a crazy idea. Why would I be interested in a family? I do like kids, just not twenty-four seven. Not diapers and food and homework and teenagers. Nope, that's not for me. How would I know where to start? We got a good thing going, why ruin it? Maybe Josh can have his need for a home and I can have a studio and gallery.

He pushed himself back to sitting, shook his head, and slowly stood, brushing off dust wherever he could reach. I'm thirsty. I need another homebrew.

Chapter Three

On the Couch

Downstairs, at the dining room table, Josh had two homebrews opened. The four ledgers rested in front of him. He slid a beer over as Andres slipped into a chair. Both were quiet as Josh turned the pages of the first ledger, through what seemed like a hodgepodge of notes, lists, financial records and receipts, with old photos and envelopes stuffed amongst the leaves.

He flipped more pages. "I can't believe this. Josef's story must be older than the house is. I can't wait to start reading this." He quickly glanced through the other ledgers. "Hey, look. Andres, here's a diary written by Uncle Manny." He shoved the ledger to Andres.

"Wonder what I'll learn about him." Andres flicked through the pages. "Looks like I'll learn a lot. Sure as heck more than I know now." He pulled out some photo albums and glanced through them. Sliding one over to Josh, he said, "Who the heck are these people? They look like holocaust victims, but the pictures were taken inside here."

Josh looked through it. "I have no idea. Obviously, they lived here. Now, put all these back, we can look at them later."

Andres stuffed the albums back in the drawer and drained his beer. He grabbed Josh's and finished it off, too. "You're driving. You've hit your limit anyway. We'll save the last two for when we come back."

"Not yet, Andres. I'm not driving that monstrosity of a van even slightly buzzed. I'm stretching out on the couch. You go rest on that recliner. It looks better than the one in the kitchen." He shuddered.

Would they keep that one? The one Uncle Manny died in? Was he superstitious? Was Andres? He decided not to think about it. At the moment, he needed to doze off some alcohol.

Stretched out on the couch, Josh—Joseph Joshua Sawicki III— shook his head in wonderment at the events of the past three days while Andres sat unusually still and quiet in the old recliner. *I'll wait till traffic dies down,* he thought. *I hate driving that big old thing; the same model of Ford that Andres has always loved as his work van.*

The two lived in a small, third floor walkup on 22nd Street in Pilsen; a one bedroom, cramped, five hundred square foot apartment with a metal ladder attached to their bedroom window as a fire escape. A place that was conveniently located for their jobs with great northern light for Andres to paint. Now, after seeing the space this old rooming house possessed, their apartment suddenly seemed even more claustrophobic. How had they managed living with all of Andres' art and supplies in such a small dump? At least this dump seemed spacious.

He yawned. *This is the same house my Grandpa Joey was born and raised in. And now I hope to live in it too.* He knew Grandpa was raised in a rooming house, but never asked or retained where it was located and his grandpa didn't speak about the house much, just his brothers, sisters and mostly about his wonderful parents. He couldn't wait to see him and Grandma Lisa when they returned from a cruise to Alaska in about two weeks. He figured they must have known Manny and they would be upset over his death. Plus, they would have been supportive through the experience. Still, he wondered why a connection had never been made between Uncle Manny and himself.

Josh's dad, Joseph Joshua Sawicki, Jr, known as JJ, never spoke about his father's upbringing and infrequently about his own life growing up in Oak Lawn, one of the close Southwest Chicago suburbs. After Josh quit playing Little League at age thirteen, his dad seldom talked much to him and even less after he said he wanted to join the swim team in high school. He didn't join. His parents said they didn't have the time to transport him to practice and all the meets, though Josh knew they would have made the time if it was baseball or football. Normal communication with Dad became almost nonexistent after Josh came out at sixteen and later, when he said he wanted to be a paralegal or an office manager, his dad sneered. "And why not a lawyer? At least you'd make some money as a pansy lawyer."

Right after high school graduation, Josh moved in with Grandpa Joey and Grandma Lisa. By then, he was already working part-time for the same law firm he was now. Grandma Lisa, an interpreter of European and East European languages who occasionally did work for the firm, told the office manager Josh would be a good office helper. Hence his interest in office and paralegal careers and his never-ending thankfulness to Grandma Lisa. Working part-time for the firm, Josh earned his associate's degree in business administration from Moraine Valley Community College. The law firm paid for his associates in paralegal studies at Wilbur Wright City College and hired him full time. They also paid half of his tuition to complete his Bachelors of Business Administration through the UIC, University of Illinois at Chicago, online completion program.

He noticed Andres was still silent, but awake. Maybe he was more buzzed than he thought. He was amazed the man hadn't started talking. "I'm sorry, I've been lost in thought. Can you believe the place is ours?" He paused. "I am so sorry about Uncle Manny. I didn't mean to be rude. It's, it's just so amazing that he would think of us in this way. Plus, it will feel wonderful to get out of the apartment and into something permanent."

Andres yawned. "I agree. I think. It's a lot to consider. Hey, I thought you were resting up to drive. I'm going to doze a bit."

"In other words, I should quit talking."

Andres grunted a short laugh.

Josh twisted onto his side on the sofa. He pondered again why Uncle Manny never mentioned he inherited the rooming house from Josh's great-grandparents. *Did he know my last name? I'm not sure he did. Maybe that first time, I did say my last name when introduced and, though drunk, he must have remembered I was a Sawicki and kept it to himself all these years. Nor did he ever mention anything about the rooming house. In fact, Andres never mentioned his uncle owning a rooming house that I can recall. We only saw him four or five times since Andres and I met, and those times were short and usually filled with tension between Manny and Art Junior. Uncle Manny never said much about his life, always asked us questions about our lives, school, Andres' art, my job. I vaguely recall him mentioning rehab or remodel jobs he was doing. He seemed so proud of the work he did. The last time we saw him has to be over five years ago, maybe even six, not too long after our college graduations.*

Once, he did mention how he hated driving out to the suburbs to visit Art Junior and Bella, Andres' mom. I remember he yelled at Art Junior for not being willing to come into the city to visit him. "Why should we come to that gang-infested place that's ready to collapse?" Art Junior sneered in reply.

Andres and his dad. Me and my dad. Our dads. That was a major area we had in common when we first met. Josh pulled an old fringe blanket over him and snuggled further into the couch as he heard Andres wriggle deeper into the recliner. *I'll never forget that first Thanksgiving at Andres' parents' house. Even more clearly, I'll never forget meeting Andres.*

~ * ~

Josh and Andres Meet

In the fall of 1999, Josh was nineteen and a sophomore at Moraine Valley. Andres was eighteen, a freshman at UIC, and already a recognized young artist. Just after graduating from high school, Andres was accepted to display and sell his work at the popular, and highly coveted by artists, 57th Street Art Fair in Hyde Park. That's where he met Aimee Yoon, a paralegal and interpreter of Japanese for the law firm Josh worked at part-time. She bought one of Andres' small pieces, gave him her business card and told him she thought some of her work cohorts might enjoy his fine art, too. He forgot to give her his card, artists aren't always the best business persons, which Josh knew he could now joke about with Andres, most of the time.

Late that September, Andres was broke, behind on his tuition, and needed to sell some work. He discovered Aimee's card in a pile of schoolwork and art supply bills and notes for classes and sketch ideas. It had her work address, 55 E. Monroe, 18th floor. He showed up late on a Friday afternoon. The firm's employees were in the conference room, celebrating the retirement of one of their longtime office-staff members. The reception counter was unattended.

The party was ending when Josh heard someone scream, "Who are you and what are you doing in here?"

Everyone rushed out to see a man, a good-looking man, Josh instantly noted, sitting on the floor in front of the reception counter, sketching. A dirty bike messenger bag was beside him. He smiled up at the employees crowding in around him.

"Well," he said. "No one was around, so I decided to wait till someone showed up. I just started doing what I always do when I have to wait. I sketch. Sorry, I kind of borrowed this picture from the counter. I hope I wasn't too intrusive."

"That's my family," the receptionist said in amazement as everyone noticed her family photograph now sitting on the floor in front of the young man. "You are good, but how the heck did you get in here? And what do you want?"

The man stood up, still smiling, as if totally unthreatened by the fact he didn't belong there. "A gentleman was coming out, so I showed him this card," he held out the bent-up card of Aimee Yoon, "he looked at my bag and didn't say anything. He even held the door for me."

"She's not even here. Why would she need something messengered? Wait. Anything messengered goes through me. What gives here?"

The man nodded, his smile weakening. "See, Aimee Yoon bought a piece of my art last summer. Said she thought others in her office might like to see my stuff and maybe buy some. I'm behind on my tuition at UIC and thought I would stop by to see if she could arrange a showing of some of my work. I'm paying my own way and not taking out loans. I wasn't trying to sneak in. The man didn't ask who I was."

"That man was Mr. Whitley, the senior partner, and he had no idea you were anything other than a messenger." The receptionist looked like she didn't know whether to call the police or laugh.

Rachel, the senior paralegal, in her usual take-charge voice, asked, "What type of art do you do? I don't know about the rest of you, but it's past quitting time, the partners have all left, this guy didn't sneak through the staff cloakroom, stealing things, or he wouldn't still be here. I would like to see his art."

"I'm Andres Rodriguez and here is a list of my awards and several sketches. If you actually want to see more of my work, I brought a notebook, too." He pulled several papers from his bag and passed them around.

"You were in the 57th Street Fair! The piece Aimee has hanging in her area is yours? She said she bought it there. C'mere, everyone." Rachel led the group down the hall and peered closely at the abstract hanging on the cubicle wall.

Josh followed the crowd. Back then, he was a lowly part-timer who was well respected and loved, not in charge of anything, though some kept saying he would be someday. He was intrigued by this Andres guy. He was so unique. Dressed in white painter-style bib overalls dotted with splotches of paint, colored pencils and brushes were stuck in the upper pockets. He wore a tight white t-shirt that further emphasized his brown skin and nice build. Gray slip-on tennies, also streaked with paint, were on his feet. More than his clothes—who shows up at a legal firm dressed in their work clothes to sell art—was the way he carried himself, the confidence, the ease he displayed. He had to recognize this was a classy law firm; the address, the views over Lake Michigan and the construction of Millennium Park, the furnishings, even the art on the walls. Josh was sure the guy wasn't any older than him.

"That's my work," Andres said calmly as they crowded into the cubicle, taking turns to examine it and read his signature. As the rest moved out of the cubicle, Josh slipped in. He realized he hadn't been in Aimee's cubicle before, so he had never seen the artwork. She had several pieces hanging; all small ones suitable for livening up a small dull space. Andres' work grabbed his attention. Against a white background, black lines angled and crossed, leaving various almost geometric shapes complimented by several curved or circular shapes. Bright colors filled several of the spaces, yet the sparseness and color contrasted in such a manner to command notice.

One of the office girls stuck her head back in. "He's amazing. This piece is like some of Stuart Davis'." Noting Josh's baffled look, she added,

"That's a compliment. Davis is long dead, but very collectible. I know. I studied art over at the Institute until I had to get a job that actually paid my bills. This kid's going to make it."

Josh shook his head. "It's hard to know what to say when you see something like that. I wasn't expecting to be gob-smacked. I love it."

The girl laughed and swatted his shoulder. "You learn that word at college? It's Australian, I think. Anyway, it fits. That's the way I feel, too."

Everyone gathered back by the reception area. Rachel asked for Andre's notebook. There was silence as she flipped through the pages, the others crowded around, looking over her shoulder or passing it around. Finally, someone muttered, "I think the partners and junior partners need to see these." No one asked the prices, after all, most of them were the lowest paid employees in the firm; not poor, legal staff positions are usually well paid, but Andres' art appeared above their means.

Andres must have sensed that. "I do other work too. Like sketches of families from photos, things that don't cost as much, yet still help me pay the bills." He waited, then started handing out his cards he remembered to bring. "I also paint houses, interior walls and ceilings, and I'm very good at painting children's bedroom walls in whatever they want: cartoons, Star Wars, princesses, imaginary characters. Last month, I did a private dining room at one of the Greek restaurants on Halsted to look like a Greek scene with columns. I wouldn't put it in my portfolio as my best art, but the owner loved it and the fee covered my van insurance and books."

Josh appreciated his humbleness. He was another kid working his way through college without parental help or loans like himself, unlike most of the kids Josh grew up with.

Several of the employees told Andres they would be calling him over the weekend and they sounded like they meant it. As everyone left for home, Josh and Andres ended up riding the elevator down together, along with Rachel, who muttered, "Maybe you two should become friends, you're both broke college kids." She winked at Josh. He blushed. It was common knowledge and accepted that Josh was gay, but he had never been on a date.

Rachel waved good bye and turned away from the guys. Walking across the marble floors, Andres said, "Well, I better be going."

"Me, too," Josh replied.

Both stopped and looked at each other. "Where to?" each asked simultaneously.

They laughed.

"I have to catch a train to Oak Lawn," Josh said. "How about you? Are you in the dorms?"

Andres shook his head and looked away. "Hey, I'm hungry for a gyro. Care to join me?"

Josh checked his watch. "I could take a later train. Where?"

"I know a great little place that's cheap. It's near Washington and Halsted, in Greek town."

"That's way to hell and back for me. Well, I guess I could bus out and back to the station." Josh was reluctant to leave this guy, but going across the Loop was not convenient and seemed a little impolite to ask of someone they just met. Still, as he would learn over the coming years, Andres had a plan. Not an ordinary plan. Andres was anything but ordinary.

"I have an idea. I know I'm a little *loco*. How about I ride you on my bike to the gyros place? Then we pick up my van near there and I'll drive you home to Oak Lawn."

Josh couldn't help but burst out laughing. He shocked himself when he heard himself say, "Umm, sure. So, *loco* one, I'll help with gas money. Where's your bike?"

It was a sturdy, clumsy bike with a back rack and saddle bags and flashing lights for safety. They giggled like kids the whole way across the Loop. Well, Josh recalled, they were only eighteen and nineteen, they *were* kids.

The gyros they rapidly consumed were excellent as they told each other about their lives. Without going into too much detail, Josh suspected they both had father issues and guessed it was because they were gay. Andres was vague as to his living quarters. "I'll show you after we get to my van," he replied to Josh's query.

Josh called Grandpa Joey and told him he had met a friend who was bringing him home. Grandpa started to ask some questions but then stopped himself and said that was nice and don't be too late. He sounded happy.

Both guys were quiet as Andres pedaled through several alleys and side streets just west of Greek town. He stopped next to an old van parked in an industrial alley that evidently few people knew of. It was deserted and felt rather scary to Josh. The van was old, probably older than they were. It was a Ford panel van, the long wheelbase model like contractors use. Other than the front doors, there were no windows on the sides and the windows on the rear doors were painted over. A large stainless-steel heavy-duty padlock secured the back doors and another was on the side doors. Ladders were strapped and locked onto the roof. Colorful dragons, boa constrictors and other strange animals seemed to grow around the lower edges, above the wheel wells and up the sides.

"It's fiberglass bondo," said Andres. "First, I started using it to cover the rust, then as the rust grew higher, I attached sheet-metal which I covered with more bondo. That's when I started sculpting. I mean, why not? It certainly is better than looking at old bondo and metal. I like the flames coming out too. Don't you?" He unlocked the back doors to show a wooden platform across the back with shelves underneath it. "That's where I carry my finished work. It's flat so they can't get damaged."

Josh could see several canvas frames covered in bubble wrap.

Andres pointed to them. "I deliver those on Sunday to several clients."

Further inside the van, along the driver's side wall, were storage bins containing paint, brushes, sketch pads, pencils, canvases, drop cloths, tools, frames for stretching canvas, hardboard, and clothes. There were shirts, painter pants, underwear, sweatshirts, socks, boots, a toiletry kit, towels and washcloths. Josh took in the pad and sleeping bag across the back platform. He reached forward and touched it. "This. This is where you sleep? This is your home?"

Andres shrugged and looked down at the gravel. "My dad wanted me to move to Plainfield with them. My poor mother, her name is Bella, had no choice, but I did. Even if it did mean declaring my independence and receiving no money from my father, who, by the way, is a well-off dentist with three offices. He's a jerk. I have friends I eat with and sleep over at sometimes. I shower at UIC, there's all kind of places to clean up and eat. I even have a heater for the van when it gets cold."

"Why? Why won't he support you?" Josh asked. He thought the

answer might be the same reason his dad didn't want to support him.

"Because I refused to go into dentistry. And-and, b-b-because I'm gay." Glancing up at Josh, then away again, he asked, "Why aren't you living at home?"

"Because." Josh waited. How much should he share? He thought about never dating, always wanting a friend who was gay, his staying away from other gay kids at school for fear of what sarcastic things his dad would say. "Because my dad wanted a boy. After three daughters and four miscarriages, my mother had me, then had her tubes tied. I was supposed to be a sports nut, a jock who would be the high school star and go to college on sport scholarships and major in civil engineering. I-I-I was supposed to be straight, too." It was his turn to look at the ground. "Maybe if I'd been straight, he might have accepted me with lesser athletic skills, or appreciated the fact I loved swimming and could have competed. Or that I love camping, hiking, kayaking and being outdoors. For him, me being gay was the straw that broke the camel's back. He hasn't totally rejected me, but wouldn't help with college unless I was in pre-engineering. He always regretted he dropped out of college. He works for the state highway department. He likes it. Inside though, I think he feels he failed. I love office management and paralegal work." He took a deep breath. "That's why I live with my grandparents now. They know who I am and accept me totally."

It was dark, late September dark. The only streetlamp was at the end of the overgrown alley. They each reached for the other's hands and stood, silent, heads lowered, staring at each other's feet. Gradually, they leaned closer until their foreheads touched. Their hands parted and moved to the other's waists. As if drawn by unseen forces, they embraced and held each other like neither wanted to ever let go. Their noses touched, their lips brushed and slowly, they kissed. A peck at first, then deeper, the longer and tighter they squeezed. Gasping, they broke for air and fought control of the urges emanating from below their waists.

"What. What just happened?" asked Josh.

"I don't know. Whatever it is, I want more."

"I do too, but I'm scared. Maybe we should just be friends for a while. Maybe I should get home."

Andres gave him a quick kiss and a hug. He loaded his bike through the van's side doors, locked both padlocks and cleared off the passenger seat. Several times on the drive out to Oak Lawn, one of them reached across the space between their seats to hold hands for a few moments.

Josh's grandparents had brownies and ice cream waiting for them, along with big smiles.

~ * ~

"Earth to Josh. Come to." Andres yanked the cover off Josh. "Where were you at, man? I'm ready to go home, still not ready to drive. Glad you are."

Josh groaned and sat up. He was okay to drive. He just hated driving the big van any time of the day. "I'm good to drive, especially as I don't have much of a choice." He grabbed Andres' arm and pulled himself off the couch. "I was remembering the first time I met Uncle Manny and he got us drunk at Thanksgiving, and I started recalling the day we first met at the firm."

"That was quite a day. I love remembering it, too." Andres gave him a sloppy hug. A happy one that said I love you and I'm still buzzed.

Both were quiet. *Life hasn't been always easy in our relationship of ten years,* thought Josh. And now, were they ready to tackle something like the old rooming house? Together? Was their relationship that stable? Yes, they were older now, stable in their jobs and in their own sense of self, but were they equipped to handle the challenges of renovating an old rooming house? Or their home and apartments? Or an art gallery? Or? He grabbed Andres' hand as they started across the worn front porch toward the street. "Wow. These three days have been incredible."

Andres squeezed his hand. "I think our lives are in for even more changes. I can't wait to go through them with you."

Josh squeezed his answer back. As he climbed into the van, he thought he couldn't wait to move into their own house. He wondered what Andres meant by their lives being in for even more changes. Did he mean moving into their own house? Had they made a decision? He turned to ask him. Andres was leaning against the window, half asleep. *Must be nice,* Josh thought as he drove off.

Chapter Four

Taking Action

Most nights, each slept facing out, away from the other. Some nights, like tonight, after Josh nervously guided the old van home, they talked a few minutes as Andres spooned and cradled him.

When Andres drifted off to a homebrew-fueled sleep, Josh was sober and wide awake. He thought he'd fall asleep soon, but didn't. He jabbed Andres with his elbow. "Roll on your right side, you're snoring."

Andres groggily complied. Andres had a deviated septum, sleeping on his left side caused him to snore, usually lightly, and alcohol seemed to intensify his sounds. At least, that's what Josh told him. Josh realized he wasn't going to sleep and slipped out of bed.

~ * ~

Several hours later, Andres jerked awake. It took a minute to collect his thoughts. Oh, yeah, the homebrew must have worn off. That stuff is potent. He stretched, climbed out of bed and went to the bathroom. On the way back, he noticed Josh dozing in the rocker, wrapped in a blanket. He didn't disturb him. *Guess my snoring got bad again,* he thought. He rooted around on the bed and was ready to fall asleep when the cries of the neighbor's baby came through the thin walls. *Dammit. That's another reason I don't want kids.* He tossed and turned and finally pulled Josh's pillow over his head.

Their building was originally a stately three-flat. As the demographics changed and the demand for more housing increased to serve the expanding Latino population moving into the Pilsen neighborhood, some owner converted the upper flats into two tight apartments on each floor. The basement housed an additional apartment, plus a laundry room and storage area for the residents. The current owner converted his first floor living room into a neighborhood bodega and sold snacks, canned goods, soda, candy and beer. Though the beer was hidden and one had to ask for it as the owner didn't have a license to sell it.

Josh's and Andres' neighbors on the third floor were a young, hard-working couple with a toddler named Pedro and another child on the way. One month before, a cousin arrived from Texas with his very pregnant girlfriend who, three days after moving in, barely made it to John Stroger Hospital, formerly known as Cook County Hospital, in time to deliver a five-pound, eight-ounce baby girl. It seemed like she rarely quit crying. Andres wondered if she was healthy.

He pulled his pillow out from under his head and jammed it on top of Josh's pillow. It didn't help. He tried to lay still, focus on his breathing and ignore the sounds of Josh slipping on his clothes, tip-toeing across the living room and quietly closing the door behind him.

I wonder what he's doing? Bet it has something to do with that crying baby. Damn him and his big heart. Andres got up, found his ear phones, plugged them into his old iPod and crawled back into bed.

The baby's cries soon turned into stereo as Pedro's wales added to the din. The toddler was quieted quickly. The infant wasn't. Andres looked at the clock. Two a.m. He sat up, turned on a lamp, pulled a sketch-pad and pencil from the night stand and began sketching. He wasn't sure what he was drawing, though whatever it was seemed filled with confusion, maybe some anger, yet some softer lines kept creeping in. He was still sketching when Josh entered the room forty minutes later. The crying stopped.

"Where the hell did you go?"

Josh half-smiled. "Walgreens; for formula, diapers and diaper rash cream. They were mixing water with their last bit of formula, trying to make it last till Saturday when Louis gets paid. Baby Angie was protesting."

"What the hell, Josh. How do you know all that? Why can't the other couple help them?"

"They're broke till payday, too." Josh slipped his clothes off and climbed into bed, pulling his pillow to him. "The reason it was so loud was because Lucia was walking the baby in the hallway so Louis could sleep. I heard her and Pedro's mom whispering how they were both broke, so I went out there." He rolled to face Andres. "Don't worry. It's a loan. Lucia insisted she will pay us back, she said they will have enough money to do so and find their own apartment as long as it's cheap. And close, like ours." He nudged Andres.

"What's that supposed to mean? You told them they could have our place? Jesus, Josh, we haven't even made a decision."

"I know, and, no, I didn't tell them we might be moving. It was just a thought. Now go to sleep. We can both sleep in as we're not working today. Remember?"

Andres turned out the light.

"Oh, and Andres, I bought them some bread, cereal, cheese, milk and peanut butter, too."

"Why don't you just open your own bodega up here? Or social work office? Or a welfare office? Go to sleep. I think that homebrew affected you."

Andres rolled over to face out. He still couldn't get to sleep. *Why did Josh do that?* He sighed loudly and wriggled to get comfortable.

Josh mumbled, "I did it so we all could get some sleep. Does that answer your question?"

Andres grunted and reached behind him to pat Josh on the hip.

I think our lives truly are going to change, he thought. *But in what ways? Our own house will be wonderful. Josh will be thrilled to not be living in paint fumes and dancing around wet canvases. His commute will be longer, not too much, mine will be as well. Our own home will be worth it. I love the idea of my own studio and possibly a gallery, though that's a big step. Is that what I meant when I said our lives will be changing? If we decide to remodel, which, why wouldn't we? He's going to drive me nuts with priorities, lists, details and concerns. Can I deal with that?* Andres readjusted his pillow and listened to Josh's soft breathing. *Well, I better deal with it, he certainly has saved my ass with his financial sense and damn lists and questions. What else did I mean by changes? Was it just the*

35

challenge of a remodeling project together? That seems a challenge, yet certainly something we're equipped to do. A gallery? Maybe. With his business sense and my artistic skills and contacts and ideas for running a gallery, I think that's doable too.

He jerked as the thought hit him. Kids. Were the spirits conspiring against him? Meg from the funeral home mentioned kids, Josh was open to at least the idea, and now, the babies crying next door. Were these omens? He'd ask his mother, she was wise in Mexican superstitions, believed in the universe working for and against us, but he knew she'd get all excited at the idea of grandkids. No way, Jose. Nope, he wasn't going in that direction. He shook his head as if to clear it and concentrated on relaxing his body, starting with his toes and slowly moving upward. Finally, he fell into a deep sleep.

~ * ~

Josh woke up to noise. His head slightly ached from interrupted sleep, talking with Lucia, and going to Walgreens in the middle of the night. As usual, Andres was energetically grinding coffee, banging bowls and spoons onto the table, pouring orange juice and rattling cereal boxes. Andres liked a mix of Raisin Bran, Wheat Chex, Rice Krispies and CoCo Puffs.

Josh stumbled into the bathroom.

"Sorry," Andres yelled toward the open bathroom door. "We're almost out of eggs. Did you give them away last night, too?"

Josh groaned and splashed water on his face. Through the towel, he mumbled, "No, I didn't give any eggs away. It's just that when you're on an errand of mercy at two-fifteen a.m., you're not always thinking of your own grocery list. When's the coffee going to be ready anyway?"

"Soon, soon. Just be patient, lover-boy. You want banana on your Raisin Bran? I'll use a table knife just to be safe, so you know I'm not hung over."

Josh slid into his seat, downed his OJ and poured milk on his cereal and banana. "Just hurry the coffee, would you? This feels almost like the first time we met Uncle Manny and he got us drunk. Do hangovers leave, then come back again? Hey, think we'll find the recipe for the beer? It did have a lot of kick. Maybe Uncle Manny was playing a joke on us. You know, get us drunk so we keep the place." He thought about his excursion in the middle of the night, but wasn't sure Andres wanted to be reminded of it. Kids.

"Maybe, but it's not his recipe. It's your great-great-grandfather's that's been passed down. I caught a glimpse of it mixed in with Manny's diary. Does that mean I'm now in charge of making the beer?"

"Wow. That's my great-great-grandfathers recipe? How amazing. Yes, it's fine with me if you're the brew master. Have we made a decision to keep it?"

That was the most pressing question on Josh's mind. He didn't want to nag, but what value was there in waiting?

Andres turned away to pour the coffee. "Maybe we should check with a realtor, find out what we could get, sell it, and use the money toward a gallery someplace closer to the Loop. I mean, how many people want to come to Back-of-the-Yards to find my art?"

"Andres. Goddammit." He hadn't meant to explode, but the lack of sleep, his desire for a home, even the needs of Louis and Luisa flashed through his mind. "The real question is how long can we survive in this tiny fleabag of an apartment with your work taking up most of the space? C'mon! We. Need. A. Home." He took a breath to calm himself. "Plus, you need space for a studio, a real studio. Did you hear me, Andres? We can't stay in this place much longer, breathing paint fumes and stumbling around stretchers and bumping into paintings hanging from the ceiling to dry. C'MON."

Andres placed a cup of steaming joe in front of Josh, kissed his cheek, tousled his hair, and wrapped both arms around him. "I agree completely. I never thought you'd see my side of things. Let's give notice to the landlord and move this weekend. That way, your new best friends with the squalling baby can move in here. God, why are you so dense sometimes?"

"Andres, you son of a bitch. You were just trying to get me riled up when I haven't slept much. Why do I always fall for your tricks?" He shoved several bites of cereal in his mouth, sipped his coffee, and calmly said, "There's a lot to do. We may not be able to move this weekend. Let's make a list of things we need to do, like…"

"Dang it, Josh. I realize we may not be able to move this weekend. We have to get all that paperwork signed over at the house, get the utilities switched into our names, schedule these utilities to be turned off, get our mail forwarded, change the address on our bills, bank accounts and personal identification, that means things like our driver's licenses and insurance cards. I get it." He sat down, laughing. "Oh, Joshy, the look on your face right now is priceless. I may have to postpone the move, you know, take several weeks to paint it."

Josh gave him the finger.

They spent the day making arrangements for their move, though Andres managed to make a quick cartoon sketch of Josh's expression at the breakfast table. "If you ever show that, I'll personally kill you," Josh said.

Early that evening, Andres began grilling quesadillas while Josh trotted down the stairs to the bodega to talk with the landlord about them moving out, and to buy some of his high-priced beer. They chatted and laughed for about fifteen minutes. When Josh returned to the apartment, Andres was still on the first quesadilla but the package of large tortillas was smaller. "Umm, Andres, have you already eaten and now you're starting mine? I thought we would eat together like we usually do. That's why I got the beer."

Andres looked away, as if embarrassed. "I got carried away, made a few more."

"Well, where are they? I don't understand."

"I took them next door. They were very appreciative. Tomorrow's payday for the guys." He turned back to the stove and flipped the tortilla in half.

~ * ~

In bed that night, Josh's mind whirred with the events of the past several days. They now owned a home together, which led to him thinking about how far he and Andres had come.

When they rented an apartment, eight years earlier, money, or how to track it and account for it, was the main source of dissension between the two of them. Andres never worried about it. When things became tight, he hustled more art jobs or scrounged up house painting work, something he rarely had to do now.

Their first years together were wonderful, except for the money. Rent would be due in five days and Josh would remind Andres for his half. "Oops, haven't got it, don't worry, I'll get it." Josh would fume and stew and worry. Not because he couldn't afford to cover Andres' half, but because he thought it irresponsible not to plan ahead and be prepared. The good, though frustrating, thing was, Andres always got the money. It might be hours before they were due to drop the 'CASH ONLY' envelope through their landlord's door slot, but somehow, Andres always had the money. He would sell a painting, collect on one from someone whom he forgot to bill, or stay up all night to paint someone's living and dining room. Andres operated on the cash-in-his-wallet system. He eschewed credit cards and checking accounts, but did have a savings account at a small, Hispanic-owned savings and loan in Pilsen.

Over time, Josh recognized why Andres handled money the way he did. His mother never had access to banks or credit cards. She was forced to ask her husband, Art Junior, for every dime she needed. She developed her own system of asking for more than she needed, hiding the balance and slowly growing that little amount to always be prepared for things that might come up. Art Junior spent freely on himself, yet was responsible for paying the mortgages, utilities and home expenses. He rarely questioned Bella regarding what she was spending money on, it was always clothes and food for Andres, or school costs. If he realized she managed to fund Andres' art supplies and lessons out of the grocery money he gave her every week, he never commented about it. If she thought Andres needed something and his father didn't, Bella would take on housecleaning jobs during the day while Andres was in school. "It's hereditary, it's how I grew up," was Andres explanation. "I learned not to rely on anyone else for money and to keep mine close and only spend what I had."

As a couple, several years passed before Josh and Andres could fully talk about and accept their differences. Josh relaxed his expectations and Andres realized Josh could help him with his lack of organization in billing and collecting. One time, he shocked Josh when he showed him a savings passbook with nine-thousand dollars in it. "I hate taking money out," he'd said. "That's why I'll take an extra job or collect from one I forgot about. It scares me to death to take money out that I might need in case of a real emergency." He'd looked at Josh and winked. "Besides, we can always live in my van."

Josh had rubbed his middle finger against his nose. "All these years and you've had a savings account with money in it while I worried my ass off."

"And a mighty sweet ass it is," Andres had replied, as he squeezed Josh's butt.

In bed now, Andres rolled over as Josh stretched, still wide awake with his thoughts. He carefully slipped out of the bed and into the kitchen where he fixed a stiff Moscow Mule. He wrapped a Bears stadium blanket around himself and curled up on the couch in their tiny living room crammed with art supplies and half-finished works.

Sipping his drink, he recalled how things seemed fine right up till they'd been together about five years and their lives seemed predictable and boring. Both were settled into rewarding careers, Josh with the firm as the office manager, and Andres teaching high school two days a week as a contract employee and selling most of his art through two galleries, plus doing exhibitions and art fairs. Josh's firm hired a new paralegal, two years younger than Josh. Abe seemed a lot like Josh and he was gay. They quickly established a strong working relationship that started to include drinks or a meal after work on the days Andres wasn't home. Josh enjoyed being with someone who thought just like he did, handled money well, planned ahead and loved swimming. His mind started to wander. Neither he nor Andres ever dated anyone else. Not even held hands with another.

One day, at an art exhibition Josh was helping Andres with, he noticed a look cross between Andres and another male artist who showed at one of the same galleries. Bingo. Josh brought the topic up that night. "Are we getting bored with each other? We've only ever known each other. I've never kissed another man, nor have you, that I know of."

Andres jerked, then blushed. "I-I have. Last week. It just happened. That's all we did." He stared at the floor.

Josh was stunned and he couldn't help thinking of Abe. He stayed calm and they spoke about their other love interests that seemed to be happening at the same time. "Many gay couples have open relationships, is that something we want to consider?" Josh asked. "It's not that I don't love you, but somehow, our lives seem so boring. Even our sex is predictable."

After several weeks of discussion, the two agreed to a three-month trial of dating others, an open relationship with extreme safety precautions. At the end of three months, they would decide whether their love was still strong enough to continue in such a relationship, go back to being monogamous, or, as scary as it sounded, separate and lead their own lives apart.

They pretended that living together while dating others was normal. They were extra polite to each other, going out of their way to make sure the other one didn't want to invite someone home for a night. If needed, Andres still had his van to sleep in and Josh had friends he could couch surf with for an occasional night. Each tried gay bars and pretended to have a good time, raving to each other the next morning about the fun they almost had. Josh told Abe he was available and was quickly invited to spend the night in Abe's condo on Lakeshore Drive. It turned out Abe, though hard-working, was a trust fund baby and thought his six-hundred thousand dollar, Lake Shore Drive condo was normal for young paralegals. Their sex was not star-bursting. The second time Josh went home with him, another gay couple showed up and Josh realized Abe was into group sex. He left and was glad Andres was at an exhibition. Andres didn't come home that night.

The following Saturday morning, they slept in together. Andres brought Josh a coffee in bed and settled down beside him, their backs against the headboard. Josh felt the tension needed a sword to cut it.

Andres blew on and slurped his coffee. "It's been almost four weeks. I don't think I can make it like this for two more months."

Josh almost dropped his coffee.

"I hate gay bars. You know the art guy I kissed?"

Josh nodded, fearing what might come next.

"I went to bed with him once. When he brought out these toys and bondage crap, I told him no deal and we ended up just jerking off, like a neighbor kid and I did back when we were thirteen." He looked over at Josh who was afraid to look him in the eyes. He nudged Josh's elbow. "You look scared. That's the end of my story. I give up. The grass ain't greener on the other side. What about you? You want more time?"

"Hell, no. Gay bars were driving me nuts, too. About Abe? Well, let's put it this way, I wished we'd only jerked off, it couldn't have been any less boring. I kept hearing the lyrics of the song one of my aunts used to play by Peggy Lee, *Is that all there is to life?* Over and over, that's all I heard. The second time I went to his place, he wanted group sex with these muscle-bound, body-building freaks, so I left."

Both set their coffees on the floor and slowly moved to embrace each other. Just before they kissed, Andres stopped. "So, does that mean neither of us learned any new sex moves we can teach the other?"

"Guess we'll have to stay bored with each other. Now kiss me."

Andres willingly complied.

~ * ~

Josh finished his drink. Damn, Mules were good. He went to the bathroom and quietly crept back into bed and fell asleep.

Chapter Five

Moving In

Josh and Andres spent the Saturday morning after Manny's burial going through the paperwork with Padre. He went through the legalities of them signing their names to the documents, and necessary procedures to transfer the utilities into their names. Even walking them over to the bank to submit the signature cards and telling them where to go at the county building on Monday to turn in the deed and request a new title in their names, which Josh did during his lunch hour.

The following Friday, both men took the day off work and packed. Their first trip to the rooming house was made that afternoon with all of the art work and supplies which they hauled into the little apartment behind the main one. Andres started to unpack and arrange his supplies and equipment.

"Dammit, Andres. We don't have time to do that now. We have to get back, finish packing, load our clothes, furniture, kitchen supplies, and clean the apartment."

Andres flipped a dry tiny paint brush at him. "Do you always have to be so task-oriented and logical? I can't wait to set up my studio. Finally, I have a dedicated space. Look at the light. It's great to start painting right now."

Josh squinted his eyes at him. "Who's being task-oriented? I'm just trying to be efficient. The landlord is giving us our deposit back, even on such short notice, and Louis and Lucia are moving in Monday. I want to be in this place sometime tomorrow morning."

"Yes, but I was hoping to get a batch of homebrew started today so we can celebrate after we move in tomorrow."

"Andres, it takes longer than one night to make homebrew beer. Now let's lock up and go."

It was around eleven the next morning, Saturday, when Andres pulled the loaded van to the curb in front of the rooming house. "Hope you remembered the keys. Did you give the old ones to the landlord?"

"Of course, Andres. Of course." Josh stretched. "Hey, I'm thirsty. We should have stopped and picked up some cold drinks. Hope there's ice in that old fridge for at least some ice water."

As they climbed down from the van, a slender black man with a head of bushy white hair and thick eye-glasses hustled across the street. He carried two extra-large green plastic glasses rattling with ice cubes. "Welcome. I'm Mr. Thompson, except most call me Mr. T. Mrs. T figured you should have some sweet tea. Said the ice will cool ya off and sugar'll give ya some energy."

He handed them each a glass and smiled as they took a long drink. Hooking his thumb at two teenage boys standing on the curb in front of his house, he said, "These two are here to help ya unload. Don't be afraid to work them, they're strong young man-boys."

The man-boys did not look excited to be volunteered or at being called man-boys. They slowly sauntered over. One appeared Hispanic. Skinny, wearing a Bulls shirt and black jeans, his dark hair was cut short on the sides, almost shaved, but long on top with the back pulled into a pony-tail. The other wore a tight Afro, stood well over six-feet tall and wore red basketball shorts and a Laker's wife beater. Both looked at the ground.

"This one is Fernando, he goes by Nando, and this taller one is Jeramiah, and he goes by Fly," Mr. T said. "Now boys, straighten up, stand tall, look 'em in their eyes and shake their hands. Ya gotta meet people the right way in this life." He waited until Nando finally looked up and slowly extended his hand to Josh.

"*Hola,*" said Josh. "*Benvenido.*"

Nando looked surprised and grasped Josh's hand tighter, then extended it to Andres, who said, "*Buenos días. Cómo estás?*"

Fly straightened up and eagerly shook their hands. "*Hola, buenos dias.* I speak Spanish, too. I'm part Puerto Rican."

The boys followed Andres as he moved onto the grass and opened the side van doors. A soccer ball rolled out. He footed it toward Fly who gave it a quick pass to Nando.

"Looks like you two know what to do with that," Andres said. "Let's get this stuff moved in and maybe we'll have time for a game when we're done."

"Let's get started," said Fly. "You got a basketball, too? I'm good at that. That's why they call me Fly."

"Ya, ya, ya," said Nando. "You think they can't figure that out? They ain't stupid, you know. Now shut your fly trap and grab this end table and don't talk their ears off." He looked at Andres and motioned with his thumb. "This one talks a good game, so you gotta keep on him."

Fly laughed and shrugged. "I'd say something in Spanish, but Andres and Josh will know what I'm saying. That's how we talk behind the T's back, they don't dig Spanish."

"That's right," Mr. T said. "But I understand face language and body language and you two ain't pulled much over on us, have ya?" He took the empty glasses from Josh and Andres. "I'll get ya some more in a bit, plus some for these hooligans. Why is it teenagers thinks they always know everything? Now, keep them busy and you best plan on Mrs. T sending something over for your lunch. We might even send some for those two as well. Notice I said might."

The boys were eager helpers and were enthralled with all the rooms upstairs when Josh gave them a quick tour after unloading the van. "What you gonna do with all these rooms? Start a group home for foster teens like us?" Nando seemed to be half-joking, half-serious.

"You think that's a good idea?" Josh replied.

"Nah, it's too many rooms. This place would be a fricking zoo if you had all them teens. Besides, foster homes are better, especially when you got good people like Mr. and Mrs. T. Fly and me are going to a group home in a few months when we turn seventeen. Hopefully, we can stay together."

"What happens after the group home?"

Fly stepped closer. "Well, if we do decent in school, graduate, we can get into independent living and the state will help pay our apartment

and college expenses. I plan to go to a city college, then maybe UIC up there on Halsted. I wanna coach and teach elementary kids."

"I want to be a mechanic, I might join the Army or Navy," said Nando. "Then go for college or more training when I get out." He paused, shuffled his feet and looked at the floor. "Hey, are you and Andres gay or something? I mean, all your clothes and stuff is all mixed together. It didn't look like you were just roommates."

Fly swatted him. Before he could say anything, Nando continued. "I'm not trying to get all personal, I just wondered. No offense." He shoved Fly back. "I ain't being rude, just wondering. You know my older sister is gay."

"I'm not offended," said Josh. "Yes, Andres and I are gay and have been together for ten years, since we were eighteen and nineteen. What's your older sister do?"

"She works at Walgreens and goes to school part-time. She lives with her girlfriend in South Holland. I don't get to see her much, but wish I could. Sis is pretty cool."

Andres showed them his studio. They quickly hung the finished works close together on the walls in the small bedroom. The works in progress, all dry, they leaned against the walls of the living area. He described how he planned his main work area to be between the south and west windows, plus the space in the middle of the bedroom he planned to build vertical shelves under a workbench to store the completed and wrapped pieces ready for sale. They were impressed with his camera and the computer he used to post them on his website or to submit his work to galleries and interested persons.

"These are incredible," Nando exclaimed. "You have several different styles, don't you? What do you call this style?" he pointed to a fairly large work consisting of bold lines and geometric shapes complimented by bright colors.

"I'm kind of a Hines 57," Andres replied. "I like modernism, cubism, realism and a bit of pop-culture, but always with my own style, such as that one you're pointing at. However, sometimes I do some more impressionistic work and occasionally some heavily detailed, realistic work, like the one of the rooming house over there. I'm still playing with

it. That's my first version, quite realistic and done in a hurry. Now look at that sketch over there. Do you see a connection?"

"Holy crap," Fly shouted. "It's like you cut it into pieces and rearranged the parts. That is so rad."

"Fly, rad is so old. How do you even remember it?" Nando punched Fly's shoulder and laughed at him. "This stuff is wonderful. I wished I could do something like this."

"Come over some time after we're settled in and I'll work with you. I believe everyone has some artistic talent, it's just a matter of figuring out what makes you buzz," Andres replied.

A voice called from the side entrance. "Is you men workin' hard or hardly workin'? C'mon, I walked over some ham sandwiches and more sweet tea."

"Good, that's Mrs. T," said Fly. "I'm starving."

Mrs. T was thin and had gray-white hair in a tight Afro and gold-rimmed eye-glasses. An old-fashioned lace handkerchief peeked out of her bra. She moved with purpose and energy as she marched into the kitchen where she set a platter of sandwiches, bag of chips and container of homemade oatmeal raisin cookies on the table. Mr. T sauntered behind with a pitcher of tea and bag of ice. "I didn't bring no more glasses, figured you found some from Manny. Hope they're clean." He looked toward the dining and living rooms. "Whatcha going to do with all that furniture just gathering dust?"

"Well," Josh said. "We're going to use most of it. Our furniture was stuff we collected from students moving away or sitting on the curb and is worse than what's here. Even if old, most of this stuff is decent, better than what we had, so we didn't bring much. Mostly clothes, books, kitchen gear and a couple of dressers."

"We left most of our furniture for the next renters. They're young kids just starting out with a new baby girl," Andres said.

"When you goin back by there?" Mrs. T asked. "I got a ton of baby clothes, girl clothes. Enough to get her to kindergarten." She pointed at the teenage boys and smiled ruefully. "After they leave, we're probably not goin to need them baby clothes anymore."

"Well," Andres said. "I'll run by there on my way to school Monday morning. I teach Art part-time at Benito Juarez High School. I'm sure they'll be thankful."

"You best start eatin'," Mrs. T said. "These here boys can help you clean, scrub the floors, do laundry, move stuff. Nando could even cook you a supper if you need. I been workin' with them."

"Slave driving us," Nando said with a laugh. "I'm good at burritos, if you got the stuff."

Mrs. T gently grabbed Nando's ear. "Yes, I been a slave drivin' you two. Ain't nobody ever said Mrs. T didn't teach her fosters how to take care a themselves and they ain't gonna start now. Even if we are older than a graveyard."

Andres swallowed a bite, took a sip of tea and said, "Nando, my specialty is quesadillas. Maybe we could start a business, quesadillas and burritos."

"Ya," shouted Fly. "We could turn upstairs into a restaurant with quesadillas, burritos and my *arroz con gandules y lechon*, it's yellow rice and pigeon peas with roasted pork and I make it real good."

Josh slammed his glass on the table in mock anger. "We are not, trust me, not starting a restaurant. I eat enough of Andres' quesadillas every week. No way are they going to be cooking above my head and me eating the ones that don't sell." Everyone laughed and resumed eating.

After lunch, Mr. T went home to wash and wax his car while Andres and the boys went outside to kick the soccer ball around. Mrs. T cleaned the refrigerator and Josh the stove. They worked in quiet unison, as if they'd known each other most of their lives, yet Josh wondered about the life she and Mr. T lived, all these years apparently raising foster children. Did they have any of their own? He wasn't sure how to broach the subject.

Mrs. T peered over his shoulder. "Someone raised you right, you sure know how to clean an oven good."

"Well, my mom tried to teach me and I watched my grandmother. I lived with my grandparents most of college, till Andres and I moved in together." He sniffed the fumes. "At least this smell is better than the cigarette smoke and urine that's in here. I don't know how we're going to get rid of that."

"Tell ya what. It's a nice day. You go around and open every window and door possible. That will freshen up the air in here." She checked under the sink, then opened the pantry cupboard and poked around. "You got some cash on ya? I'll make a short list and send Nando down to Jorge's store. I'll put them boys to work, they been outside playing long enough. Say, that Andres sure is good with kids, ain't he?"

Josh nodded and pulled two twenties out of his pocket. "This enough?" He wanted to say more, but didn't know how he felt in his own mind about being good with kids.

Mrs. T grabbed one of the twenties, pulled a stubby pencil from her dress pocket along with a scrap of paper and began making a list while Josh called the guys in. "Here, Nando," she said. "Run down to Jorge's and get this. It's vinegar – a gallon, three bottles of hydrogen peroxide, 'bout three big boxes of baking soda, and some activated charcoal."

"Oh, good, we going to grill out?" Nando said.

"No. An' don't go bringin' us a bag of charcoal. Back by the cleaning supplies, look for a box, it'll say activated charcoal, it's a powder. Now, you gotta open your eyes and look good. Don't be like a typical man, you ask some woman for help if you can't find it. Jorge keeps it 'cause of all the old houses around here that need airin' out."

"Can Fly go with?"

"No. What I been tellin' ya? Two boys are worth half of one boy and three are none at all."

Josh laughed. "That means don't even think of taking Andres along. By the way, where is he?"

Nando took the money and list from Mrs. T. "Okay, I'll hurry." He glanced at Josh. "I think he and Fly went downstairs to look for the still."

Mrs. T straightened up, marched over to the stairway leading to the basement. "Fly and Andres. We got work to do up here, not down there."

Andres looked a bit sheepish as they entered the kitchen, like he got caught sneaking out on his chores.

"Bet you wantin' to make some homebrew, huh? Well, when you get this place ship-shape and you're all moved in, I'll send Mr. T over to help you. He took lessons from Manny, and at his age, he's limited to drink only one. Maybe, if you two young ones act right, maybe someday, you could have a half each. Under supervision." She shook her head in mock disgust. "I'm older than dirt, but I ain't a Puritan or naive about sixteen-year old boys. Now, we got work to do." She glared at Andres. "I was just sayin' how good you do with kids. Don't make me change my mind." She laughed at the surprised expression on his face.

Nando and Fly were very helpful. They moved furniture, some of it to the basement, set up Josh's and Andres' bed, and helped rearrange the dressers. They hung the men's clothes in the front closet until the one in their bedroom could be emptied and scrubbed. With only a few complaints, they jumped to Mrs. T's commands. Wiping down the woodwork with wood soap, washing the ceilings and walls, plus the inside windows, sprinkling baking soda on the aged, flowered rugs, and vacuuming with the ancient Kirby discovered in the front closet.

Josh and Andres worked on their bedroom closet. It was under the stairwell, deep and narrow and the ceiling angled down. They were surprised how few clothes Manny actually had. Or anything else. While Josh scrubbed the ceiling from a step-stool, Andres carried Manny's clothes to the basement where they started a pile of things to discard or donate to the Salvation Army. He didn't return right away. Peevish, Josh changed the water in his bucket and went down to the basement in search of him. He found him sitting on an old chair, bent over, still holding Manny's clothes, his face buried in an old winter coat. "What's the matter? You coming back up to help or what?"

"Of course. Sorry. I didn't mean to run out on you. It's just that…"

"C'mon, Andres. Let's get this closet finished, scrub the bedroom down and make up the bed so we can at least sleep in a finished room. You know I hate living in chaos."

Andres' head snapped up. There were tears on his cheeks. "Dammit, Josh. Just God dammit. Do you have to be so fucking task-oriented? Besides, you claim you've been living in chaos for years with me. What the hell's another ten minutes? Can't a man think about his uncle for a minute? Huh? Should I make an appointment? Set a time for grief? Keep it on a schedule?"

"I'm sorry, Andres. I didn't realize what you were…"

Josh stepped carefully to the side as Andres jumped up, threw the clothes onto the pile and stomped past him toward the stairs.

Josh quietly followed. He avoided looking at Mrs. T or the boys. He began scrubbing a side wall, Andres the low walls at the end of the closet.

Wow, Josh thought, *that was a side of Andres I rarely saw before, plus, I was acting task oriented, again.*

Silently, they finished the closet. Andres changed the water in the bucket as Josh slid the bed away from the wall. Andres stood on a stool to do the ceiling while Josh cleaned the wall. They moved almost in accord. Next, they moved the bed back and attacked the outside wall. Still not speaking.

All at once, the sounds of Benny Goodman filled the home. Both of them set their rags down and moved into the kitchen. The music emanated from the living room. Fly, Nando and Mrs. T stood in front of an old console TV with a built-in stereo.

Mrs. T snapped her fingers and swayed. She smiled gently as Josh and Andres approached. "Swing music is good for you. It always picks my spirits up. Did for Manny, too. Couple a times, we brought him over some greens and corn bread and he was listenin' to this or other big band records. He liked that Cuban jazz, too. Always made him feel better, even if he was down." She looked at the teens. "The Mr. and me used to dance to this. Swing dance, all the different kinds. We was good, too. Dang good."

"What kind a dances were they?" Nando jigged around to the beat.

"Well, not quite like that, young man. Swing dance goes like this." She kicked her canvas shoes off and demonstrated the rock-step-behind, then the slides to the left and right. "Now, you start with your left foot rockin' back and I'll start with my right goin' forward." She pulled Nando into a loose hold and began guiding him.

After he seemed to catch the basics, she grabbed Fly and taught him. Looking at Josh and Andres, she said, "What you two waitin' on. You're a couple, get started. We ain't washin' walls all day."

"I'm Polish with two left feet," said Josh. "I can't even polka well."

"Andres, you start switchin' with the boys, while I work on Josh."

Andres easily began moving in synch, laughing and switching off with Nando and Fly. Josh, self-conscious, couldn't keep the count, or the steps. He stumbled around, trying to avoid Mrs. T's toes and stay upright.

"Boy," she finally said, "you need a whole lot of work. More than this old lady can give ya today. Why don't you go pour us some sweet tea?"

"Finally, something I can do well." He ducked Mrs. T's mock swing at him.

The five sat around the living room, sipping their iced tea and listening to the LP albums Fly discovered in the old console. There were many of them, most from 1940's, '50's and '60's. Josh wondered where Manny's CDs were.

"These young men did me proud today," Mrs. T said, smiling at Nando and Fly. "The living room is finished. The dining room is finished, plus the ceiling and walls in the kitchen are. Mr. T and I are goin' to church tomorrow morning. These two will be over between ten and eleven to do that kitchen floor. I already gave them good instructions on how, same as in the bathroom. Why the good Lord didn't design you men a better way to aim is beyond me. I'm thinkin' that's one of the questions I just might ask him, but after I'm all the way through those Pearly Gates. The first question is gonna be why he closed my womb up." She shook her head, sipped her tea and looked out the window. Glancing at the boys, she said, "Guess I kind of know that answer, don't I?" She stood and slipped her shoes back on. "Well, I been neighborly enough for an old woman. I'm goin' home. You two boys be home at five, I got an old hen in the crockpot."

She stepped over to Josh and pulled him to a stand, did the same with Andres. Putting her arms lightly around them, she said, "You two are gonna be just fine. Movin' is always stressful, especially after a loved one dies. Be patient with each other and you'll do good." She squeezed their shoulders, making them step closer, turned and marched out the door, humming *Blue Skies.*

Josh and Andres hugged, picked up their glasses of tea and, elbows touching, moved back to their bedroom and resumed scrubbing. The music stopped and they heard Nando and Fly talking quietly as they worked in the kitchen. It sounded like one of them was going through the dish cabinets and the other the pantry. "Hey, can I use my own judgement out here?"

Josh and Andres stepped into the kitchen. Nando was pulling out dishes and cleaning the shelves. Fly waved them over to the pantry. "So, what is the oldest food you want to keep?" He grinned as he handed them a tin of cocoa. "This one says 1979. Unopened. Wanna try it?" He pulled a can of pepper out, looked at it, and said, "Hey, we're getting closer. This is 1997. Brand new, too."

"Umm, I think it's fine to be extravagant and throw anything out of date into the garbage. Josh and I brought our food supplies and I'm sure it's all current."

Josh raised his hands and waved them around. "Well, most of its current. At least not decades old, maybe a few spices Andres bought from some little old lady at the farmers market are on the edge."

The boys grinned.

"C'mon, Andres, let's get our bed made and move our clothes from the front closet, then everyone is finished for the day."

After they finished, Andres set cold Cokes on the kitchen table. "Come on, guys, sit down. Let's drink a Coke, then go see if you're still as good with a ball. Hopefully, all that cleaning hasn't ruined your skills."

"You guys are great helpers," said Josh. "How long has Mrs. T been training you?"

"Well, we'll finish up tomorrow. Just because it's put away, doesn't mean you can find anything," Nando said. "Mrs. T's trying to get us to put stuff away in the same place. She says we drive her nuts sometime when she can't find things."

"We been with them a little over a year," said Fly. "We came at the same time. They're about the best foster parents I ever lived with. I lived with a lot. They're getting old and thinking of retiring from kids. Nando and me will be all right. Now. We probably wouldn't have been ready for a group home or independent living if we hadn't been placed with them."

Josh didn't know how to respond. Finally, he said, "Well, I can tell you've learned a lot. You can be proud of yourselves because you can certainly do more around the house than I was doing at your age. Thank you."

After a game of soccer with Andres, the boys went home. Josh and Andres walked to Jorge's neighborhood grocery store. They met Jorge who seemed surprised, yet pleased, when they asked him about his mother-in-law who the two priests went to see immediately following Manny's funeral. He said she was fine and was again working in his deli, but now needed blood pressure medication. He also expressed his condolences regarding Manny. "The two priests keep us all updated, they're good folk in this neighborhood. I heard one of you is an artist. Me? I can't draw my own name, but I love looking at art, especially locally done stuff."

They bought some Modelo beer, glad the selection was mostly Mexican. They also picked up some fresh corn tortillas, vegetables, Queso Fresco cheese and ready to go seasoned taco meat. Both men were too tired to cook much. Back at the house, they stretched out in the living room and relaxed, sipping their beer, listening to the sounds of the old house, the kids playing around the neighborhood and the street traffic, which was a lot softer than at their former apartment.

"You know there's a whole house fan over the outside side door, don't you?" Andres asked.

"No, I wondered what that was. How's it work?"

"You open some windows, preferably on the cooler side of the house, leave the door open from the kitchen to the back stairway and turn it on. It draws the cooler air through and exhausts the hot. They're great at night."

"I'm getting us another beer, then let's start reading Josef's diary. It's going to take us a while."

Chapter Six

The Rooming House Plans

On Sunday morning, Andres cooked a big breakfast of sausage, pancakes, eggs, juice and fruit. He timed it to be ready for when the boys appeared. "Can you handle two breakfasts?"

"Of course. Mrs. T fixes us a big breakfast on Saturdays, cuz she likes to get all ready for church on Sundays and we was both too lazy to cook today, so we only had cereal. This is great," said Nando.

After breakfast, the boys finished the kitchen while Josh and Andres scrubbed the bathroom. "Umm, I think this room needs to be the priority when we start some renovation." Josh was on his hands and knees, scrubbing behind the toilet, while Andres banged around in the shower. "I think this floor might be a little soft. In fact, I'm thinking the only thing holding the floor together around the toilet is a zillion layers of linoleum."

"A zillion?"

"Well, maybe I exaggerated. Just don't jump up and down near the toilet and make sure of your aim, we don't want to add to the moisture content. It's a little spongey."

They sent the boys' home at one-thirty, thankful to the two for getting so much accomplished. Arrangements were made for them to come back later in the week when Andres would be home during the day to work on the other three bedrooms. Andres, then Josh, showered in the almost sparkling bathroom. "Hey," Andres said, "have you seen the garage? We put our bikes in the basement because I couldn't figure out which key is to the garage. Let's explore. Grab that wad of keys."

It took several minutes to find the right keys. The single-car garage had concrete block walls and two heavy-duty steel doors that swung sideways with two deadbolt locks securing it. "Why so much security on an old garage?" Josh groaned as he pushed the door open.

"Oh my God. That's why this place is like Fort Knox. Look. Joshy, look. Is this another secret?"

A 1956 Ford Fairlane, four-door, V-8, shiny, but covered in a thin layer of dust, gleamed at them. "Here, in this bunch of keys is a Ford set. Open the door. I can't believe this." Josh was surprised he was so excited over an old car until he recalled going to car shows with his Grandpa Joey and realized some of the excitement must have stuck with him. "No wonder this was locked in. Manny must have made sure it stayed safe. Grandpa Joey will be shocked when he sees it."

Andres slid behind the wheel and turned the key. Nothing happened. Josh went to the front and found the release lever. Cautiously, he opened the hood. "Umm, Andres. I'm no mechanic, but it looks like it needs a battery."

"Wait, there's a car battery and a charger in the basement. One of the boys saw it and asked about it. I'll run and get it."

While Andres went to the house, Josh poked around in the car. It was spotless. He opened the glove box and spied the title. He pulled it out and saw it was signed over to him and Andres. Next, he saw the registration and realized the tags were current, good till May of the following year. *Manny took care of everything,* he thought. *Well, probably Padre helped.* He watched as Andres set the battery in place and hooked it up.

Andres slid into the driver's seat. He shouted as he turned the key to on and saw the dash lights flicker, "Holy cow. Seventy-eight thousand miles is all." He cranked the key and the engine fired up. He eased it into reverse and slowly backed into the alley. "We can't go far till we get plates and tags."

"No, we can go as far as we want. The car tags are good till May next year, and the title has been signed over. We both just need to sign it."

They took turns driving slowly around the neighborhood. Josh stopped in front of the Thompsons and tooted the horn. Andres jumped out and ran to the front door and rang the bell. "Would the boys like to take a ride in our new car?"

Mr. T peeked around Andres and yelled, "Don't care about those boys. Great timing, we just got back from church. Let me get my hat." The boys ran out with him and the three jumped into the back seat as Andres eased back into the passenger side.

Mrs. T stood on the porch and waved. She hollered at Andres' open window, "You boys have fun, now."

That evening, crawling into bed, Josh said, "Can you believe our first two days here? We're way more settled because the Thompsons and their two foster boys helped us. A classic car in the garage ready to go, our own home with no mortgage

"It is amazing. I can't get over the Thompsons, them taking in foster kids all these years. I couldn't do that. No way."

"Maybe someday, it does make me wonder." Josh hoped he didn't sound too interested, even though he knew he was.

Why, he hadn't figured out yet. He hoped he ran into Meg from the funeral home some time. She indicated she wasn't interested in kids either, but later, she changed her mind. Why?

"Go to sleep, Josh. I don't want to wonder about kids. No way. Now give me my good night kiss so I can sleep like a baby."

~ * ~

Josh and Andres spent the rest of the summer adjusting to their new home; the creaks and sounds, the space. They set up a guest bedroom, Andres rearranged his studio and built the storage shelves, they worked on the lawn and flower beds. They talked about paint colors for the walls once they stripped the old paper off, new floor coverings or refinishing the hardwood, and wandered through the rooms upstairs. Their consensus was to renovate the two floors into an art gallery and studios. Andres agreed they needed some professional advice, but still loved knocking out some of the walls between the bedrooms. "I'm sure these ones won't matter," he said when Josh came home and found him excitedly swinging a sledge hammer. Both recognized it might take time to do as much of the work themselves on a pay-as-they-went basis; neither wanted to take on a mortgage, at least to start with. About once a week, they got together with the Thompsons to share a meal, grill out, or sample the homebrew that Mr. T helped them make. Nando and Fly were in and out, helping when needed, but became less available once school started.

~ * ~

Thursday, September 10, 2009

Josh jumped off the bus and walked briskly toward South Justine. He always walked fast, even after work. Andres was always yelling at him to slow down and smell the roses. *Typical artist way of thinking,* Josh thought. He always replied, "If we slow down, we'll never get the bushes planted to get any roses for you to smell, now c'mon, keep moving." Usually, they both laughed.

True to form, his mind raced even faster than his feet. Denny James, the architect who specialized in renovating historical buildings, was coming to meet with them at five-thirty. He visited the place several times while the men were at work and said in an email to them that he had a lot of ideas and questions. Josh hoped Andres remembered their meeting and hadn't taken off for some project elsewhere.

He made a mental note to warn, or advise, Andres, how abrupt Denny could be. The man was considered a genius when it came to community redevelopment, building preservation, and converting the old to new uses, yet wasn't known for his tact. Josh also wished he and Andres would have time that evening to discuss the first diary of Josef Sawicki They finished reading it the night before and it was freaking amazing.

The home was quiet, which meant Andres was either in the back apartment, now his studio, or out somewhere. At least he wasn't upstairs, tearing down plaster or banging out some of the walls. Josh feared him knocking out a support wall and causing more expense in the long run. Besides, they didn't even have plans to follow. He hoped Denny could guide them to an architect who could give them some practical advice at a low fee.

He crossed the worn linoleum between their kitchen door and the studio's and heard a brassy-sounding bell ring as Andres yelled, "Holy crap, that's loud." Josh opened the door to see him holding an ancient, wind-up alarm clock. "Look what I found in the basement. I set it so I wouldn't forget our meeting." He seemed pleased as punch with himself. "Isn't it cool?" He gave Josh a hug and a quick kiss. Josh tried not to move during the hug and quickly stepped back as Andres let go. He asked, "Did I get any paint on you?"

Josh looked down the front of his suit and tie. "Nope, not today." Both men laughed. Josh looked across the room. On an easel rested an acrylic painting of the rooming house. "Oh my God, Andres. That is wonderful and captures the essence of this old place perfectly. I love the progression you've made from your first sketches you made before we moved in."

"Thank you. I started it outdoors, then moved in to work on it. I need a little more time. It's my third one and even more realistic. Look at the fine detail."

The front doorbell rang and Andres dashed to open it.

Well, thought Josh, *I didn't warn Andres about Denny.*

Built like the short, stocky, college wrestler he once was, and still wearing a flat-top, Denny rushed in, glanced at the piles of papers, ledgers and photos on the dining room table, sat down at the kitchen table and began pulling papers and notes out of his briefcase, along with a laptop. "You're supposed to have coffee ready," he barked. "Sit down. No, I don't want that instant crap and don't start brewing some now; I have another meeting near Midway."

Josh grabbed a notepad and pen and sat down next to Andres who looked startled.

"Okay, I have lots to tell ya, so pay attention. One, your idea of turning this place into an art gallery with studios is wonderful, even if you don't know what the hell you're doing."

Josh winked at Andres.

"Two," Denny raised his hand, making circles with two fingers. "I've been looking the place over while you've been at work—here's your key back—and this place is well built. You could probably put two more stories on it, but you don't want to, and I'll tell you why. Either of you know anything about historical buildings or the National Register of

Historic Places?" He watched them shake their heads. "Didn't think so. Know the old Goldblatt Brothers Department Store building at Ashland and Forty-Seventh? That's on the list. Up on Pershing Road is the Central Manufacturing District. Cornell Square and Davis Square are too. So is the Old Stone Gate at the Union Stockyards."

He paused as they looked at him in confusion. Jumping up, he pulled a glass out of the cupboard and filled it from the kitchen faucet, took a long drink and refilled it. "Coffee would have been better." He sat down. "Okay, where was I?" He checked his notes. "Oh, yeah. Next, have you two got out into the community yet? Met any movers and shakers? People who know what the heck is going on around here?" He watched them shake their heads. "Didn't think so. Well…"

Andres interrupted, "I kinda see why we might want to meet some community people, but what's the historic register stuff got to do with us?"

"Maybe a lot, maybe nothing, it's something we're going to talk about. First, I'm getting back to you two meeting people around here. Andres, I'm sure you know some artists and struggling galleries close by, but you two have an opportunity to be part of a bigger picture."

He spent the next fifteen minutes telling them about community development and the ups and downs of the Back of the Yards neighborhood. After that, he talked for fifteen minutes about the idea of being on the National Register, the attention it brought, the possible restrictions to rehabbing that could be part of their efforts. He asked them about their ideas for financing the art gallery. "I asked ya in my email. Did you do anything yet?"

"For cripes sake, we're still trying to figure out the place and neighborhood," Josh snapped, feeling a bit defensive.

Denny ignored his tone. "See, I'm a visionary. I think if you formed a nonprofit, got this place listed, and worked with the community leaders, you would have a marvelous opportunity to be a part of this community as it tries to revitalize itself. That synergy will result in opportunities you may not have considered yet. Like public and private grants, even tax credits. Plus, I know of no other old rooming houses on the register in the Chicago area." He paused and pointed his stubby finger at each of them. His voice softened and his pace slowed. "I honestly mean this. I think you two are the ones to pull this off and you will be a tremendous asset in this neighborhood." He stood up and began pacing. "This is about more than showing off the art of you and some of your derelict artist friends, as good as they are, and providing space for studios." He smiled. "This is about offering art lessons to kids and families and seniors. This is about having your exhibitions and other ones for people from this community. This is about getting local people involved with painting murals in the underpasses and public spaces, part of the work you love to do. Am I correct, Andres?"

Andres nodded.

To Josh, his face looked perplexed, as if wondering how Denny knew so much about him. They never met or spoke in person.

Denny marched into the dining room and began poking around at the ledgers and photos Josh moved from the buffet to the table. "What the hell is this stuff? Where did you find it, and what are you going to do with it?"

Josh and Andres scurried across to stand next to him. Josh answered, "Those are everything we found in the buffet. There're diaries in those ledgers. We just finished reading the one written by my great-great-grandfather who built the place and here's the butcher paper he and my great-great-grandmother sketched the plans on."

Denny pulled a chair out and sat down heavily. He inhaled deeply and let out a whistle. "Good grief. Do you know what you might have here?"

"A lot of history, we're thinking," said Josh. "Do you want me to tell you about how the building was built, with a back addition added on shortly after the front foundation was set?"

"I already figured that out." He tapped his foot several times. "I think you have something of historical importance here and maybe you should consider a historical component to the gallery. Now that would be bloody unique; an art gallery, a community art center, plus with the history of the building. My God, what a concept. You two better get your asses out and start meeting people. I'll be back Monday, same time. Damnit, have some coffee ready, at least. Maybe even a sandwich. You two get your heads out of your butts and start thinking big. This ain't going to be some flea-bitten, half-assed grubby gallery run by a bunch of nitwits. Nope, this is going to be great." He jumped up, stuffed his papers away, grabbed his cases and tore off. "My God, what an opportunity." he cried as he slammed the door. He reopened it. "Track down Mona Smith and Enrique Salzmon. Try the community development office, they'll know how to find them. Don't wait." The door slammed again.

Andres pulled two beers out of the ancient fridge. They sat down at the kitchen table and took long swallows. Andres exhaled a deep breath. "My God. He is intense. Does he act that way around everyone?"

Josh nodded and took another long draft.

"Did you get all that? Did he really think we wanted to run a flea-bitten gallery for a bunch of nitwits?" He scratched his armpit and chuckled. "God, that almost hurt. He did get me thinking. Just how firm were our ideas? How were we going to accomplish them? You know," he paused to consider his words. "Isn't it your supervisor who always says, 'failure to plan is planning to fail.'? How realistic were our plans? Had we thought this big? This guy thinks big and seems to plan well."

Josh shook his head. Something made him feel uncomfortable. "No, I hadn't thought much about the needs of the community. I was still excited over inheriting this place, having a place to call our own home, to display your work, plus the work of other young artists. How we were going to do that, I wasn't sure. I first wanted to make sure the building was solid, which we now know it is. Yet," he paused, trying to identify what was niggling at the back of his mind. "I think some of my dreams, and yours, for the place still fit. Don't you?"

Andres gave a slight nod and took another sip of beer. "I have to admit, though, Denny is obnoxious. A real turn-off, yet he just pushed me into a larger realm, expanded my universe. Now what the hell do we do? You're the planning man, I like to float." He grinned and winked.

Josh was quiet, thinking. "I guess I agree. My head is spinning. We need to track down this Mona and Enrique, get more info. I'll google them after we eat. Maybe they can help us better understand the idea of being on the National Register of Historic Places. Tell us how that might affect how we live here and what we can do to the place. Say, you threw something in the crockpot, right?"

"Umm, I got a little distracted with painting today. Sorry. How about my famous quesadillas?"

"Sure, Andres. This will be the third day in a row. Yup, sure, they are famous."

Josh was glad to change the subject, still uncertain as to his feelings about involving the community in their home.

"Well, we could ask Fly over to make his burritos for us."

Josh shook his head emphatically.

While Andres made his famous quesadillas, Josh googled the community development center and began making notes on who to contact. He found several newspaper articles about Mona and Enrique and realized they were active in the efforts to re-energize Back of the Yards and the overall New City area. He also googled how to form a nonprofit organization, and considered asking for additional help from the law firm.

"Andres, this is a lot to consider. I'm not sure I can grasp it all or sense the complexity of Denny's crazy ideas."

"Yeah, my head is still spinning, but I'm truly interested in learning more about the historic registry idea, plus being a part of the community. It's kind of mind-boggling." He flipped the big quesadilla onto a plate, grabbed a fork and shoved them over to Josh. "Tonight is black bean and chicken."

"What was last night?"

"Umm, chicken and, and, pinto beans?"

"They were black beans. Monday was pinto. Hand me some of your homemade salsa out of the fridge, please."

"We ran out, here's *Chi Chi's*. Guess I'm a failure, huh?" He handed another beer to Josh, held onto Josh's hand, and bent over to kiss it. "I'm sure glad you liked that ride on my bike ten years ago."

"That was only because I hadn't had your famous quesadillas yet."

After eating, they showered together in the oversized shower that looked like it was added for an invalid. The markings of an old free-standing tub were still visible on the floor. "Wanna mess around?" Josh wanted a distraction and wrapped his arms around Andres and began kissing his neck.

"Yesss but I thought we were going to discuss Josef's diary. Stop it, unless you're prepared to follow through."

Josh reached out, grabbed a towel and stepped onto the rug. "You're right. I almost got my priorities out of place. After reading Josef, does it seem that horniness may be heredity? Is it something in this house that affects everyone?"

He hoped discussing Josef would ease the uncertainty he was sensing about their future in the old place.

"Yes. Both. I just hope whatever we talk about is important or I may rearrange the priorities."

Josh looked at Andres stepping out of the shower and moaned at the sight. "Oh, to hell with it. You and I need to be a priority right now." He took his hand and led him to their bedroom, both still wet.

After making love, still cuddled in each other's arms, Andres said, "Reading Josef's diary, I realized I am actually a first generation American, at least on my mother's side. I never thought about that. What your great-great-grandparents went through to come here and build this place and establish such deep roots is amazing. But…"

"I know," Josh said, "think about what your mother went through to come here illegally, have you and raise you. I think that's equally amazing. Don't you?"

Andres wriggled out of Josh's arms and sat up. "Mom is amazing, I think I need to tell her that more, and I want to ask what she remembers from crossing into the country with the coyote, the extortionist guide, her mother dealt with." He lightly touched the mole on Josh's left cheek. "Did you notice the mole almost in the same spot on the photo of Josef?"

"I did. Apparently, it skips generations. Josef, Grandpa Joey and me. Hank and Dad didn't have them. How the heck does that work?"

"And your eyes are set slightly close together, too. We should line up photos of you, your dad, grandpa, Hank and Josef to compare."

Josh sat up. "Yes, we should, but right now, I'm still hungry." He looked at the smile spreading across Andres' face. "No, we are not having your famous quesadillas again. I'm ordering a pizza." He jumped up and pulled on his shirt and pants. "Somehow, I want to hear the story of your mother. All of it. You truly are part of the immigrant experience, much closer than I am. I think Josef's story is as poignant as your mom's, still, but somehow, hers seems important to hear. Especially when we're so moved by Josef's story. Think she can come by at the weekend?"

Andres called his mother. "She's been dying for us to invite her and says she's thrilled she won't have to sleep on our old lumpy couch, sniffing paint fumes. She'll bring the train in tomorrow, meet you at the office and come home with you."

Chapter Seven

Bella Briseno Rodriguez

Andres' mom was tiny, maybe five-feet tall, and looked like she was in her mid-thirties, not forty-five. She fell in love with the old place and exclaimed over and over about all the space they had and their idea to turn it into an art gallery. She was enthralled with the old photos and information about the diaries and secrets. Andres didn't tell her much about the community art center idea. It was too soon, and he knew Josh had some reservations. That Friday evening, after dinner, they met in the living room over wine.

"Mom," Andres began, "can you tell us your life story? Until reading the first diary, I never grasped I'm actually a first-generation U.S. citizen. Can you tell us what it was like, coming here, how you met Dad and when you had me?"

Bella paused, and sipped her wine. In a mix of Spanish and English, she began talking. "I guess knowing a bit more about this place does make my story seem less trivial. I just know so many people, mostly Mexicans, who have similar stories that I've never thought much about it. Also, I didn't have time to when you were little. I was too busy."

She took another sip of wine. "My maiden name was Bella Briseno and I am seventeen years and six months older than you." She nodded at Andres, he smiled back. "I arrived in Chicago from the barrios of Mexico City. There were many poor people there and struggling to survive seemed normal to me. My mother, your Grandma Briseno, had almost a full high school education and knew there was life beyond the barrio and wanted better for myself and her. I don't remember my father; he disappeared when

I was little. In 1970, when I was seven, my mother borrowed two-thousand dollars from a distant cousin in Texas who arranged for us to be smuggled into the country. He contracted with a coyote. It would take Mother, with my help, eight years to pay the debt off. The cousin was not a nice man. He had friends in Chicago who collected for him."

Bella leaned back on the couch and stretched; her face somber, like she was remembering the hard times. "The trip was horrible. We were crammed in the back of a big truck with little air. People tried to take my water bottles away from me, or steal our food, but I stayed awake. In the middle of the night, they dropped us off and began sneaking us in small groups across a low spot in the river. I don't remember the name of the farm community in Texas. I do remember sneaking into some barn where we refilled our water bottles, slept in the hay and straw and, before it got light, we got into a camper trailer pulled behind a pickup truck. It was very crowded. At least the windows could open and we got some fresh air. We never got out. When the truck stopped for gas, we had to be quiet so no one would know there were people riding in the trailer; that was illegal. I think people may have been riding in the back of the pickup, too. It had a top over it. The little bathroom in the trailer soon flowed over so the place stunk. We were glad when we were moving, at least there was fresh air coming in."

All three were quiet. Andres wasn't shocked, but near to it. He'd heard snippets of similar stories as a child and just now realized how little he truly knew of his mother's journey and the hardships she endured, as did many others in their Pilsen community. He wondered if Josh had heard of stories like this, and if he knew anyone who experienced such a trip. He glanced at Josh, who looked stunned.

"God, I can't believe how much I took for granted, growing up in the suburbs," Josh said. "I now know better what my great-great-grandfather went through, but to hear your experiences and to realize they are so recent…" He shook his head as if he didn't know what else to say.

Andres, with tears in his eyes, said, "Mom, you have never told me this story with this much detail."

"Why would I? Back then, even today, it's not that unusual. At least, it didn't seem that way until I moved to the suburbs and met all these people who have no idea what many Mexicans and other foreign people have gone through to live here. I began telling my story to kids at the library and the elementary school. Anyway, let me continue before I get too emotional."

Bella stretched and rearranged herself on the couch. "One of Mother's jobs was cleaning the dental office of Art Junior Rodriguez."

She gave a rueful look at Josh. "Beginning to see a connection?"

Josh nodded.

"She did such a good job, he asked her to clean his apartment above the office. His staff of hygienists, receptionists and assistants, all good-looking women, referred to his apartment, some from first-hand knowledge, as the Pilsen Playboy Mansion. I've been told I grew into a tiny, beautiful young woman."

"Um, Mom, you're still beautiful."

"Yes, thank you, it's taken me years to realize that. Your father was not very complimentary after we married. See, I never attended school regularly and could barely read or write Spanish, let alone read or speak much English because I was so busy helping Mother clean the dentist's office, his apartment, plus other homes and businesses. The coyote debt was a huge amount to pay off. She knew she couldn't be free till it was. I was shy and, as I hit my teen years, I saw little future beyond cleaning other people's homes and businesses, marrying someone poor and making babies. Not what my mother originally imagined, but then, Chicago wasn't the promised land Mom envisioned, yet she was always thankful because it was still better than where we came from."

Josh stood. "I need to get another bottle of wine. Your story is making me emotional."

Bella waited till he returned. "I was shocked when the dentist, your dad, who was twice my sixteen year old age, started paying me attention; complimenting me, bringing me little trinkets or jewelry when I was cleaning his apartment and office. Mother and several of the staff warned me that all *El Doctor* was interested in was between my legs, that he would eventually drop me like he had most of his staff. At first, I tried to ignore him, yet I was also intrigued by him. He was very good-looking and charming."

"Must run in the family." Josh winked at Andres.

"Now, Joshua, you be quiet and let me finish. He told me he was in love with me and I was soon enamored with him. One night, he snuck me off to some fancy restaurant. I'd never even been in a real restaurant. He brought me back to his apartment and made tender love to me. I was thrilled." She paused. "I was so naïve. Only sixteen, never dated, watched a lot of Mexican romance shows on TV when I could. Here was a strong, good-looking man with money, telling me he loved me and couldn't live without me. He drove me to this fancy restaurant in his fancy car and the waiter put a white cloth napkin on my lap. Afterward he bowed, scraped and treated us like royalty. My God, I thought I was in heaven and life with him would be like that every day. Of course, I wanted to make love to him. It was so romantic."

Andres opened the bottle of wine. Handing Josh a glass and taking a sip of his, he motioned with his glass for his mom to continue.

"For the next two months, in the evenings and overnight, he acted like I was the only person in his life. I was so in love with him, even though, during the day, he ignored me. 'We told you so,' the other girls and Mom said. I just smiled. I may have been in love, uneducated, even simple, but I was not stupid. I knew how biology between a man and a woman worked. I knew he didn't consistently wear protection, and I soon knew a seed was planted deep inside me. Even after *El Doctor,* I still call him that, appeared to be tiring of me, I simply waited. At first, I was hurt because I realized Mom and the girls were right, but I refused to show it because I knew I was carrying his baby. When I was around ten weeks along; I quietly told Mother and several of the girl staff members. They started to cry or act upset. I told them not to be and that I had an idea. They were shocked but, still, they gave their approval. One day, they watched me slip upstairs shortly after *El Doctor* went home after work. I purposely left the door ajar so they could hear me tell him I was pregnant." Bella shifted in her seat and gave the men a rueful smile. "*El Doctor* hollered, 'Get rid of it. That's your problem. Get an abortion. I'll pay for it, like I have for others.' 'No. I shouted back very loudly so the others could hear me downstairs. You will marry me.' He was so shocked that this quiet little mouse dared yell at him, he roared back at me, 'The hell I will.' He raised his hand as if to slap me.

I screamed. My mother and four angry female employees flew up the stairs, each with a pointy dental instrument clenched in their upraised hands, ready to strike. Each were screaming where they planned to jab their weapon into his body and cut off his manhood."

All three laughed at the image of five angry women ready to attack the man.

"Well, he froze, sat down and said, 'I have to think about this.' The office manager said, 'Good. Now think about this. My husband's brother is a cop. He's patrolling about two blocks away. He hates rapists.' *El Doctor* yelled, 'I'm not a rapist.' and the lady said, 'Bella is only sixteen. He would be glad to arrest you for statutory rape. Think about your practice when that news gets out in this community.'"

Andres laughed, shook his head and looked over at Josh as they sipped their wine. Josh shook his head too and grinned.

Bella smiled, a look of pride on her face, and continued, "We were married at city hall on my seventeenth birthday. There was no celebration. We went back to the apartment and I moved my small bag of clothes into a tiny back bedroom then went downstairs and started cleaning after the last client left. I kept the apartment as well as the clinic spotless and helped my mother on other jobs. You know what?" The men shook their heads, almost giggling at her big grin. "I never quit smiling. No matter how large my tiny body became, I kept smiling like there was no tomorrow."

"Mom, did you want to get pregnant?" Andres asked.

"No, in some way, I loved him, maybe still do in some odd way. I didn't feel as if I purposely trapped him, though that's still his claim. I was definitely naïve. When I realized I was pregnant, I quickly thought up a plan that would be best for my child. I knew it would be a cold, dead marriage, but that there would be income to support my child. That was better than raising a baby by myself, especially when I was young and uneducated. In some ways, some would say I gambled. I did, but I won. Thank God."

Andres' eyes began to tear. Josh shook his head in amazement, reached over and patted Andres' arm. Andres nodded for Bella to continue.

"*El Doctor*, your dad, was delighted when I birthed a son at Cook County Hospital. He acted like he wasn't before, just dropped me and my mother off when I started labor and left. He sure was excited when he brought us home." She paused a moment, as if to think how to say what she wanted to say next. "You see, boys, even if I couldn't put it in words back then, down deep, I knew he would not deny his own flesh and blood. Like his father and grandfather, he was a very proud man. Most proud men want to be seen as providing for their children, even if they don't like, or are unfaithful to, their wife. As long as he didn't physically hurt me, I knew he wouldn't throw me and the baby out. He would never want it said he abandoned his child like his father did his half-brother, your Uncle Manny, God rest his soul." She paused, wiped her eyes. "Andres, I'm so sorry I couldn't figure out how to get here for Manny's funeral. Your father didn't tell me he died till the morning of the service and I couldn't even get a taxi on such short notice. He told me on his way out the door for work."

"Mom, I understand. I knew you always liked Manny and respected him and would have been here if you could. My dad is such a jerk."

Bella nodded. "Let me continue. See, I knew he was always embarrassed over how his father treated Manny. Even though he didn't really like Manny and was very much like his father, I was certain he would not throw his own blood and the mother of his son out on the streets. That was my gamble." She stood up and walked over to Andres.

He stood up.

Hugging him, with tears in her eyes, she added, "It was the best gamble I ever made. His bad attitudes toward me were nothing. Even when he wasn't the best father to you and didn't accept your being a homosexual, I knew he would never disown you. Do you know every time your art or name is in the newspaper, he clips it out and posts it on the bulletin boards in his offices?"

"You gotta be kidding me. Really? The man who hasn't said anything good about me to my face in over ten years follows my art career?" Andres slumped down into his chair and rubbed his eyes, astonished at the fact his father was proud of his accomplishments.

"*Si, si*, son. He does. I think someday, things will get better between you two. He has started asking me about my life now. Not often. He actually attended the ceremony when I became a citizen." Bella pulled Andres' shoulder for him to stand back up.

"Mom, I didn't see him there."

"He was, he stood at the back of the room and snuck out as soon as it was over. He even waved at me."

"Maybe he just didn't want to see me up close, then. This is hard to believe."

"Son, you had to leave right after the ceremony, remember? So, we had little time to talk and I probably didn't tell you."

"Well, I'm still not holding my breath, waiting for him to change."

"No, son, you shouldn't, but neither should you blind yourself to the idea that people can't change. Now, I am tired. I want to go prove that your guest bed is better than your old couch and there are no paint smells in the room. Tomorrow, I will continue my story, there may be more surprises."

~ * ~

In bed, Andres snuggled into Josh's arms. "I can't believe what my mother went through. I'm not sure how to respond, or what to say to her. My word, she is so strong; and so smart. Can you imagine figuring out a plan of action at sixteen when you're pregnant, don't speak English, have little education and little future? It's mind-blowing."

"Andres, your Grandma Briseno must have been strong, too. I mean; to go into debt to someone who could be ripping you off, to risk your life and that of your young daughter's." Josh squeezed Andres. "Obviously, that strength carried down. Look at your life."

"Hell, I've done little compared to them. There's no comparison."

"Ya, ya, ya. Declaring yourself independent at eighteen, living in a van, graduating college in four years without borrowing a dime. Go on, kid yourself. No, you didn't wade the Rio Grande, but you could have frozen to death in your van. I don't see much difference."

Andres turned in Josh's arms and kissed him. "Yup. It took a lot of strength to fall in love with a suburban white Polack, too."

~ * ~

Bella was up Saturday morning when Andres walked out to the smell of coffee. Bella had eggs, bacon and toast lined up, waiting to be prepared. "Son, sleeping in a nice double bed with clean sheets, a pillow and not smelling paint fumes was fantastic. Wait till I tell your father what you plan to do with this place."

"Like he'll care."

She tousled his hair. "Now listen, I want to go to a Mexican store and stock your house up with real Mexican food. Then I will leave some stuff for you in the freezer tomorrow so you will remember me when I go the long way back to Naperville." She laughed. "Actually, I have come to like Naperville, a number of Hispanics moved there, plus other immigrants are scattered around. We have kind of a group that meets at the library. Even your father is surprised how busy I keep myself, now that I don't clean houses to help you through college."

"Mom, I could barely get to sleep last night, thinking about all you told us. You and your mother are amazing. I wished Grandma Briseno was still alive to see how your life has turned out."

"And yours, son." Bella grabbed a napkin and blew her nose. She sat down and poured them each coffee. "There's not a day goes by I don't think of her, or sense she is with me. Sometimes, it's like she's on my shoulder, whispering in my ear. Good things. All good things. Moving to Naperville from Pilsen was a huge adjustment for me. There's no way to get around easily, no buses at the corner, we moved to a subdivision where you can only get around by car or bike or walking a long way. After a few days of feeling sorry for myself, it's like she said, 'Get out of the house. Talk to other people. Help others. Tell your story. Make yourself legal.' So, I did."

"Mom, I still don't know what to say. I love you so much." They stood and hugged.

Josh stumbled out, wiping sleep crumbs from his eyes. "What am I missing?" He sat down as Bella filled a cup for him.

"Coffee, and my son being nice to me so I'll start cooking."

"That's not quite why I was being nice, but I am feeling hungry. Hey, Mom, this just crossed my mind. Does Dad even realize how much you helped me? Not only growing up, mostly me in college? You didn't give me huge sums of money. It was the little things you kept doing for me that were so wonderful. The twenty-dollar bills you'd mail somehow when I was most broke, even the coupons for soap or deodorant were extremely helpful."

"Son, I'm not sure. I think he does. Your father is getting older and is beginning to realize he's not the young stud he thought he was. He's even been paying me more attention, why, he asked to take me out to dinner last week. He was shocked when I told him I had plans. And I did." She laughed. "You should have seen the expression on his face, like he never conceived of the idea his little wetback wife has a life."

After breakfast, they walked toward Jorge's store. On the way, Bella began where she left off the night before. "Andres, when you came home from the hospital, I started to nurse you; but he grabbed you away from me and carried you downstairs and showed you off to the staff and clients. He drove you over to his father's home, next his mother's, they divorced when your dad was in college. Your grandmother Maria sent him home, told him he was a fool, that you were hungry and needed your mother. She yelled at him, 'Next time, bring Bella with you.' The next week, he again brought you over without me. Your Grandma Maria told him he was acting like his *pendejo* father. He only wanted a child to show off and from then on she would visit you with me at the apartment so she knew the baby wouldn't be howling from hunger. I guess your dad just shrugged and left with you still screaming."

Josh put his arms out to stop them as a car sped out of an alley. "Go on, this is fascinating."

"Soon, your father tired of you and only paid attention when you achieved a milestone; crawling, first teeth, first steps, first time you said Papa, threw and kicked a soccer ball. *El Doctor* never took me to any social events, or out to dinner, or took us on a family vacation. I was basically a live-in housekeeper and childcare attendant who he failed to tell others was his legal wife, especially when he brought other women into his bedroom. He rarely yelled at me, unless I wasn't home with something he needed immediately, and he only spoke to me in short sentences, like I was mentally challenged."

Josh looked perplexed. "Andres, have you heard this before? This is amazing. I never knew this."

"I'm amazed too. Mom never spoke much about her relationship with Dad, never complained. Obviously, as I grew older, I could tell what was going on. I knew she didn't want to say anything negative about him. She was very smart in that she let me make up my own mind about him based on my own experiences." He hugged Bella's shoulders.

Josh shook his head. "Bella, Mom, I still don't get how you dealt with such cold treatment. I mean, your husband bringing other women into his bedroom. That must have been humiliating."

"Josh, I tried to take a long view of my life. For Andres' sake, mostly, but also for mine. I always smiled and asked politely when I needed money for groceries or clothes for Andres. *El Doctor* would hand me a wad of bills. He knew I could do little else with the money. I was an illegal who wouldn't leave him without Andres, who was legal along with his father. I was thrilled when Andres started preschool, then kindergarten."

She put her hands out to stop Andres and Josh from going into the cross walk. Neither had noticed the 'don't walk' signal.

"So, every day, I studied each page, each tiny book and each coloring sheet with him. After he was in bed, I stayed up, reviewing the letters, the words, the numbers. I started taking him to the library for children's programs. His teacher told me about them, she told all her students' parents about the programs, apparently to help us become more literate as families. At first, I never asked about books for myself, only for him." She glanced at them as they crossed the walk. "I remember how sometimes the librarian slipped in a little more advanced book and when we returned it, she would ask me if Andres was able to read it. The librarian smiled the first time I replied, 'he couldn't, but I could.' Of course, I covered my mouth in embarrassment, like I'd been caught doing something I shouldn't."

Outside the store, Bella looked away for a moment, a look of surprise on her face, as if she was still astonished at her life.

Inside, Bella loaded the men down with bags from all the food she bought. Exiting the store, she said, "You boys need a good grocery cart; especially now that you don't have three floors to climb and such a nice store so close. I like this store. Maybe I could drive my scooter in here to shop, but I don't think I could carry much home on it. Besides, it would take a long time on the back streets to get here."

"Your scooter! Mom, what the hell are you talking about? I knew you had a bicycle, but a scooter?"

"Yes, I bought a scooter. It's a used one, an old Honda with a fifty-something engine. I keep it in the lawn mower shed and use it when your dad is working. It's very handy." She laughed at the expressions on the men's faces. "How else do you think I get to the library and schools for my volunteer work? I even have a license and a helmet. Next, I'm going to get a car-driver's license and tell your father to give me a car. He doesn't need three anyway."

Andres began laughing so hard, he sat down on a bus bench and slid his bags to the sidewalk. "Oh my God, Mother. You are the bravest, strongest woman I've ever heard of. And Dad doesn't know?"

"He does now. He saw me drive it from the house on my way to the train station. You should have seen the look on his face." Bella giggled and sat down beside Andres as tears of laughter and love rolled down both their cheeks.

Josh stood, laughing and shaking his head. He looked like he was trying not to drop his bags, since he carried the eggs.

After stocking the cupboards and brewing a pot of strong coffee, Bella sat down at the kitchen table and broke several churros into pieces and pushed the plate into the middle of the table. "Sit down, boys. I will tell you more of my story, then I will start cooking for you."

Andres looked at Josh. "That means we'll have enough to eat for a week. Maybe we can get her to come in every weekend so we never have to cook again."

"No, that won't work. Most Saturdays, I tutor Spanish to high school kids. Now, let me see, your grandma died when you were eight, a stroke, she was only forty-five. She was so proud of your school abilities and artwork and the fact I was learning with you." She sighed, blew her nose and added, "That was a rough time with no family around and *El Doctor* so wrapped up in his own world."

Bella took a sip of coffee. "About the time Andres was two and a half, I thought it was time to have a second child. So, I bathed myself in bath oils and wrapped a towel around me. I was once again slender and beautiful after weaning that one," she pointed at Andres who smiled. "One evening, I slipped into *El Doctor's* bedroom. I had not entered there, other than to clean it, since before we were married. 'What do you want?' he asked. I dropped the towel and said, 'it is time Andres had a sister or brother. I think we should try enough times till I know a seed is planted.' At first, I thought he was interested. He eyed me up and down then he looked away from me. 'You dummy,' he said. 'I had a vasectomy six months after Andres was born. Never again will a woman try to claim me with a child. Now go back to your room and never try this again.' I was very disappointed, but refused to let him see that. Still, I didn't know what a vasectomy was. He glanced at me, noticed my confusion and said, 'My God, you are stupid.' He uncovered himself, and tugged out his ball-sack and made the motion of scissors. 'Snip, snip. Those little seeds can't get out anymore. Comprehend?'"

Josh jumped up, almost spilling his coffee mug. "Jesus, Andres. Uncle Manny was right. Your dad is an asshole in as many languages as can be spoken."

"You're right. I hate to say it, but it's true. Grandma Maria says he turned out almost the same as his father. Anyway, let Mom finish."

Bella continued, "I know those feelings very well. Anyway, that was a long time ago. I was very hurt at the time. I just nodded, pulled the towel up around me and slowly walked out of the room. At that point, I didn't realize such a thing was even possible, though when it happened, I was very sad, knowing I would never have another baby to grow up with Andres." She giggled. "I could tell they hadn't cut anything off on the outside, so it must have been something on the inside of his parts. I wondered, why would a true man want to do such a thing? Years later, in the library, I learned how a vasectomy works."

"Some people thought I raised my mother, but that was never true," Andres said. "She was remarkable; learning along with me without me realizing it till I was in fifth grade. We started teaching each other, almost like a competition. By then, she wasn't as embarrassed for others to know she wanted to learn and she would ask my teachers for old textbooks, even the next years', anything she could get her hands on. Early on, Grandma

Maria told Dad to speak English to me, and Mom, Spanish. That's why my English is decent, plus I taught Mom so she speaks well enough now."

Josh interrupted, "How's Grandma Maria doing? I liked her so much at her holiday parties; she acted like she knew me her entire life. Now she has dementia."

"Maria is in a nursing home. She doesn't recognize anyone now. It's so sad. She was such a vibrant person," Bella said. "Anyway, back to Andres and me. I think we kind of raised each other. Sometimes it feels like I'm still raising your father." She laughed and jumped up to grab the coffee mugs and put them in the sink. "Enough of this memory stuff, I have work to do. I will cook. Andres, you should go make art, and Josh, you should go make your bed, start the laundry. Next, you can do the dishes as I dirty them."

The men looked at each other and laughed. In unison, they said, "Yes, Mother."

~ * ~

In the basement, sorting, spraying stains and loading the washer, Josh thought about losing a grandmother, a maternal one, at age eight like Andres did, and how Bella, an immigrant, an illegal in a cold, loveless marriage, still raised an outstanding child.

He wondered how it must have been for his great-great grandparents, Josef and Walentina Sawicki, immigrants from Poland, their language problems, adapting to a different culture, the stockyard smells, building this house, and the many miscarriages Walentina had. *My mother, Marge, could speak to those,* he thought. Only on one occasion did she mention the miscarriages in such a manner that Josh realized the emotional pain and loss she suffered.

Now, hearing Bella's story caused his mind and emotions to rock and roll. He couldn't believe how fortunate he was to know someone like Bella, Andres, and his grandparents. Soon, he would read the rest of the old diaries and learn even more about people of strength. Not magical people. Just hardworking, do what it takes to survive and succeed, people. He rarely used the word blessed. *Religious people overuse it*, he thought. As if some

God somehow reached down and touched their lives, but few, if any, of the others around them. Thankful. Thankful is the word he decided on. Thankful and astounded, yet blessed.

~ * ~

Several hours later, Andres was in his studio, leaving the studio door and the kitchen door open so he could hear his mom if she needed anything. Josh was in the basement, doing laundry. Andres heard the front doorbell ring and Bella trot off to answer it. He moved into the kitchen, enough to see his mother greet Mrs. T at the front door. Mrs. T held a plate of fresh cookies. She said, "Well, this is a surprise. I just baked these for Josh and Andres and there's plenty for you too. I'm Mrs. T. Me and Mr. T live across the street and try to make sure these two keep on the straight and narrow."

Andres watched Bella laugh, wipe her hand on her apron, and stick it out to shake Mrs. T's. "Hi, I'm Bella, Andres' mom. The boys mentioned you a couple of times. I'm glad you live close and keep track of them. I live out in Naperville and don't drive a car. Come on in, I'm making tamales."

"Tamales? Them's those things in corn husks, right? Mr. T picks them up over at Jorge's grocery sometimes, we love them, but then he bugs me to make them. Are they hard to put together?"

"No, come back and I'll show you."

Andres moved back into his studio, still leaving the doors open. He didn't want to break his concentration by getting involved in any conversation. The two talking wouldn't disturb him.

He sensed the two chattering away as they mixed, soaked corn husks and steamed the tamales. Mrs. T told Bella about her years fostering nearly ninety children and the two teens they currently had. Bella talked mostly about her life in Naperville, volunteering in the schools, at the library, tutoring and helping with election days. Bella must have handed Mrs. T a platter of tamales. "This is eighteen; think that will be enough to feed your hungry husband and those big boys?"

"Oh, Lordy, yes. The men are goin' to think they died and went to heaven."

"Mom, are you taking the food out of our mouths just to feed the neighbors?" Andres stepped into the kitchen, a wet paint brush in his hand, as Josh followed with a basket of folded laundry.

"*Muchacho*, when have you ever gone hungry? Look at all those we made to freeze, and these right here are to eat tonight, along with the *sopa de fideo* I'm ready to start." Bella shook a mixing spoon at him. She looked at the expression on Mrs. T's face. "*Sopa de fideo* is Mexican noodle soup. I'm making my own chicken broth from the chicken I cooked for the tamales." She waved the package of noodles she purchased at Jorge's store. "Use these noodles, not spaghetti ones. I don't use bouillon or broth out of a can or box. I only fix the real stuff." She stepped closer to Andres and tapped him with the spoon. "Mrs. T was just telling me how good you two are with her foster boys. You got lots of space now..."

"Mom. Don't go there, you don't need grandkids." He tweaked her cheek and went back to his studio.

Andres heard his mom address Josh. "You think the same way?"

He wanted to hear this. He stood and moved close to the door, enough to see across the landing into the kitchen and he noticed Josh blush and glance around as if to see if Andres was still in the room. "I'm not adamant about *not* having kids. For some reason, it keeps coming up and Andres doesn't seem too receptive to the idea." He smiled. "Yet, anyway. Besides, we got a lot to do with this place." Josh turned and went into the bedroom.

Andres heard Mrs. T whisper loudly to Bella, "Them two would make great parents. Just you wait. I betcha you get grands someday. Jist be patient. Now, I got to be gettin' home. Next time you come in, tell Andres to let me know and we'll have you over for soul food. Bet you don't get much of that out in them fancy suburbs."

"I heard that," Andres called out.

Damn, he thought, *it's getting to be a conspiracy for me to have kids.* He let his mind wander again as he worked with acrylics on a large canvas, an abstract. Often while painting, he thought about other things than what his hands were doing. It was like his mind operated at two levels, his hands with brushes and his mind with something seemingly unrelated. Yet at the end, the brush strokes interrelated and interpreted his thoughts.

Today, he couldn't help but think about his mother's life. As he painted, he imagined her living in the dark barrios of Mexico City, riding on the floor of a camper trailer, bouncing along with the smells and the fear of being apprehended; of arriving in a new city where her language was only spoken in a small area of it; the grayness of Chicago, how she created color and beauty in her life.

He mixed several colors on his well-used palette; then made more strokes with different sized brushes and the new colors. For some reason, greens and blues began to dominate the foreground against a backdrop of dark browns and grays. What about his father? How does one explain a dad who willingly forced his son into independence without a blessing or any support? Who sneered at his art, called him a pansy, even when he won city-wide high school awards. Now he proudly posted clippings of Andres' art achievements, yet had still to communicate that pride to him. What would his dad think about their gallery plans once he heard them?

He started to recall the day he told his father he was gay, but stopped. He shook his head to stop those thoughts. That pain went too deep. He laid his brush down and looked at his painting. At the soothing greens and blues against a cold dark background. He started to smile until his eye caught the slashing red lines and geometric shapes scattered around, some changing from red to orange and purple, not dominating, although definitely a factor in the work. He sighed. Wow, maybe I should see an art therapist. I bet they'd have a field day with this one.

He turned to see his mother standing in the doorway. She softly said, "You're a good story teller. I want to see it again when you've finished it."

"That's funny," he said. "I thought it was finished."

She smiled and walked away.

Andres stood staring at his canvas. I think it captures the darkness she came from, the travails of her trip, the darkness she came to and the gradual color of life she built in spite of everything. He studied it harder. Maybe she was right. Maybe there was something lacking, but what was it? He decided this piece was going on the wall with his unfinished works.

Chapter Eight

The Dots

Sunday morning, both Mona Smith and Enrique Salzmon groaned as they stood up from the kitchen table. Mona exclaimed, "We came for a meeting, not a Mexican Sunday Brunch. I am so stuffed."

Enrique hugged Bella. "What do I tell my wife and kids? I promised to take them out for Sunday dinner today. Now, I'm too full to eat anything."

At the door, they each shook Josh's and Andres' hands. "We are so excited to hear some of your ideas for this place," Mona said. "And we will support you in any way possible. Tell Denny hi, and keep us in touch with your progress." Enrique nodded his agreement and patted his stomach.

Monday, at five-twenty-three p.m., Denny barged into the kitchen, sat down and drained a glass of lemonade. "Now that hit the spot, but you better have some coffee. What the hell's up with these tacos? Tacos are messy. I can't wave my hands around in a meeting and talk with a bloody taco in my hand. I said sandwiches. Jimmy Johns is great for meetings." He crammed half a taco into his mouth and chewed rapidly. Wiping his greasy chin with a napkin, he mumbled, "Oh, damn. Damn, these are good. I forgive you. The beans, those are real beans. Cooked, not the canned crap, right?" He inhaled five tacos and two large helpings of beans and rice before jumping up and clearing off the table as Josh and Andres valiantly rushed to finish eating.

Josh watched Andres, as, still chewing, he poured Denny a large mug of coffee, placed it in front of him and covered the steaming brew with his hand. Denny looked up in surprise. Andres seemed to nervously swallow before saying, "You can thank my mother for most of the food. Now, before you ramp up talking or asking questions, I want to get a word in edgewise and share what we have done since we met last Thursday."

Josh snickered when Andres removed his hand as Denny nodded and lifted the mug to his lips and blew on it. Mimicking Denny, Andres pointed his first finger and made a circle with it. Denny smirked.

"First, we did some talking and I agree we were not thinking big. I agree about your ideas of a community art center, gallery and family history center. Thanks for the direction. Two." He sat down, still with his hand up, both fingers now making circles, just like Denny usually did. "We met with Mona Smith and Enrique Salzmon…"

"Aren't they great?" Denny almost spilled his coffee in excitement.

Josh tried to keep smiling. Yes, they met, and yes, it was exciting, but there was still something floating at the back of his mind that caused him personal concern. He wished he could better articulate what it was so he could talk with Andres about it.

Andres continued. "They are thrilled we contacted them. They heard we inherited the place, knew I was an artist and wondered what our plans were. They came over Sunday morning and stayed three hours. Mom fed them, which probably influenced their decision to get involved. Mona is going to help a lawyer and us with the nonprofit process. Enrique had a few ideas for board members, though we already have several ideas from our contacts. A couple of my artist friends are dying to get involved." He held up his hand toward Denny who appeared ready to start talking. "Three, we did some research into the historical registry component. Mona and Enrique were also thrilled with that idea and want to help with that as well. You need to get us some more info about what we can and cannot do. We've heard some stories that sound quite restrictive."

Josh hoped his nod seemed in full agreement.

Denny stood up and began pacing around the kitchen. "Can I talk now?" He didn't wait for an answer. "Okay, that's fantastic. Now, here's the deal. I can answer all your questions, in due time. I know the horror stories, but in your case, I think the covenants will not be too restrictive. Now listen, I've been doing some thinking and want to get involved more, a lot more with you two; especially now that your brains are headed in a good direction. If all you want is a personal gallery for your nitwit artist friends, tell me now and I'll leave."

A small shudder ran through Josh as he wondered what the heck Denny would say next. He glanced at Andres whose eyes were huge. It looked like he was biting his tongue in order not to explode at Denny's comment.

"Good." Denny continued, seemingly oblivious to how his comment about nitwit friends might be insulting. "I talked with the three owners I'm currently doing restoration projects for. The bottom line is they will allow me to spend up to ten percent of my time on your project. Down the road a way, it may require more of my time and I'll need to charge you then, but it will still be way less than you'd pay with someone else. Plus, I have the contacts and these owners have many more. So, if you want, you now have an almost free architect who will sit on your volunteer board as a consultant on renovating historical structures, plus be the architect of record for this sorry old place." He grinned, pumped his fist and belched.

Andres appeared even more stunned at this latest proclamation. Josh stared at Denny in shock.

Denny glanced at them in wonderment. "What the hell? Don't you understand my English? I just said I want to work with you on this project and three major property owners are so excited over this idea, they will sponsor part of my time!"

Andres let out a huge sigh. "We heard you. You're kidding. Right? For real, you want to help us? Just like that?" He tried to pull Denny into a hug.

Denny lowered his hands and stood there like a stone Buddha.

Josh stepped over and cautiously extended his hand to shake Denny's. Denny laughed, grabbed both men and pulled them into a tight hug. "There're some types of people I only do group hugs with." He slapped their backs hard enough to make them wince. "God, you two are stronger than I thought." He laughed again at the looks on their faces. "Okay, I'm serious now. I know I'm rough around the edges, but my word is gold. Ask around the city and you'll hear the same thing. I would have made a great coach, but I'm one hell of a restoration architect and community developer. Now, I'm not going to be at all your board meetings, especially if it's filled with a bunch of artist friends. When you're talking building stuff, I'll be there. I don't have the time to waste getting waylaid with small talk like most boards do. Second," he stabbed his middle finger into each of their chests. "Josh, you keep the minutes of each meeting and you keep the checkbook and pay the bills. Andres can help if he's any good at that stuff. The message is, don't turn those two functions over to volunteers, especially just starting out with a new board. Got it?"

As they watched Denny turn and whirl out of the house, Josh and Andres nodded like they understood perfectly.

Josh quietly said, "I feel like I was just in a tornado and can't decide if I've survived or not."

"Oh my God, Josh. I feel spun around too, but at least we now have direction for this place. That's wonderful."

Both men sat back down and remained silent with Josh thinking how their lives might never be the same again. He figured Andres was thinking the same thing. Eventually, they stood and put away the food, rinsed the dishes and wiped the counters and table off.

On their way to the living room, Josh pulled the ledger containing Mae's diary. Mae Sawicki was his great-grandmother who was married to Hank Sawicki. The two had ten children. Josh vaguely recalled his grandfather, Joey Sawicki, mentioning two of the boys, the oldest and youngest children, died in wars a little over twenty years apart. After reading his great-great-grandfather's diary which Mae interpreted from Polish, Josh knew she had a marvelous sense of humor and a deep mothering instinct. He and Andres sat next to each other on the couch and began taking turns reading aloud to the other. Josh loved her wit and directness, but something darker kept entering his mind; something about the house.

The following week, they met with the lawyer Mona and Enrique directed them to. He would help them set up a nonprofit, free of charge. He explained the process, their need to develop a board of directors, what they could and could not do as a nonprofit and excitedly spoke of the need for a community art center.

"There are two ways you could do this," he said. "One is to form a nonprofit, and lease building space from someone, like yourselves. The second way would include the building as part of the nonprofit. In other words, the nonprofit would own the property, not you. Actually, this makes the most sense because you own the building and planned to make it into a gallery anyway." He paused and studied the men for a moment. Smiling, he added, "I'm sure the nonprofit could designate living quarters for the directors. That way, you wouldn't be paying property taxes and rent, plus you get a tax donation for gifting the building."

Holy crap, thought Josh. *Now, I know what's been bothering me, what it was I couldn't articulate.* He kept glancing at Andres, trying to catch his eye, warn him this was a big step. Maybe they should go back to their original dreams of a home and art gallery for Andres and his friends. At least focus on leasing out the upper two floors to the nonprofit. Andres was so intent on discussing the paperwork and ideas for forming the board of directors, the time frame and the community that he barely looked at Josh.

Over coffee with the lawyer, Andres said, "I am so excited to get started. We even have a top architect with sponsorship to work with us. Just think what this will mean for the community. I'm beginning to see the need, and love the idea to be involved with something bigger than we originally thought. I think the nonprofit should own the house. It makes the most sense. Start drawing up the papers."

Josh was too stunned to interject his idea to focus on leasing the upper floors.

Why wouldn't it work if he and Andres owned the building and leased the top two floors out to the nonprofit? They would get their own home and could do anything with it they wanted, plus the nonprofit would have a long-term lease for a gallery. That seemed to make so much sense. Why was Andres so quick to jump on the second option?

Both men were quiet as they walked home. Andres skipped and smiled while Josh stared at the ground, wondering if he was wrong to have such misgivings. It felt like they might be giving up their forever home. How was he going to approach Andres who was skipping along on cloud nine? Why didn't he state his feelings during the meeting? After all, he usually took the lead in legal and important situations.

At home, Josh boiled eggs and started putting a Greek salad

together. He warmed some pita bread in the oven as Andres kept chattering about being a part of the community and his new vision for the place. Finally, he asked, "You've been quiet. In fact, you haven't said a word since the lawyer's office. What's wrong?"

"What's wrong? You ask what's wrong?" Josh felt his face flushing, but couldn't stop his rant. "You're running around, babbling about turning this place into a community art center, about turning our home, our home, Andres, into a place that will no longer be our home. Our home! A home we wondered if we could ever have; a home where our roots go back forever. And you wonder what's wrong?" Josh yanked a beer from the fridge, popped the cap onto the floor and took a long drag. He banged it down onto the table, picked it back up and took another slug.

Andres stared at him in shock. He opened the fridge, grabbed a beer, flipped the cap onto the floor and watched it roll around till it landed close to Josh's feet. Josh footed it toward the waste basket. Andres took a long drink, wiped his mouth and sat down at the table. "But I thought you liked the idea of making this place into a community art center. I-I thought…"

"You thought what? Had you truly stopped to think that we could be turning over our home to a nonprofit board of directors who determine the future for this place? A board of directors who could determine our future? A board of nitwit artist friends of yours? Have you…"

"My artist friends are not nitwits! How the hell dare you say that?" Andres jumped up. "God dammit, Josh. What the fuck is going on with you?"

"I'll tell you what the fuck is going on. I have never sensed being at home anyplace I've lived. The best place was Grandpa and Grandma's, and that wasn't my home. It was theirs. Finally, we fall into a place that my great-great grandparents built, that your uncle lived and died in. Now it could be ours till we die and pass it on to our kids. You're all for turning it over to a bunch of people, including some of your nitwit friends, who have no sense of history or belonging; people whose blood doesn't run through the walls here like ours does. And you wonder what the fuck is going on with me?"

"Joshy, oh my Joshy. I don't know…"

"Don't you Joshy me. God damn you, answer my questions."

Andres sat down and patted the table. "Sit down, Josh. Calm down. Let's talk about this."

Josh continued to pace the room. "Josh. You're always the calm one of us two; the one who always says to talk things out. Now," his voice strengthened and became authoritative. "Josh, sit down now."

Josh sat down across from Andres. "I'm sorry. I think I've been letting these feelings build. I couldn't quite identify what was bothering me till that lawyer stated it was better if we turned our house over to the nonprofit. Then it clicked and you seemed to jump on the band wagon without even a thought of what we were doing."

Andres waited a while before speaking. "I guess I didn't realize how deep your feelings were for this place." He paused and took a sip of beer. "You see, I have pretty much felt at home since I met you. I never truly felt at home with my father; my mother, yes. Once they moved out of the city and I met you, well, I knew I was at home. Being together with you is home for me. Where we sleep doesn't matter." He grabbed a napkin and blew his nose. Josh did the same. "Neither of us ever saw this place till the day *Tito* Manny died. I guess I hadn't thought of it as deeply as you. Or felt it as intensely as you. I—I don't know what else to say right now. I've never seen you this upset."

They were both quiet, looking at their beer, the floor, anywhere except at each other. Josh knew Andres was right. He never exploded like this before. What was wrong with him? How had this old wreck of a house burned so deep into his psyche that he blew up when he felt it was threatened? Hell, they only lived in the place a short time, months, not even years. Were his desires for a place to call home so great and yet he never recognized them before? He glanced at Andres who also glanced quickly at him. A tentative smile crossed Andres' face. Josh half-smiled back. "I-I'm really sorry for losing it like that. I'm shocked at myself. I don't understand it. Something about this place being our forever home must have wormed pretty deep." He looked at Andres again and saw the tender, loving look he got on his face whenever he was concerned about Josh or those close to him. "I did hear what you said about being with me felt like home, wherever that is. That was very kind and loving. Part of me feels the same way, but I think part of me wanted a permanent structure to share with you."

Andres stood. "Yeah, I've never got the impression you wanted to spend eternity living in my van." He pulled Josh up from his chair and into a tight hug.

Josh gradually relaxed into the embrace. He nuzzled Andres' cheek. "Thank you," he whispered. "You're right; I didn't want to live in that van." He gave a low chuckle. "Maybe I transferred all my fears of living in your van to the security of this house and now that it may not be our home, I became afraid of living in the van again." He squeezed Andres and kissed his cheek again.

Andres pushed back, but kept his hands on Josh's shoulders. "I think we need to talk some more, take our time. Maybe do one of those things you talk about. What do you call them? A cost to benefit ratio or grid; you know, write down all the plusses and minuses of each option."

"I agree. Though tonight, I just want to be held, drink some wine and read Mae's journal together. Okay?"

Andres opened a bottle of wine, grabbed two glasses and led Josh to the living room couch where the journal waited.

~ * ~

They didn't speak of the house until two weeks later when a large brown envelope arrived in the mail from the lawyer. During that time, they hadn't been tense with each other. Both seemed cognizant of the issue and were able to set it aside as they made plans to form a nonprofit, focusing on recruiting a board of directors; whether their home became part of the new organization or not, both felt the need to help form a nonprofit community art center. Josh kept telling himself there were lots of options to explore that would allow them to keep their forever home. He wasn't sure what those options were, and thus he avoided writing anything down.

When Josh arrived home from work, the envelope sat in the middle of the kitchen table, unopened, the only piece of mail that day. Andres had a chicken roasting in the crockpot and rice on the stove, with the table set. A yellow lined pad and a pencil sat next to each of their placemats. A big plus and minus sign were at the top of each pad. Andres hugged Josh, patted his butt, and said, "I think it's time to talk about the house."

Josh slowly sat down. He wanted to shout, 'hell no, it's not time. We have plenty of time. Let's put this off a while, get all the facts.' He didn't. Instead, he said, "Can we each make our own list to start and then compare?"

"Of course, that's fine." Andres sat down and began making notes.

Josh crossed out the plus and minus signs. *I can't think in those terms yet,* he thought. *I simply want to make a list of the issues, then assign them a plus or minus.* He began his list. After several minutes, he realized each item he was writing down could be a plus or a minus. Inwardly, he frowned. He re-read what he listed. *Oh, I can address this in another way; I'll use the SWOT method we sometimes use with clients: Strengths, Weaknesses, Opportunities, Threats.* He got busy again: Writing, making small notes, drawing arrows. He shook his head. He was going in circles. Why was this so hard? He looked up to see Andres slide a glass of water across the table to him.

"You look like you could use this."

"Thanks. This is harder than I thought. My mind goes all over the place, and everything I note seems like it can go many different ways. No outcomes are perfect and none are all wrong. See, I was really leaning toward us owning the building and leasing out the upper floors. Except the last few weeks other things have hit me."

"Like what?"

"For one, what happens when the lease ran out and the gallery didn't want to renew? Say they needed more space? Do we want to have to find another tenant and be in the property rental business? Two, what happens if the nonprofit can't sustain itself financially or needed to borrow money and has no equity to borrow against? They could go out of business and we'd be back in the property business. Three, what happens if we want to leave the nonprofit; not be a part of it, and move away. What happens then?"

"Just a minute," Andres said. He ran into his studio and returned with a piece of jagged old wallboard; a hand-written saying painted on it. "Maybe this will help. I saw this yesterday in one of the school classrooms, snapped a picture, came home and painted it. I wasn't sure why, but now, well, maybe it's important." He read it out loud then handed it to Josh.

By Steve Jobs, Stanford Commencement Address, 2005
"You can't connect the dots looking forward; you can only connect them looking backwards. So, you have to trust that the dots will somehow connect in your future. You have to trust in something — your gut, destiny, life, karma, whatever. This approach has never let me down, and it has made all the difference in my life."

Josh stood and walked around the kitchen as he read it over several times; the last time out loud. "Since when did you follow entrepreneurs and management gurus? I remember seeing the video of him saying this. I was at an office managers' conference. It's powerful. I think I realize it's not about facing backwards. It's about occasionally looking back to see how well things worked out, then moving forward in some type of faith in the unknown." He plopped into his chair. "My problem is; how far do I trust my gut? Even harder, which way is my gut telling me to go? Insist we keep the house in our name? It's a family tradition. Or let it go and become part of something much bigger than us?"

Andres stood behind Josh, placing his hand on his shoulder. "Sitting here, making notes, I was going in circles, too. I was trying to figure out what was best for you. Not me, not us; mostly you. I remembered this and I realized our dots have connected pretty damn well in the past. Based on that, my choice is to turn the place over to the nonprofit. I think our dots; everyone's dots, will connect in the future, maybe even better than in the past." He squeezed Josh's shoulder. "I know that's a harder decision for you." He lifted the wallboard from Josh and kissed him on the cheek. "Maybe it's because you have so much Polish blood in you. Can we eat? I'm starved."

"So am I, plus, I think you're right. There is something in my family history about owning your own home. I think it started in the old country."

They spoke of other things over dinner. After the table was cleared and dishes done, Josh said, "Can we wait and open the envelope tomorrow?"

"Of course. Have you decided what you want to do? We both must decide together. It's a big step. We each may have to compromise, but with the idea that whichever we choose, we're both equally committed to it."

Josh remained silent, his mind not whirring in circles; which surprised him. Their dots connected well in the past. Why wouldn't they in the future? Still, it was frightening. "Basically, the issue is to include our living quarters with the nonprofit which provides more space and opportunity for the gallery or keep it carved out as our home and rehab the house as we can afford to? Is that the bottom line?"

"That's it." Andres thought for several minutes. "I could certainly live in chaos for a long time until our living quarters are finished. Something is telling me we are on the cusp, how's that for a fancy word, Mr. Legal Man, of something big. Keeping the house could ruin the momentum. Also, the opportunity for confusion between the nonprofit and ourselves will always exist. Would our home ever be truly 'our home'? As scary as it is, especially for you, I still think we need to jump in, turn the whole place over, live on faith that our dots will continue to connect." He paused. "I'm still willing to listen to your arguments against doing so."

Josh's first thought was: *Is this the same carefree guy I fell in love with over ten years ago? Now he's quoting Steve Jobs and sounding like an organizational consultant, a good one.* "Mr. Art Man who sounds like a management consultant, I still have butterflies, big ones, and probably will for some time. I'm with you. Let's jump." He took a sip of wine, looked at the dark grayness outside the window and shuddered a bit. "You know what I feel right now?"

Andres shook his head and raised his shoulders.

"It's a dumb analogy, but I feel like I'm a snowball at the top of a big hill, just starting down. I know I'm going to go faster and faster and get bigger and bigger and I can't stop myself, yet part of me feels that instead of hitting a tree, I'll roll onto smooth, flat ground and the snow will melt quickly and I'll be fine." He sighed and looked down.

Andres' arms encompassed him. "We're both in the snowball, and even if the landing isn't smooth, our dots will still be connecting. Together."

Chapter Nine

The Board of Directors Meeting, May, 2010

By May, the board of directors was formed and met three times, the nonprofit status was achieved and the application for the Historical Register was in process. Denny's initial plans were enough for Andres and Josh, plus several volunteers including Nando and Fly, to begin tearing out the non-supporting walls on the upper floors.

Tonight, the evening before their fourth board of directors meeting, Josh sat at the kitchen table, his fingers flying over his laptop keyboard. Making notes, punching numbers on the keypad, working on a spreadsheet of the construction costs already incurred, and the projected future costs, based upon preliminary reports from Denny. "Sweet man, we're going to run out of money unless this board gets moving."

Andres stopped washing dishes and stepped over. He leaned over Josh's shoulder and pretended to peer at the screen as he slid a wet, soapy finger into Josh's ear.

"Damnit, Andres. I don't need a wet willy. We need money. Quit farting around. This is serious." He shook his head in frustration as Andres pulled a chair out and sat down next to him.

"Yeah. I know. I thought a little soap might clean the gears a bit." He sighed. "Neither of us has started an organization before or worked with a nonprofit board of directors before. Between the money Uncle Manny left and the forty-grand you and I contributed from our savings, are you telling me it's all gone?"

"No, we're down to about fifteen-thousand. When we tell the board members that tomorrow, some of them will think that's a lot of money to play with and the ones that know it's not won't speak up. Jesus, organizing a nonprofit board is the hardest thing we've ever done." He stood up and started drying the dishes. "Right now, drying these seems more logical than beating my head into the table over money. Hey, I need a program report, a paragraph in writing of the contacts and ideas you are forming as Senior Program Director. We need something to report at tomorrow's board meeting. I'm going to pick up some cold cuts and cheese and bread for the meeting. After feeding them fajitas last month, these people are starting to expect a complete meal and we spend more time sharing recipes than discussing finances and development."

"Senior Program Director: what a joke? You're the Executive Director and Chief Finance Officer. I thought boards did more than just give out big-sounding titles."

"Well, half of them are your artist friends. Why are you surprised?" Josh didn't mean to sound peevish, but he was.

Andres gave him the finger and headed toward his studio. "Just don't call them nitwits," he muttered.

Ten members of the board of directors from the now official nonprofit named 'The Rooming House Art Gallery & History Center', squeezed around the dining room table, along with Josh and Andres. Three of the members were community citizens recommended by Mona Smith and Enrique Salzmon from the Community Development Council. Four members were artist friends and contacts of Andres who were excited to get involved. None had been on a nonprofit board before. Jorge, from the neighborhood grocery store, was the president. He was active in the community and supported local art and area beautification projects. He opened the meeting, asked for approval of last month's minutes and welcomed the two new board members recommended by Denny James and approved at the last meeting. Denny was absent. Both new members were women, which brought the total board members to ten with six males and four females, plus Denny as a consulting member. Jorge asked the new members to introduce themselves and tell a bit about their backgrounds and interest in the gallery.

"I'm Synoma Tidwell. I grew up and live here in the community, one of the remaining Eastern Europeans. I'm a consultant for nonprofits,

I'm on the local community development board—that's how I know Mona—and I have a Masters in Organizational Development from Benedictine University. After meeting with Andres last week, I am intrigued by the possibilities this place might bring to the community."

Josh flashed a surprised look at Andres who winked at him with a look that said, 'Guess I forgot to tell you all that'. Josh grinned and winked back. He forgot to tell Andres all the details about their next new member.

"I'm Quianna Morgan. I also grew up in this area, in fact, Synoma and I attended grade school together. My parents were one of the early black families to move into this neighborhood as many of the white families were moving out. Synoma's family welcomed us with open arms."

Synoma laughed. "Well, my grandmother's arms weren't very open. Eventually, she came around after Quianna's mom brought over some peach cobbler and gave her the recipe."

Everyone laughed.

Quianna continued. "That was so true, but she never would try my granny's greens. Anyway, I work in finance at South Shore Bank and I also still live in this community. I hope to bring some expertise in accounting, finance and grants, plus I am fascinated by the historical aspects of the people who lived here that Josh and Andres seem to be discovering. Josh, thank you for sharing some of those photos you've discovered and are still wondering about. I love mysteries!"

"That's wonderful. Welcome, you two," Jorge said. "I remember my family moving into a white neighborhood. First thing my parents did was plant the Virgin Mary in the front yard. Nobody bothered us because most of the neighbors were Catholic, and they had a bathtub Virgin Mary in their yard, too. So, as we walked to the Spanish mass, we'd pass them coming back from their English or Polish mass."

Quianna replied with a smile, "I don't think that would have done much for us. Granny was a staunch Pentecostal and would have had a heart attack if we put a Virgin Mary in the yard."

Jorge smiled, stretched, leaned to his side and pulled out his wallet. He sorted through an assortment of bills and receipts crammed in together. "You mentioned finance and it reminded me I have this bill." He selected a receipt and dropped it in front of Josh. "I ordered a sign to hang off the porch so people would know we exist. It's for, let's see, it's for three hundred and eighty-nine dollars. Josh, next time you're writing checks, just make one out to me. The sign will be delivered next week and you guys can hang it. It won't take much hardware."

Josh looked at Andres in surprise, who, in turn looked just as surprised and shook his head. He didn't know anything about it.

Jorge stuffed his wallet back together and picked up the agenda. "Okay, next item here is a program report from Andres. Let's hear it."

Josh noticed a look of amazement pass between Quianna and Synoma as they looked around the table and noticed no one was questioning the purchase. "Excuse me," Synoma said. "I read through the last month's minutes Josh provided and don't recall a sign being discussed. Was it?"

Josh shook his head as Jorge said, "Well, I guess it wasn't. The guy gave me such a good deal, I figured we'd need one eventually."

"Wait a minute," Sharie snapped. "My background is in graphic design. How will this design fit with our overall plan to have a consistent image? We're not even ready with professional letterhead and envelopes yet, and now we got a dang sign. What gives here?"

Jorge shifted uncomfortably, took a sip of his Coke and said, "Well, I am the president and I thought we needed something to identify us better than rusty old numbers on the porch of this relic."

Voices erupted around the table.

"Unfair!"

"Board presidents can't do stuff like that!"

"How'd you get elected, anyway? I thought you had experience on local boards, that's why I voted for you."

"Man, we don't know what the hell we doin'. I jist want to get some art stuff going for the kids around here. Do we need a dang sign to do that? Them monies coulda bought art supplies and Andres could be giving kids lessons."

Synoma waved her hand till everyone stopped talking and looked at her. Her voice calm, she asked, "What are the policies and procedures for expenditures? Are there job descriptions for board members?" No one had an answer.

"See, we don't know what the hell we doin'. I never heerd of no job description."

Jorge jumped up and grabbed the receipt from in front of Josh. "Screw this crap. I got a grocery to run. I'll cancel the order and get my money back and you all can find a new board president. Call me when you want some donations for snacks and goodies for the kids, but I'm off this board." He slid his agenda over to Ricardo. "You're the Vice President, take over. Just don't go buy a goddamn sign."

There was silence. The members stared after Jorge as he stormed out.

Josh didn't know if he should run after Jorge, take charge of the meeting, tell Ricardo to adjourn it, or what. He'd never been the Executive Director of a nonprofit before. Getting these board members seemed easy and all of them were so enthused. His supervisor's phrase ran through his head, failure to plan meant planning to fail. Just how the hell did you plan for something like this? He glanced at Synoma and Quianna. Neither looked too shocked, although both seemed sad.

Haltingly, Ricardo asked Andres to give his program report. There was little to report and no questions. Aaron, the treasurer, asked Josh to give the financial updates; still no questions. Josh wondered if they didn't understand the reality that the people sitting around this table were responsible to get this organization running. Or what? He wasn't sure.

Synoma smiled at him. She tapped her pen to get attention. "People, I can tell we are all new at this board stuff. This is normal behavior for new organizations with fantastic ideas, but I sense we need some direction. How about if Quianna and I bring some materials next month on board organization?"

Quianna nodded vigorously. The others did too, very half-heartedly.

"Sure," said Ricardo. "Let's do that next month. I move for adjournment."

"First, someone needs to motion that Ricardo be acting President," Synoma said.

Everyone stared at Ricardo. He shrugged. "Sure, just as long as it's not very long. I mostly like to make art."

Someone made the motion. The vote was called for and was unanimous. Someone else quickly made a motion to adjourn.

"Seconded," someone said. There were no objections and no further discussion was made as everyone stood to leave.

So, Josh thought, *that's the end of our fourth board of directors meeting.* Thinking everyone left, he closed his eyes, lowered his head onto the table and covered it with his arms. With a big sigh, he mumbled, "Dammit, Andres. What the hell are we doing? Why is it the people you selected, your artist friends and Jorge the grocer who sponsors street art, all know jack shit about anything but art? We aren't going to make it with this bunch. Your friend Aaron, the treasurer, does he even know how a checkbook works? He's clueless as to a balance sheet. For cripes sake, he sleeps in a hammock in Ricardo's garage and showers over at UIC. You said he'd be a good treasurer because he has an associate's degree in accounting that his parents made him get. That, plus his being one of the best young sculptors in the city, qualifies him to be a fucking treasurer? Jesus, Andres…"

He paused as he realized Andres wasn't responding. Lifting his head, he saw Quianna and Synoma still standing at the table with Andres, who was trying not to burst out laughing. He felt the heat rise on his cheeks. "Oh, God. I'm so sorry. I thought everyone left and I was venting on Andres. Can I just crawl in a hole now?"

"No. How about a beer? Would you two ladies like one? We also have wine. Maybe we can drink Josh's funk away until I kill him for his unkind, devious, malicious words about my friends, most of which were true." Andres pulled out beer and a bottle of wine, plus some glasses and guided them to the living room.

Synoma took a sip of wine. "I'm sure you want to start all over, but the facts are that the same thing might happen again. Plus, this board now has legal entity and responsibility for this place. You do understand that, right?" She looked sharply at Josh. "The bottom line is you don't even own your own home. It appears that this level is currently designated as staff housing, yet technically, the board can fire you and you'd have to move."

Josh slumped further into his chair.

"That's a touchy subject," Andres said. "We do know that. For me, it wasn't that big of a deal. For Josh…Well, I guess he has more family blood spilled here over the years than I do."

They were quiet for several moments before Josh said, "He's right. For some reason, this place quickly absorbed me. I didn't realize how long I wanted a permanent home till we inherited this place. Logically, I've come to the conclusion that turning over the building seemed simpler than forming a nonprofit and leasing the space. Logically."

"I get it," Synoma said. "That is a big step and I appreciate your sacrifice to the community. Plus, I understand you both donated a lot of money toward developing the building in addition to gifting it." She paused and looked encouragingly at Josh. "The good news is I think you're quite secure living here. This board isn't strong enough or together enough to do anything. That's why you two must take more leadership and guide the board. You start making the decisions and let them think they have. At least till it's a stronger group."

Josh tried to smile as he realized they hadn't seen the latest version of plans that included the first-floor apartments. He motioned for Synoma to continue. There was no sense in getting them involved in his intermittent angst.

Instead of Synoma continuing, Quianna stood and refilled her wine glass. "See, you two need a crash course in board and organizational development, which is what Synoma can provide. You also need to move ahead on fund development, which is something I can help with. How many grants have you written, or found someone to write?"

"None," said Andres. He looked dejected.

Josh's mind whirled. *Holy cow, why did we think that just forming a board would automatically begin the fundraising process? What the hell have we gotten ourselves into?*

Synoma noticed their hang-dog looks. "Here's what I suggest, and I think Quianna will agree. She and I have been dying to work on a project together and were thrilled when Denny said he recommended us both to the board. Now, we don't want to take over. If we did, everyone else would drop off and the fact is that some of the members are exactly what you need for the short term. You two need some help and we'll call it crash boot-camp training in board development and grant writing."

Josh and Andres shook their heads to focus and managed to smile in agreement. The four spent the next three hours talking board development and grant writing and made plans to meet weekly. Losing their home still gnawed at Josh, but he needed to remind himself that it was a done deal; that and the excitement of developing something much bigger than himself.

That evening, Josh and Andres went to bed earlier than usual. Neither could get to sleep. Josh sat up and turned on the night stand light. Andres twisted to the end of the bed, sat cross-legged facing Josh, and asked, "That hit you hard again, didn't it? This place not being our forever home."

"Yup. It comes and goes. I get so excited and charged up over what we're starting and then, once in a while, giving up the house kicks me in the gut again." He looked at Andres, gently smiling back at him. "I guess it's something that will just take time. I don't mean to be a bitchy drag about it." Both were quiet, deep in thought for a while. "You know what's been hitting me lately?" Andres shook his head. "What will my grandparents think? We didn't discuss this with them. We both inherited something that has been part of our family for years, decades, over a century in my case. What did we do? That's why I sometimes feel sick."

Andres whispered, "I've had similar thoughts. What would Uncle Manny think? Over fifty years in this place, thirty as the owner."

Josh was silent a minute. He remembered his outburst, what he said about leaving the place to their kids. Swallowing hard, he said, "Also, when I thought of a home, as you know, a few times I've thought of kids, too, which is crazy. I think that slipped out when I was ranting several months ago."

Josh was surprised when Andres calmly replied. "It did. I picked up on that right away and as far as I'm concerned, it's crazy. I know we got all these bedrooms, but they're not going to be bedrooms once this place gets turned into a gallery." Andres jumped abruptly off the bed.

Josh wondered if maybe he was surprised too soon at Andres' calmness. What would his reaction be when he returned to the bedroom?

Andres returned with two glasses of wine. He handed one to Josh, still not smiling. "You know," he said as he carefully slid onto the bed, holding his glass, "I think your history with this place is different, plus you have sisters and come from a huge family. I have few relatives that I've met and only Uncle Manny had a history with this place. You have three generations before you who lived here." He paused, glanced quickly at Josh and away before mumbling, "Besides, I'm still not sure about raising kids. I mean, look at my father and grandfather. I just don't want to talk about it right now. Sorry."

Josh decided to not engage the subject anymore. He wondered though, when or if they could get back to talking about having kids. He noticed Andres shift his body and look at him. He refocused his attention on him and forced a smile. "Well, buddy, it's obvious we can't have children unless we both want them and we have a place for them."

Andres nodded and continued, "While getting the wine, I kept thinking about what Uncle Manny might say. Somehow, knowing his heart just a little, I think he would be glad to see people using this place. See it busy again with people from the community, kids and adults and old folks. He often asked about my art, and one time, he said..." Andres' face now glowed. "Remember our first Thanksgiving when he got us drunk? Well, while you ran to the john, he refilled my glass and said, 'Thank God you're not going to be a dentist. I hope lots of people see your work. Art makes the world go around.' So, I'm not so sure he would be upset with what we're planning."

Both were quiet as they sipped their wine. Josh finished his, climbed off the bed, went to the kitchen and returned with the bottle and refilled their glasses. After several sips, he said, "I agree with you on Manny, I can see him excited as hell over this place becoming a community art center. As for me, realizing how deep my history is connected to this place, it's so hard to see the future, especially our future anyplace else." He took another sip and looked at Andres. *My God,* he thought, *I still love this man, but it's hard to quit thinking about having children someday. Why would Andres, who loves working with children, after all, he's an art teacher, not want to raise children?* He distractedly climbed back onto the bed. *What brought this out? Why now?* It hit him. Andres didn't want to be a father the same way his dad and grandfather parented. He smiled to himself. *That's it. I can live with that for a while. Eventually, I hope I can find a way to move him away from his fear.* "I need some time to adjust to giving away our inheritance. Would you like to split the remaining drips of wine?"

Andres' face lit up. He held out his glass. "Hey, I'm still hungry, I can barely eat during those meetings. Let's go make a sandwich. I need something to absorb the wine you've been forcing down me."

They fixed sandwiches and continued to discuss their feelings about not owning the place. They didn't mention children again. Gradually, Josh became more excited about the community art center as they spoke of their upcoming meetings with Synoma and Quianna. Their need to take hold of and guide the board members to develop a shared vison and mission for their fledgling organization became stronger as they talked.

For me, Josh thought, *it's going to be a roller coaster before things level out. Guess I best hang on tight for the ride. As if possibly raising kids wouldn't be a roller coaster.*

Chapter Ten

Josh and Meg

Several weeks later, on a Saturday morning, Josh came out of the bank after making a deposit of a small donation check and ran into Meg from the funeral home. "What a surprise. I've been thinking about you two," she said. "Hey, you got time for coffee? We've got no roomers today, so I don't have to rush back."

Josh laughed. "It took me a moment to catch what you meant by the word roomers. Yes, I have time."

Over coffee, Josh updated Meg on the plans for the rooming house, although he didn't go into detail about it now being owned by the nonprofit. Meg was excited and thought one of her daughters might be interested in volunteering with the children's programs when they began operations. Josh gathered his courage and blurted out, "Meg, you once said you didn't want children, but changed your mind. What happened? How long did it take for you to change?"

She looked surprised, but she smiled.

"I'm sorry," he added. "I've wanted to talk with you about that a long time. I didn't mean to change the subject or be intrusive."

She laughed. "You are not being intrusive, but it was an abrupt topic change. You're correct. I didn't want children and Roxie did. Over time, she challenged me, nicely, to consider my reasons and fears. It might have taken a good year, maybe year and a half. Looking back, it was a good process. First, I got some help and then we both went to the counselor." Meg sipped her coffee and stretched her long legs. "Why are you asking? Does one of you not want children? Which one?"

"I'm open to it. In fact, I keep thinking about it more and more. Andres doesn't. I think…" he paused to gather his thoughts. "I really think Andres is worried that he might parent like his father and grandfather and doesn't want to put children through the same stuff he experienced."

"Was he abused?"

"No, not physically or sexually. It was more indifference and lack of connection or full acceptance. His dad believes Andres' mother trapped him into marriage by getting pregnant. Get this, she was sixteen and he was thirty-two. Anyway, I think that's his main fear."

"What does he do? Doesn't he work with kids a lot?"

"That's what's crazy. He teaches high school art half-time and is planning on including kids classes at the art center. He's incredible with children. There's just this reluctance…"

Meg was quiet a minute. "You know, I majored in psychology in college, got my Masters, became a certified psychotherapist and never planned on going into the family's funeral home business. Things happened and I ended up being the fourth generation to continue the ownership. I found my educational background and therapy experience came in very handy while working with grief-stricken families." She sipped her coffee. "Although when it came to kids of my own, I had to force myself to consider why I didn't want them. I'm a bit masculine, but lots of masculine women want and have children, so I knew that wasn't it. When I finally got some help, the therapist helped me identify a couple of blockages that occurred through interactions with my parents. It wasn't physical abuse or necessarily emotional abuse. I was able to recollect several interactions and words from my parents that sank deep into me and made me decide I never wanted kids. Gradually, I came to realize my personality and situation was far different than my parents and how I didn't have to parent like them." She waited a few moments before asking, "Do you think Andres would talk with someone about this?"

Josh remained silent, thinking. Finally, he said, "I honestly don't know. In some ways, he's very proud and doesn't like asking for help, yet he has learned to usually trust my opinions and suggestions." He thought some more. "That has been mostly in the areas of organizing his art business and recordkeeping. I really don't know if he would consider a counselor. I'll have to think about it. The reality is we wouldn't have the time or the space for kids right now."

"Space? I understand the time, but space? Good Lord, you've got three floors of rooms. How many bedrooms do you have in just your place? Three? Four?"

Josh held up four fingers. He hadn't meant to bring that issue up. On the other hand, he felt like he and Meg quickly established a trust relationship. She almost felt like an older sister or aunt. "Well, that sort of slipped out. The reality is," he quickly sipped his coffee. "The reality is, the nonprofit, the Rooming House Art Gallery, owns the entire building which includes our current living quarters and Andres' studio. Eventually, we will most likely have to move out." He gave her a rueful smile and shrugged his shoulders.

"Wow. With all the history you two have tied up there, that is a surprise. I don't know what to say." She shook her head in disbelief.

"It is. It feels like this is so much bigger than just us. We discovered several diaries and tons of photos, so we're thinking of including a space that tells the story of the place. The diaries and photos are fascinating and we think will be of great interest to others." He grinned. "Of course, we still don't know where the hell we will live." He checked his watch and stood. "So, in some ways, thinking about kids may be premature, but I needed to talk with someone who's been through something similar, you know, being gay and having kids. Thank you for taking the time to listen. I will think about how to approach Andres regarding a counselor."

"This was no bother. I'm honored you trusted me and will keep everything confidential. However, you might consider both going to counseling." She turned toward him and touched his arm. "Please realize, having, and raising, children is one of the best things that ever happened to me. I have no regrets. Is it easy? Hell, no. Worth it? Hell, yes."

They stepped out onto the sidewalk and turned to hug. Meg slapped her forehead. "It just hit me. Me and my big mouth! Did my comments when you guys were getting out of the van after the funeral set Andres off? Did I start this?"

Josh laughed. "Um, the answer is yes, but don't take it personally. I think those feelings were deep and would have surfaced anyway.

Especially as the desire in me for kids started the minute I realized the place was ours. Either way, we would have been dealing with this eventually."

"Well, I'll understand if he never speaks to me again. I'm sorry."

"Don't be. I think your words just struck a nerve he hadn't dealt with. Thanks for talking and listening. I'd like to do this again."

"So would I. Take care."

On his way home, Josh thought about Meg considering her issues with children. Andres was totally different; still, they had time. He decided not to nag at him, but not to hide his interest either. Somehow, things would work out. If it was meant to be, it would be.

He stopped in Jorge's Grocery to pick up some fresh tamales and horchata. Several days after the board meeting in which he suddenly left the board, Jorge had come over and apologized and said how he hoped he hadn't offended them by resigning so suddenly. He loved the idea for a community art center and would support it, Jorge told them, and he realized he wasn't good board of director material. "I'm too used to making decisions and acting on them," he said. "When I see something that needs to be done, I do it. I don't make an agenda, form some committee and discuss it forever. I'm a good independent businessman, but I'd be lousy in a corporate office somewhere."

Today, he greeted Josh warmly and shook his hand. Josh laughed as he asked, "Jorge, we had a committee meeting and decided Andres and I need some tamales and horchata. Can you approve that decision?"

Jorge wrapped one beefy arm around Josh's neck and gave him a knuckle rub on top of his head. "*Senor* Josh, I think I need to take that to my committee. Come back in three months to see if it's approved."

Walking home, Josh kept rethinking his conversation with Meg. *Why wait to bring it up with Andres? What were the advantages?* He couldn't think of any, but didn't want to hit him over the head about kids. Yet, to Josh, this was an important subject.

That night, over the tamales, horchata, chips and salsa, he tentatively began the conversation. The one he'd been thinking about all afternoon, in between updating the nonprofit's books and preparing the next month's board agenda. "Andres, I ran into Meg from the funeral home today." Andres frowned, yet nodded for him to continue. "I updated her on this place and I asked her something I've wanted to talk with her about since we met."

"Let me guess. You want to move Uncle Manny's urn?"

Andres took a big bite and chewed a moment as Josh wondered if this was going to lead to an argument. He considered dropping the subject, but decided to continue.

Andres swallowed and winked. "You want to prearrange our funerals. Is that it?"

Josh shook his head, trying to smile.

"Oh, I know. It was about having kids."

Josh nodded. "Yup. Please listen, I'm not looking for a fight. Just something I'd like you to think about."

Andres put his fork down. He didn't look angry or happy. Josh took a big breath. "See, I've wanted to talk with her since we met. She mentioned she didn't want children at first and I wanted to know why and what changed her mind. She said there were several experiences with her parents that left an impact. She didn't say what they were, other than that it wasn't physical or verbal abuse. Whatever was said, she decided she didn't ever want children." He paused and looked at Andres.

Andres had his elbow on the table, head resting in his hand, a sober expression on his face. "I'm not sure why you had such a conversation with someone we barely know, but yah, I can relate. Go on."

"I get not knowing her well, but somehow we meshed. She felt like an older sister. Anyway, she said Roxie encouraged her, nicely, to think through what her objections were and to consider talking to someone; a counselor or therapist. That's how she discovered the roadblocks, the interactions she had with her parents that affected her so deeply. I'm not trying to force you into anything. It's just that, someday, I'm strongly interested in considering a family and your abilities with children are phenomenal. You have to realize that. That's all I'll say. I'm asking you to consider it and get some help if needed. Just on that issue, I'd be willing to do it jointly if you wanted. Okay, I'm done." He picked up his fork and attacked his, by now, cold tamale.

Andres looked out the window for a moment. "I'm not mad at you for bringing this up. I'll think more about it. Maybe I do need to identify my hang-ups." He slapped his palm on the table, rattling the plates and glasses.

Josh jumped, his eyes wide, his shoulders starting to tense. With a mock glare of anger, Andres said, "Dammit, that's the only subject I would consider talking with someone else about." He slapped the table again. "Because. I. Am. Perfectly. Normal. And. Don't. Need. Any. Other. Psychological. Help." He stuck his first two fingers in his glass and flicked horchata droplets at Josh. "Now analyze that, counselor."

Josh jumped as Andres roared in laughter.

Chapter Eleven

A Diary Found and Returned—Fall 2010

Other than several supporting posts, the third floor stood open all the way to the walls of the efficiency apartment at the rear. The exterior walls were waiting for insulation to be installed, then dry-walled. Highlighted by the new energy efficient windows and skylights, dust still floated amongst the space. The rear outside decks and stairways were torn off and footings staked out for an addition on the rear, another area waiting for more funds.

"Why don't you tear out the efficiency room walls?" Kate Kozlowski asked Josh and Andres as they entered the old apartment.

Kate, now nearly eighty, was a single pregnant teen in 1950 when Josh's great-grandparents, Hank and Mae, rented her the efficiency apartment on the third floor. Back then the floor was for women. Kate's daughter, Krys, was born in Hank and Mae's bedroom. Kate and Krys lived in the one room, cold water efficiency and shared the toilet closet down the hall. After seven years, they moved down to the rear apartment, now Andres' studio. They lived there until Krys was sixteen. Years later, in 1980, both Kate and Krys were present, along with Manny, when Josh's great-grandmother, Mae, died. According to Josh's Grandpa Joey, his mother always called them her adopted kids. More than once, he reminded Josh that family wasn't always determined by blood.

"Oh, my goodness." Kate exclaimed. "This looks much as it did when Manny moved down to be closer to Mae, I think in the seventies. I can't believe it." She walked around, smiling at the huge, fading sunflowers and Mexican designs painted on the walls and ceiling. "Andres, I think some of your talent comes from your uncle." The ancient refrigerator was a mix of colors resembling a tortoise shell and the small range painted a similar design. "I remember helping Manny paint these walls about a year after he moved in and finished upgrading the other rooms. Krys, look, here's the flowers you painted. Oh, what memories."

Kate's daughter, Krys, and Krys' husband, Tim McGuire, had also come to view the progress at Josh's invitation.

"Aunt Kate," he said on the phone. Josh never knew any other title than Aunt. "Andres and I want you, Krys and Tim, and if your grandkids, Lacie and Nate, are available, to come visit us. We discovered something you might be interested in, plus we'd love to see your reaction to the renovation plans."

"Oh, my goodness, Josh," she said. "Whatever have you found? I heard you have a wonderful architect and can't wait to see the plans."

Josh didn't tell her what they found, but they did arrange a date convenient for the three to come over. Krys' and Tim's son, Nate, was away in college and their daughter, Lacie, was unavailable due to work and grad school. Kate insisted on bringing corn beef sandwiches and potato pancakes from Manny's Deli on South Jefferson. "It was a joke over the years between Andres' Uncle Manny and the family," she said. "He always teased that he owned the place and was the silent non-Jewish owner the family disavowed. He loved their food, 'almost as good as Mexican,' he'd say."

"To answer your question," Andres said, "the plans did call for tearing these walls out. However, when we got this far back, we couldn't keep going."

"For some reason, we both have this feeling that this room should be used for something different," Josh said. "You see, we keep finding things, like photos…"

"Maybe this could be your family photo room," interrupted Krys, her fingers lightly touching the flowers she painted fifty years ago. "Would you keep the walls painted like this? Could they be brightened up?"

"We're not sure. I think all our minds are running the same way, toward keeping this room or at least some of the space available for family remembrances and history," Andres said.

Reaching to the top of an old armoire, he felt around. Not finding anything, he stood on his tiptoes to look across the dusty top. He shook his head in surprise. He opened the doors and ran his hand over the shelves, then opened the drawers. Shaking his head, he said, "We found something we thought you'd be interested in. Both Kate and Krys." He scratched his head and looked at Josh as if asking if Josh put it somewhere.

Josh shook his head. "No, last time I saw it was on top, up there."

Andres turned to Kate. "The neighbor boys and I were pulling this armoire loose from the wall and something fell down. I glanced in it and noticed it was written by you. I set it back on top; or at least thought I did. I told the boys what I thought it was and how excited you'd be when I told you. That's when Josh called and invited you over." He shook his head, an expression of frustration on his face. "Can you give me a few minutes? I'm going to check downstairs just in case I forgot I carried it down there. If I don't see it, I'll run see what the boys might know." He frowned. "I'll be back shortly. Sorry for the confusion." As he walked through the doorway, he smacked his fist into his palm.

Josh looked confused, too. "I'm sorry to drag you out here. Hopefully, Andres figures out where it went." He glanced at the door as Andres hurried down the hall. Rarely had he seen Andres smack his fist into his other hand. He must really be upset.

Kate stared at him for a moment, a glimmer of recognition on her face. "It couldn't be…It couldn't be my old diary. Could it?" Josh nodded. "Oh, my God. That would be wonderful. Just who are these boys Andres mentioned?"

"Their names are Fly and Nando. They are foster boys who live across the street, about sixteen or seventeen, good kids. They've been helping us do some of the rough tear-out work. It's hard to believe they'd take something, but I guess one never knows. Both boys have been through a lot. Still…" His voice trailed off as they heard the front door open and several pairs of feet stomp up the stairs.

Andres, Fly and Nando crowded into the tiny space. Fly held a faded red leather diary. "I-I wasn't stealing this," he said. "I know it looks like it, but please listen to me." He thrust it toward Kate. "You must be Kate. I am so sorry it wasn't here." He lowered his head then shook it as if to clear his mind. "You see, it went down like this. Nando and me and Andres found this when we moved that dresser thing away from the wall. Andres looked in it, seemed all excited and said he knew whose it was and bet they couldn't wait to see it. Then he told us it was an old diary from someone who lived here years ago." He stepped closer and gently placed the diary into Kate's hands. She hugged it to her chest, swallowed, and looked at Fly and Nando as if she was going to speak.

Nando broke in. "Yeah, and while we was working, we started talking about people who might have lived here. You being a woman surprised us. We thought only men lived here. So, we take a break and Fly starts reading some out loud. For a couple of days when we was over here, we'd work, take a break and read a bit more." He stopped and smiled at Kate. "Man, lady, you sure had some life."

Kate, her eyes moist, nodded for them to go on.

Fly started in. "Anyway, early in the week, it was time for us to go home, but we just read about those black dudes comin' over to pick up your boyfriend and go back to the army base and the problems of traveling while black—or Negroes—back then. We didn't want to go without learning more. So, I took it along and told Nando we'd finish reading it at home and bring it back the next day. Well, we didn't work over here the next two days and I didn't know you was coming over today. I'm so sorry. Honest to God, we wasn't tryin' to steal it. We just had to know how things turned out."

Josh listened closely. He noticed Andres doing the same, as if he wasn't sure to believe the boys or not. It was hard to read Andres' expressions or manner, especially when he brushed his hand across his shoulder like something was there. *What did that mean? Was he angry? Embarrassed? Not sure how to react?* He wondered how Andres approached the boys. *What did he say? How did he say it? Were these behaviors something to do with children?* He watched Kate stand and pull both boys over to her. She stared up into their faces as they shifted uneasily on their feet, each of their expressions wondering what this tiny old lady would say to them.

She handed the diary to Krys who also looked like she had no idea what would come out of her mother's mouth. "Boys," Kate finally said.

"I've worked with a lot of people in my eighty long years and I'm a pretty good judge of who's bull-shitting me." She smiled at the shocked look on everyone's faces. "And." She paused as the boys shuffled more, paused as if she wanted them to suffer a bit longer. "And...I believe you." She reached her hands around their necks and pulled their lanky bodies into a hug. "Now, what have you two learned from this experience?"

Krys laughed. "That's my mom. Always looking for the teachable moments in life."

Nando looked at Fly. "I think, I think we should have told Andres or Josh we was reading it, been ready to quit if they said no. But, dang, lady, that's one hell of a story. How could we just up and quit once we started?" He looked at Josh and Andres. "Honest, you two, we're sorry. We should have never opened it. Still, it was like dope, man. Once we started, we was hooked."

Everyone except Andres laughed out loud, though he smiled.

Kate pulled out a dusty kitchen chair and sat down as several tears seeped down her cheeks. "Boys, I'm glad you learned something. Diaries are considered very private, but after nearly sixty years, I'm not sure they should be kept under lock and key. Heck, I even find them for sale in antique shops, so there's no damage done here." She wiped her cheeks. "Yes, I remember this. I thought I lost it and for the life of me, couldn't figure out where." She clutched the leather-covered book to her chest and shook her head, a look of wonderment on her face.

"We found it behind the dresser, between the wall and back, like it fell down there on top of that cross piece nailed to the wall," Fly said. "That piece was hard to get loose, too."

Kate opened the diary. Her eyes moistened again as she glanced through the first few pages. "I think I need to take this home and read it where no one can see me cry. My mother gave me this for high school graduation. She had to sneak it to me so my father didn't know she spent the money on it. Oh, me, oh, my." Turning to her daughter, Krys, she said, "Honey, this is all about meeting your father and our years here till we moved downstairs to the back apartment." She looked around the room and looked at Josh and Andres. "You know; if you're thinking of making this room a family remembrance area, once I read this I'll keep it at home but

I'm open to making copies for you."

"Geez," Josh said, "That would be great."

Fly raised his hand and waved it around like a kid in class with an urgent question. "Can, can you tell us about it sometime? We want to know more about you. You was almost like a foster kid with your parents being so mean and all that." Fly looked surprised when everybody laughed at him. Hanging his head, he said, "Maybe we should just go. I don't wanna embarrass myself anymore."

"Boys, as far as I'm concerned, you have no reason to be embarrassed. I will be glad to come back someday and tell you my story. You should hear about Krys' story too, and Tim's." Kate hugged each boy and led them out of the room. "Now, go tell your foster mom she loves you and so do we."

The five people poked around the third floor, toured the second, looked at the plans, and ended up standing by the dining room table in Josh and Andres' apartment. The table was filled with the ledgers, numerous packages of photos arranged in date order, plus several packets of letters. Kate, Krys and Tim gasped in unison and looked at the guys in confusion.

"Kate," Josh said, "your diary is not the only thing we've found. We're thinking all this stuff might go in that room upstairs. Maybe tell the story of this old place."

"Guys, my brain is spinning with everything I've seen and learned today. I have some questions. Is it all right to change the subject?" Krys asked. When everyone nodded, she continued. "I'm an accountant and Tim and I have done a lot of rehab and renovation work. Just how much is this going to cost and how the heck are you paying for it? I mean, counting the two apartments on the first floor, you must have nearly five thousand square feet and the plans show a sixteen by twenty-four addition with three floors, so that's another thousand square of new construction." She looked at them with a mixture of concern and wonderment.

Andres waved his hand at Josh to signify he would answer the question. "First, this home is now a registered nonprofit. Close your mouths, we'll get back to that in a moment. Second, by the end of the year, we are quite sure we will be approved to be on the National Register of Historic Places. Third, we have received several small grants which are keeping us going, using volunteer labor to do most of the grunt work in tear-out and another one paid for the windows. Fourth, we think a grant is coming through to help us hire a part-time grant writer and development person…"

"Andres, I hate to interrupt," said Krys, "you know I'm a CPA and I want a bottom line. I'm thinking you are looking at four to five-hundred thousand. Am I close?"

Andres stood and asked if anyone wanted water or beer before he said, "Krys, we think you are close. It's going to take a lot of work and our board is slowly moving toward the reality of such. What we haven't shared with them, but plan to at the next meeting, is that as a nonprofit, we can sell something called tax credits through a broker, whereby for-profit businesses buy them which gives us funds and lowers their tax liabilities. We think we will still need to raise at least three-hundred thousand, though." He grinned and looked at Josh. "How'd I do, Mr. CFO?"

Josh gave him the thumbs up.

"Tax credits?" Tim and Krys spoke in unison.

"What a marvelous idea. Do you need some help? I can research the process and provide more information or back-up. It gets quite complicated. My God, what a great idea." Krys jumped up and gave Andres and Josh a hug.

They talked more about the financing issues and ideas for programs. Andres shared they had a small grant to soon start offering art classes in their living and dining room for neighborhood children.

"Just how are you going to do that without getting paint and glue all over your furniture?" Kate demanded. "Not that it's brand new or stylish, but it's still part of your families."

Josh looked at the floor as Andres said, "Most of the furniture is going to the basement for storage. The TV is going into our bedroom. We're clearing out the small bedroom between the dining and living rooms for our office and one bedroom will be for guests. My mom loves to visit us. The other one will be for art supplies."

"How can you do that? Who would expect you to give up your living and dining rooms and a bedroom? This is your house. Can't you wait till you have space upstairs? Plus, they'll be using your bathroom. Can't you just use the little apartment?" Kate looked perplexed.

Josh answered her. "Andres has to have a studio, a place to do his art, or he's not making any money." He paused. This was going to be harder than he thought. Taking a big breath, he said, "First, please understand this whole building and land is now owned by the nonprofit." He scratched his head. "That decision still affects me, but it is our idea, no one else's. Us having the money to transform this place would have taken a long, long time, and second, now we can begin programs in the community to build interest and excitement for what we want to do. This place is going to be more than a gallery. It's going to be a community center for art."

"Third," Andres said, "and this is the part hardest on Josh, eventually, we will move out so this floor can be renovated into classrooms and offices."

Josh looked away, his eyes blurry.

For several minutes, the only sound was the ticking of Mae's old red Aunt Jemima Breakfast Club clock on the kitchen wall. "Wow." Krys exhaled. "I knew you formed a nonprofit, but that element totally escaped me. I don't know how to feel. Part of me is sad that this place isn't truly in the family anymore. Although I understand there is no way you two could quickly fund a major renovation yourselves."

"We're broke," replied Josh. "We each sunk twenty grand into this place, plus most of the money Uncle Manny left us. That's fine, we have no regrets. This place can be something so much greater than the two of us ever imagined the day Manny died." He paused, then whispered, "Folks, this idea is taking off and it's going to be fantastic, not easy, but fantastic. We need our families behind us all the way. Grandpa Joey and Grandma Lisa are; everyone else's emotional support would also be helpful. Somehow, this place felt like a home I wanted forever. Now..." The only sound was the ticking of the clock.

That noise was broken by Kate. "Guys, I think I can speak for the three of us. We were so excited about your double connections to this place; the fact that Manny was like a son to Hank and Mae. You two met and fell in love not realizing, till Manny died, the connections you had. Well..." She took a breath and smiled at them. "Anyway, to see this place stay in the family and now to realize it technically isn't..." Her voice trailed off a moment. "We are also so proud of you two and want you to know we are behind you all the way. What a blessing this will be for the community."

"Besides," Krys said, "including the family history room actually tells the story and continues the Sawicki and Rodriguez spirit. In fact, it will actually spread it even further than it already is."

Kate looked at Tim and winked. "Mister Lawyer, you're changing my will to include this place, too. My two grandkids still won't be hurting when I kick off."

Andres took the three outside and showed what the addition would look like: Where the elevator, accessible bathrooms, kilns for pottery and fused glass, and the storage for art would go.

Back inside, Josh showed them the copies of the diaries they made and placed in three-ring binders. He quickly showed them some of the photo albums, but not the one whose photo dates said they were from the '80's and '90's and all the people looked like folks from concentration camps. The setting was definitely the rooming house. He hoped they found out what the pictures were all about after reading more diaries. Another secret about this old place.

Kate, Tim and Krys left with plans to visit periodically to see the progress on the building. As Josh and Andres sat down in the living room, Grandpa Joey phoned. "Sorry we couldn't be there with Kate, Krys and Tim. I got an idea. I've mentioned Arnaud before, my half-brother, did you realize he's also an accomplished consultant for start-up nonprofits?"

"I'm surprised he's still alive," said Josh. "How old must he be?"

"Well, he's gotta be crowding ninety. Anyway, I think he might be an asset to you two as you try to grow and raise money. I'll call him and update him on the old place and tell him about you two. Don't be surprised if gets in touch with you and wants to help."

"Thanks, Gramps. We'll take all the help we can get. Kate, Krys and Tim are really interested also and want to help in some way. Take care."

Josh and Andres went for a walk around the neighborhood. "I'm wondering about your feelings regarding Fly and Nando," said Josh. "You looked quite upset when you left the room to find the diary. Were you angry?"

"Yeah, I was upset. My mind was running with how I wanted to yell at them. Tell them how disappointed I was. How much I trusted them and they broke that trust." He nudged Josh. "Something told me to shut up and just ask if they'd seen it, even though I knew they were the only ones who knew where it was. As soon as I asked them about it, I could see it wasn't my idea of theft. They insisted on personally giving it back to Kate and explaining." They stopped walking and stood under the soft yellow of a streetlight. "While they were telling all of us about it, I still felt this urge to yell at them and then I grasped how I was hearing my father's words running through my mind. Like he was sitting on my shoulder. I thought about how I didn't want to react the way he used to, so I just listened and truly heard what they were saying. They didn't mean it as anything wrong. Kate handled it so well, she is so amazing. Should we let the boys read the other diaries we copied?"

"Did you know that while the boys were talking, you reached up and brushed your hand across your shoulder? What did that mean?"

"No. I didn't know I did that. I'm not sure what it meant. Maybe I was trying to brush my dad off my shoulder." His face scrunched up in surprise. "Wow! Think that could be it?"

"Andres, I don't know. I think that's an interesting insight to keep in mind."

They began to walk, each deep in their own thoughts. Josh wondered silently if Andres' revelation might affect how he thought about children. Wait and see, he decided. They started to pass by a loud and exuberant volleyball game being played in the front yard under an assortment of lights temporarily strung from the porch and trees. "C'mon and join us," someone called. "We know who you are and where you live, just not your names."

The men joined in and stayed for several beers. This area feels like home, thought Josh. Still, what happens when we have to move out of the house? He took Andres' hand as they walked home in the dark.

~ * ~

Email from Arnaud Sawicki Aubuchon Johnson

September 30, 2010
Fr: Arnaud Sawicki Aubuchon Johnson
To: Josh Sawicki & Andres Rodriguez

Greetings from your ancient great-uncle in Colorado! I recently had a magnificent time speaking with Josh's grandfather who updated me on the two of you and what you are doing. I adore your efforts in turning the rooming house into an art gallery with a room for family memories. After hearing a few snippets of those memories and secrets, I wonder if one room will be enough. I spent one night stay there in 1934, up in one of the rooms. Those memories are still vivid.

I have been successful in real estate development, cattle brokering, horse training, and investments. I now spend most of my time, along with several other ancient persons, consulting for nonprofits, particularly new ones trying to get their boots on the ground, so to speak. I have talked with two of my comrades and we agreed we would love to help you, pro bono. This project is obviously of personal interest to me, but also the idea of developing an art gallery and community art center in a diverse, needy community intrigues the three of us beyond measure.

I will mail several packets of manuals and surveys for you and the board to review. Should you like what you see and complete the surveys, your board of directors will see their strengths and weaknesses in better light.

Now, don't worry. Joey told me some of your frustrations with some of the board members. While some of the current members may not be true board of director material, you will need their help on program and community development committees. Matching up well-meaning volunteers with the right job is important so that both the organization and the individual feels successful and useful.

My two colleagues and I still have enough brain cells left to help you, and thanks to Skype and technology, we can start next week on Friday. That is if you're interested in my help. Now, I know your big worry is about raising more funds and the tax credit details. However, you first must get your cattle in the chute. You probably say get your ducks in a row. Unless you get a plan of action first, you will be running around like drunk cowboys. Making lots of noise and busy, but absolutely ineffective.

Joey mentioned the family records room being your last priority. However, I think it gives you a unique angle for publicity and fundraising. To that end, I am donating some Apple stock to use as a matching gift program. In other words, once you are better organized, your board can approach potential funders and say we have this much already donated, provided we can raise twice that much. That way, you raise money toward the rehab, plus you have the family room funded. Don't worry, I will work with you in any way needed to ensure your success. Also, one of my colleagues is experienced with the tax credit process. What a great idea. I hope you accept my offer and I can't wait to meet Denny James as well. He sounds like my kind of man - benignly obnoxious.

So, round 'em up. We don't have a lot of time and I need to stay alive long enough to be at your grand opening, whenever that is.

With love,
Arnaud Sawicki Aubuchon Johnson

~ * ~

Email reply from Josh and Andres

October 3, 2010
Fr: Josh Sawicki & Andres Rodriguez
To: Arnaud Sawicki Aubuchon Johnson
WOW!!! We are blown away by your kind offer. We checked out your website and are so impressed with the consulting work you have done. YES! We accept your help and your offer to fund the historical room with a matching grant is incredible. We look forward

to Skyping with you this Friday.

Thank you from the bottom of our hearts.

Chapter Twelve

More Discoveries—Marge Sawicki

January 2011

Andres drove the van down the alley toward the back of their home. Light snow covered the back yards and gardens. "Who's that parked in our drive?" he asked.

Josh craned his neck to see a dark sedan with its motor running. "I don't know. Hope it's not someone waiting on a drug deal. Oh, wait. My mom drives a car like that."

Andres pulled onto the cement pad that remained from the garage they and the boys had torn down late in the fall to make room for the addition. Grandpa Joey now cared for the '56 Ford in his garage. Josh climbed down and peered in the sedan. It was his mother. She gave him a tentative smile as she rolled the window down. "Is it okay if I come in?"

"Sure, Mom. I hope you're not cold. This is a surprise."

Josh's mother had not visited the rooming house, nor their former apartment. About once a month they spoke on the phone and caught up on the basics of their lives without going deeper. It wasn't as if they had a big blow-out or major issues. It just seemed that after he left the house to move in with his grandparents, things grew into a cool, unemotional rapport. Growing up, even after he came out, he got along well with his mom, even though she seemed hesitant to confront his father when he made sarcastic or mean remarks. Josh thought it might have embarrassed his mother to tell friends and relatives how Josh moved to his grandparents. Cripes, it sure was more convenient for transportation into the city. Besides, lots of kids moved in with their grandparents during college.

Andres tried to break the tension. "Hi, Marge. Good to see you. Hey, can you give us a hand with some of these groceries? I'll come back out for the construction stuff we picked up."

"Sure, Andres. It's good to see you, too." Marge grabbed several bags and huffed and puffed behind them into the house.

Marge Sawicki looked like an average, short, pudgy, suburban mom or young grandmother. She kept her hair dyed brown, wore loose tops that hid some of her weight, full cut slacks and practical hiking shoes, good for winter wear.

"Mom, would you like a tour of the place as soon as we finish putting the food away?"

"Sure. My God, Josh. I remember this table from when Mae was still alive when your father and I, along with one or two of your big sisters, stopped by to visit her. It surprised me, because your dad never spoke much about his grandparents or where they lived. I only met her a few times, usually at weddings. Why have you kept it? It looks like you've kept some of the other old furniture too."

Josh forced a smile. "Mom, it's better than what we had. I'm a good Polack, remember? Why get rid of it if it still works?"

Marge was quiet as he gave her the tour and explained the plans. Josh couldn't figure out if it was because she was impressed, worried or had something else on her mind. Why did she drop in? Back in the kitchen, he poured coffee for them as they heard Andres pounding on something on one of the upper floors. Both sat down. Josh looked at her expectantly.

His mom sipped her coffee, set it down and gave a big sigh. "I suppose you wonder why I popped in?" Josh nodded. "Well, Grandpa Joey and Grandma Lisa stopped over last week for a drink and they started to tell us all about what you and Andres are doing with this old place. After learning all about your plans, they were so excited for you and kept chattering away. I was so glad to hear all you are doing, too. Your dad, JJ, sat there and I could see he was getting more and more tense. Finally, he said, 'You know we got three other kids, why ain't you talking about them?'"

She shook her head, sipped her coffee, all the while watching Josh intently. He shrugged.

"Anyway, Grandma Lisa stood up and said, 'Listen, son, we just spent New Year's Day with the two of you, your three daughters and their husbands and your four grandkids and we are just as proud of them and if you'd have listened, you would have heard us say so.' Oh, Josh, I tell you, Grandma Lisa was hot. Then she said, 'And who wasn't there that day? And why not?' She even stomped her foot. 'I'll tell you why. Because your only son doesn't feel welcome in the home he grew up in. Because you belittle him and Andres, make snide comments about flaky faggot artists and girly office managers. When your daughters, Josh's sisters, try to change the topic or tell you that's not fair, you yell at them or storm off and sulk somewhere. Now you tell me why Josh and Andres should come for family holidays when you behave that way.'"

Josh smiled. "Wow, Grandma was on a tear. What did Dad do?"

"Well, he started to get up to stomp off, but your grandfather told him to stay put. Grandpa Joey said, 'Son, here's the bottom line. We're going to hold the next holiday get-together at Easter and you are not invited. I don't want to see your face at any more family events until you can act decent and respectful to your son and his partner. I never want to hear you say anything about girly Josh or call Andres a flaky faggot artist. Now, run away and pout someplace, just not at a bar.' Oh, Josh, I feel so terrible about all this."

"Wow. That's pretty amazing. Why do you feel so terrible? You've never been mean to me like Dad."

"Because, son, I've enabled your father for all these years. Trying to excuse his behavior without making waves, trying to keep the peace, speaking with everyone on the side behind his back, I feel like a tug of war rope stretched both ways." She looked at Josh as if to gauge his reaction. He waved his hand for her to go on. "The worst thing is I realized how cool I've been to you all these years since you moved out. That wasn't fair and I'm sorry." She wiped her eyes and blew her nose.

"Mom, I'm not sure what to say. At some level, I realized you were in the middle, that you loved your husband and son, but couldn't make things work. I'm not sure I've been angry with you, just sad that we haven't been able to keep the close relationship we had when I was growing up and through high school. You seemed supportive of me moving to Grandpa's and Grandma's house. After that, things did get cool. You were hard to read." He paused, noticed Andres standing in the doorway and realized he'd heard much of their conversation. He motioned for him to join them, poured a cup of coffee and slid it across the table to him. "I'm glad you came to tell us, but what does this mean now? Has Dad changed recently? Can you tell me he's a new man who wants to know all about his gay son?"

Marge blew her nose again and pulled a fresh tissue out of her clutch to wipe her eyes. "No, I can't tell you he's a new man, though he might be a lonely one. I packed a suitcase and came here. Can I stay with you guys for a few days? Long enough to see if he truly heard me and will start listening to me. On the way out the door, I told him his attitude had to change toward you and Andres, that I couldn't take it anymore. I was leaving him the space and time to think things over. If he doesn't, well, I'll figure something out…"

Josh jumped to his feet, bumping the table, spilling his coffee. "What? You left him? My God, Mom, that's drastic for you."

His mother stood and grabbed the dishrag from the sink and began wiping up the spilled coffee. "Yup. It's very drastic. For me." She tossed the rag toward the sink and started to giggle. Next, she broke into a hearty laugh. "Oh, God. I shouldn't be laughing. This really isn't funny, but it felt so good to see the look on his face when I walked out with my suitcase. He looked like a little boy who just learned Santa Claus isn't real and he didn't know what to do."

Josh and Andres stood and started laughing. Shaking his head, Andres walked over to her. "Mrs. S, you just grew some *cojones*. Some big ones." She giggled as both men pulled her into a hug. "Of course, you can stay here. From what we're learning, you're not the first runaway to stay here."

Their laughter subsided as they hugged tighter. Josh broke away. "Mom, you can stay as long as you need. I do hope this shakes Dad up enough to realize what he has in you. On the other hand, if he doesn't, we could use some good Polish cooking. I'm getting tired of Mexican." He winked at Andres.

"Oh, son. You're just like your father. You only want me to cook and clean up and still work full time as a bank secretary." She smiled at him, then grew serious. "I do apologize to both of you, especially Josh. I should have jumped down his throat when he first got nasty about you being gay. Maybe now I wouldn't have to take this drastic of a step."

"Mom, we forgive you. I'm just glad to see the real you back. Can you handle some pulled pork for dinner? Andres made a great coleslaw, Mexican style. It might make your mouth happy."

The three were quiet for a few minutes. Josh wondered if his mother meant to leave JJ permanently or just long enough to shake him up. He hoped the latter. A thought flashed through his mind. "Mom, I can remember when Dad seemed so excited to spend time with me. I was little. Maybe around kindergarten or early grade school. Why did he change? Why did he become the way he is with me?"

Marge sighed, sat back down and sipped her coffee. Josh and Andres quietly sat down too. "Josh, I've had time to think about this. You know your father was young when we married, eighteen, just eighteen, right after his high school graduation."

"Marge, how old were you?"

"I was twenty-two, almost twenty-three. No, I wasn't a cougar. I was a young widow with three daughters."

"Wow. Josh, did you know this? You never told me." Andres jumped up and began pacing. "So, Josh's sisters aren't really his full sisters? I'd never have guessed by the way everyone acts, even their looks."

"That's because JJ adopted them shortly after we married…"

"I never thought of them as adopted," Josh said. "I guess I'd heard that, or knew it since I was little, but it meant nothing to me. When I was growing up, they were just my big sisters. We were all JJ and Marge Sawicki's kids with the same last name. By the time I was old enough to know what happened, no one else ever brought it up, like my cousins or aunts and uncles." He motioned for Andres to sit back down.

"That's right," Marge continued. "See, Andres, I married Tony, my first husband, right after high school. We grew up together in the same neighborhood, which also included JJ who was Tony's little brother's best friend. We all knew each other, all lived within two blocks, and ran around together. I even babysat JJ a few times when he was nine and I was fourteen. I knew Josh's grandparents, Joey and Lisa, very well. I think I even stayed with them a few times when my family had to go somewhere, probably a basketball tournament for one of my brothers or something." She stood, emptied the coffee pot into her cup and started another brew. "Anyway, I got pregnant shortly after our marriage and Sara Marie was born one month before our first anniversary. Tony and I were just nineteen. Six months later, I got pregnant again." She snickered. "Guess we weren't too consistent with our birth control attempts. The twins, Lisa and Emily, were born when we were both twenty, almost twenty-one. We didn't care. We were young, in love, and Tony had a good job with the family glass business. We lived upstairs in the flat over his parents. We had all these neighbors who helped us, almost like a village. By then, JJ was around fifteen and he was in love with the girls. Whenever he had spare time from football or working, he stopped in. Sometimes he'd help me with the babies, other times he went with Tony on emergency call-outs to replace a window."

Andres poured everyone more coffee and sat, gripping his mug tightly. "How did Tony die?"

Marge waited a moment and took in a big breath. "He was on Southwest Highway, driving one of the glass trucks. You know, those vans modified to hold big sheets of glass on the back?" Andres nodded. "He was coming home, southbound, and just before 111th Street in Worth is a long curve. A guy driving northbound in a pick-up with a big freezer of steaks and seafood in the back swerved into Tony's lane. Tony might have survived the crash, except that the freezer had a broken hinge and the lid snapped off and flew through the windshield and hit Tony in the head. We showed his body at the funeral, but it wasn't Tony." She shuddered. Josh jumped up and grabbed the Kleenex for her. "Give me a minute please, I need to get rid of some of this coffee and pinch my cheeks." She stood and went into the bathroom.

"Did you know all this?" Andres whispered to Josh.

"I don't remember all this detail. I was vaguely aware growing up that Mom was a widow with three little girls when she married my dad. I don't think I ever put it into a timeline perspective or realized he was so young. Man, what a lot of responsibility at eighteen. Plus, I know he started college."

Marge sat down. "I caught what you just said, Josh. Yes, your father took on a lot of responsibility and most people in the neighborhood thought we were crazy. Both of us. Him for marrying a widow with three kids so young. And me for marrying an eighteen-year old kid when I was almost twenty-three with three toddlers."

"Wow." Andres said. "How did Tony's family deal with you marrying again and so soon?"

"Not well. They were so grief-stricken and expected me to mope around with them. I quickly realized their depression was not good for me. Not that I wasn't grieving, but with three babies, I had to go on with life. If not for me, then for them. Plus, I wasn't looking to date that soon. The thing with JJ just happened, gradually for us, though it did seem fast to others, which I understand." Marge paused to wipe her eyes. "Anyway, they sold the business and moved. My letting JJ adopt the kids hurt them. Eventually, they realized the need we felt to be a unified family, plus, they always loved JJ. We kept in touch till the parents died and we still do with Tony's brother."

"What did Grandpa Joey and Grandma Lisa think? They've never mentioned it to me."

"Josh, they accepted the fact that their seventeen-year old son, their only child, fell in love with me. If they had any qualms, they sure hid them well. They knew me well, knew the girls and acted like everything was fine. Which it was. The only thing they asked was that we wait till JJ was eighteen to marry and we try not to get pregnant first. By then, I had a little more self-control with birth control. We managed to wait a year after marrying to start you." She sighed. "Of course, then I had four miscarriages. That was rough. Before, with Tony, I only had to look at him naked and I was pregnant. Your dad worried there was something wrong with him. Plus, he wanted a boy so badly. Especially after he dropped out of college and took a job with the county road department. Later, he switched to the state, IDOT."

"So, Mom, my recollection is right. Dad didn't get frustrated with me until he realized I had little interest in traditional sports, which were his favorites. Is that why he was so bored when I got into scouting and swimming?"

"I think so, son." She took a long sip of coffee. "Your father was an outstanding athlete. Football was his main sport, but he excelled in all. He turned down a full four-year football scholarship to Northern Illinois University in order to stay home with me to play basketball and baseball for Moraine Valley Community College, which is where you went."

Andres gasped, "A full ride? That was a huge sacrifice."

"Yes, it was. I don't want to diminish his love for me and the girls, but I do think he put a lot of hopes and expectations on his only son fulfilling his dreams. I'm not trying to make excuses. Sometimes there are reasons, whether right or wrong. I think the reasons for the poor relationship between you, Josh, and your father are due to his extreme expectations that you would bring the college glory to the family name that he wasn't able to. The fact is, I don't think anyone else in the whole Sawicki family cared about the glory, which only adds to the sadness. Grandpa Joey tried talking to him as it became apparent you weren't going to be a Heisman Trophy Winner, but he wouldn't listen." She paused and thought a moment. "Josh, I love your father deeply, and I hope my departure wakes him up a little. I don't intend to separate, just give him a nudge and hope he relates it with not being invited to Easter. It may take something else. I have no idea what that might be. I'm just taking things one day at a time for now."

"I love you, Mom. I hope this helps Dad change, but I'm not holding my breath. Thanks for sharing all this. A widow, four miscarriages and a husband who is nasty to his gay son because he's not a jock; I don't know. You sure have dealt with a lot."

"I agree, this is amazing. We'll help you anyway we can," Andres said.

"Thank you, boys. You kids, you two and Josh's sisters, have made life more than worthwhile. The fact is, JJ and I love each other deeply, but this has become a mole hill that grew into a mountain. One I won't deal with anymore."

In the shower before going to bed, Josh couldn't stop thinking about his father. How could he be such a jerk about Josh being gay and still be such a good father to his half-sisters? Half-sisters. He never thought of them as that. They were his sisters. They accepted him and supported him as he was. As he always was. With his dad…Maybe…Maybe, Josh being gay was the straw that broke the camel's back. Maybe his father's frustration was over not having a son that could fulfill his dreams, more than him being gay. It didn't seem fair. In fact, was wrong, yet after talking with his mother, Josh got a different sense of what made his father tick. All the sacrifices he made for his wife and family and the only thing he wanted; a son who loved football and sports and engineering, he didn't get. Couldn't have. What a shame to live with those disappointments, even if they were self-inflicted.

Josh dried off and slipped into his winter night clothes, baggy flannel pajama bottoms and a t-shirt. *Dad. My dad. I still feel resentment and hurt, but I do have another perspective on him. Guess life isn't all black and white like I want it…*

That night, it started to snow hard. At four in the morning, Josh awoke to the sound of a snowplow going down the alley. Andres jumped out of bed. "What the heck? The city doesn't plow alleys first. They don't usually get to our street till it's almost melted."

Both stumbled out into the kitchen to peer through the windows. "That's not even a city truck. What the hell is going on? Why would a state truck be plowing our alley?"

Marge joined them and started laughing. "Maybe because Josh's dad works for IDOT. He usually plows I-55, the Stevenson Expressway. That's his truck. I bet he figured out where I'm at and made a little detour. I'm sure he wants to make sure I can get home."

"So, Mom, does that mean you're leaving this morning?"

"Oh, heck no. It's going to take more than that. I'd call that a snow job, wouldn't you?"

Andres put his arm around Marge's shoulders. "I'd say. For all of us. Josh, now we have two vehicles plowed in to shovel out."

All three laughed and headed back to bed.

~ * ~

"So, is the reason you're gay because you had three older sisters to baby and cuddle you?" Andres asked Josh as they snuggled under their blankets to get warm after standing in the cold kitchen with Marge.

Josh snickered. "Of course. Isn't the reason boys turn gay because they have big sisters to mollycoddle them? I don't remember. I've been told they were extremely excited to have a baby in the house. Girl or boy. I was also told how quickly that changed when I started walking and getting into their things." He pulled the covers tighter around his neck. "Being five years younger than the twins pretty much kept us in different worlds. In one way, it wasn't like being an only child, but it wasn't like having siblings close in age either. I always figured we were just a family. I never caught a whiff from my dad that he wasn't my sisters' true father. And they never truly remembered another dad. As we got older, I could tell my sisters were not always happy with the things Dad said to me. However, by the time I hit high school, they were pretty much out of the house and couldn't run interference for me." He yawned and pulled his pillow tighter. "I'm tired, I love you. Good night, again."

Andres squeezed Josh and rolled over to sleep. His mind whirled with the realization of Josh's family situation. JJ, an eighteen-year old kid getting married right after high school and adopting three little girls, giving up a full-ride athletic scholarship, giving up college and a civil engineering career to drive road trucks, then seeing your only son have no interest in the things that were most important to you. It was a lot to absorb. It was frustrating.

He worked his pillow around as he heard Josh's steady breathing. Must be nice not to worry about snoring. He smiled. *Our dads. Guess I never thought deeply about our dads being so similar with their gay sons. I knew we shared similarities, but never fully grasped the depth of those parallels, and the differences. My dad didn't want a kid, felt trapped into marriage, yet developed strong ambitions for me to be a dentist, the third generation. He couldn't understand that my bent was different, just like Josh's was, and neither dad could adjust. It was like each of them was on a one-way train track with no sidings or interchanges or curves to other locations. How sad.*

The real issue is how will I parent? There's no way in hell I want to raise children with all those heavy expectations. Would I? Would I want them to be artists? Or like Josh, organizing everything? Would I always be smacking my hand in my fist when I became frustrated with them? I wouldn't care if they were gay, straight, trans or purple. Would I talk to them about other things the way my father yelled at me? Have all kinds of expectations built up in my mind about what they should do, who they should be? Will I refuse to help then financially if they want to become an accountant, a salesperson, a truck driver? Or if they knock up someone or get pregnant at a young age?

He never fully slept, tossing and turning until the alarm blared.

Damn kids.

What an idea, anyway.

~ * ~

On Wednesday, the men came home from their jobs at about five-thirty to find no one at home. Andres peered out the kitchen window. "Josh, your mother's car is gone."

"I know, here's a note and she left us a plate of freshly baked muffins." Josh stood next to Andres so they could read the note together.

Josh & Andres,

JJ and I spoke at great length this morning on the phone. I think me leaving him and his dad's words about not being welcome at Easter have had some effect. At least enough that I feel comfortable returning home. I do love him and know he loves me. He was in tears several times during our talk. I'm not sure he fully grasps how his actions have hurt the family, but is trying to. That's a start. He knows I will not tolerate any more snide remarks about either of you. I know he's deeply hurt about not being invited to Easter. I'll try to tell him why and how he can change that by his actions after I get home. Change is hard. I can't tell you he's a different man, but I sense a crack in his thought process.

Thanks for everything. I love you two and am so proud of you. I can't wait to come back again!

Mom

Andres put his arm around Josh. "Well, what do you think? How do you feel?"

"I think I have my real mom back. I hope Dad comes around. If he doesn't, he doesn't, and I can't control it." He stepped to the sink, poured a glass of water and took a long drink. "I hope she comes to visit soon so she can cook some Polish for us. Do you realize we went a whole week without quesadillas?"

Andres laughed as he rubbed his eye with his middle finger.

Chapter Thirteen

Friday, April 1, 2011

Padre An tugged the squeaky metal door open and pointed into the dimly lit storage room located on the backside of the church school. "Take what you want. This has been the place where broken tables and chairs go to purgatory. I think it was meant to be a temporary space, like a hospital, where they could be repaired, you know, out of sight, out of mind."

Josh and Andres squeezed into the dank-smelling room. Andres found a light switch and one long florescent bulb flickered on, giving the room an even more garish look. "How many can we take? Do you want them back?"

"Andres, the only way I knew about these was because I'm nosy and found a ring of old keys and tried each one till it opened. I think you'll find enough decent table tops in here and you can scavenger the legs from the other ones. As for the metal chairs, well, sort through them. I'll bet some twisting, a few washers and nuts and good scrubbing will resurrect enough to help you out. Like this one." Padre yanked a chair onto the driveway. He opened it, wiggled it and sat down on it. The chair gradually sunk backward, like the Titanic going down. "Guess not like this one." He pulled another out of the tangle and bounced his butt on it. "See, this one is fine, I think it just got old and rusty. A can of spray paint will make it look new."

Josh sighed. The following Monday, spring break for most of the schools began, and they were starting community art classes for the children. They delivered flyers to the local elementary schools and Jorge passed them out at his store. Josh took this week off as vacation to prepare for the classes, plus the next week to help with registration and whatever was needed. He was physically and emotionally tired. The living room, dining room and one bedroom were completely cleared out and an office set up in the small bedroom between the dining and living rooms. As usual, Andres kept saying not to worry about tables and chairs. Finally, Josh asked him, "Do you expect them to fall from the sky like manna did in the desert for Moses?"

Andres had looked at him with a quizzical expression. "You know, that's a great idea. I've been looking for used ones to buy and they're hard to find. I wonder if Padre and Father Frank have any ideas."

Padre An pulled another chair out. "This is so exciting. What do you think, Josh?"

"Manna from heaven, Padre. Manna from heaven."

Josh grabbed the end of a table, nodded for Andres to grab the other end and the two hauled it out.

"I'm running to the van for my tools. I can repair the tables and chairs right here, and paint them at home." Andres glanced at Josh and winked. "Should be easy painting, now that we have all that empty space." Josh scowled at him.

Three hours later, the men had eight solid folding tables and thirty-six chairs, an office chair that only needed castors, plus several bookcases that Andres quickly rehabilitated. With Padre's assistance, they made two trips to get all the stuff home. Once unloaded into the living room, Andres led them to the basement and pulled out three homebrews and waved them toward the couch and easy chairs that used to reside in the living room. "Have a seat, Padre. You too, Josh. We have plenty of comfort down here now."

Padre looked at Josh. "How you doing with all these changes? This is a big step. Giving up your living and dining room to offer art classes is a real sacrifice."

Josh looked at the floor a moment. "I won't lie, Padre. It has been painful emotionally. When we first inherited the place, the idea of a permanent home sunk in deep and quickly. My head knows this is the right decision, but when I started moving my great-grandparents furniture to the basement and squeezing Manny's records and CDs into our bedroom, well, it really hit me." He took another draft of his homebrew. "On the other hand, I'm excited to know we received a grant to get started with classes and we have about twenty kids registered for next week, plus Andres has almost the same number of volunteers who want to help."

Padre An smirked. "You do realize people in this neighborhood don't always register on schedule, don't you?"

"What's that mean?"

"It means don't be shocked if more kids show up." Padre winked at Josh and stood up. "I've got to run and act like a priest now instead of a junkman. I'll plan on helping you scrub, then paint for several hours tomorrow. I'll see if Father Frank has time. The promise of a homebrew might be enough to entice him away from preparing his homily for Sunday or, at the least, help him keep it short. The man gets long-winded sometimes." He headed toward the stairs, then stopped. "Hey, I might know where there's some bulletin boards you could mount on the walls to show off the kids' artwork. Interested?"

Josh groaned as Andres jumped to his feet. "Of course. C'mon, I'll drive you back and pick them up."

Josh went up the stairs and walked around the bare dining room, empty bedroom, and the living room stacked with old St. Bobola's tables and chairs. *What a loss,* he thought. *What a change of my life. Our lives, I mean. We only have a kitchen and bedroom now. Even our bathroom will be in use by rug rats running around with painty hands. Our kitchen sink will now be used to clean brushes and fill buckets. Who knows what else?*

He eased himself into the recliner they kept in the kitchen, the one Manny died in. *Manny, oh, Uncle Manny. I bet you're laughing your ass off if you can see us. If you can't, then I bet you would be. Heck, you'd be out here, fixing pozole for everyone, or sneaking homebrews to the volunteers. And laughing. I didn't know you well, but I do remember your laugh, especially when Andres and I told you about our follies of being college students and first living together.*

He stretched back in the recliner. *Maybe I'll call Grandpa Joey and Grandma Lisa to see if they want to help scrub and paint tomorrow and Sunday. They are amazing people, accepting my dad's young marriage to a woman with three kids, being so supportive of Andres and me with this old place, plus our desire to turn it into a community art center. Instead, maybe I'll just invite them to stop by next week during classes. Grandma will probably bring a truckload of cookies for the kids and volunteers.*

At the sound of the front door opening and Andres yelling, Josh sat up.

"Hey, Joshy. These are fantastic. Some are even cork. Even a chalkboard. Get out here. I can't wait to fix these up too."

Josh smiled and said, "More manna from heaven? I'm coming."

~ * ~

By four o'clock Sunday afternoon, the volunteers were gone. The third bedroom was now a well-organized art supply room, the little bedroom a neat-looking office, the dining and living rooms transformed into bright and shiny classrooms with freshly painted, brightly-colored tables and chairs, along with bulletin boards mounted on the walls. Andres found some floodlights he aimed at the ceilings to provide extra light. The chalkboard was refreshed and said welcome in English and Spanish with sketches of kids around the edges.

"This is stunning. What a change." Josh kissed Andres' cheek. "I didn't think we'd get everything finished on time."

"Oh, Josh, you always worry." He poked his elbow into Josh's ribs. "To be honest, I was ready to rent tables and chairs which is expensive, then you thought of the manna. Guess God works in mysterious ways after all." He took Josh's hand and slowly walked him through the rooms. "Hey, let's go out for pizza tonight."

"I'm up for that, especially because I can't fix you a formal candle-lit meal to consume in the dining room anymore."

Andres pulled him into a hug and kissed him on the lips. "Oh, Josh, I know what this place means to you and how many dreams you've given up for this project." He kissed him again, deeper, and ground his hips into him. "I love you and I'm confident our dots will keep connecting. I just know things will work out for this place and for us."

Josh stepped back and took a deep breath. "Is it only the dots you want to connect?" He led Andres to the bedroom. Later, they ordered a pizza delivery, and watched a movie from their bed.

Monday, April 4, 2011

At nine a.m., Andres went over the expectations and the projects with his volunteers, a mix of high school and college students, along with several board members. He gave them the names and ages of the twenty-one children signed up and mentioned they might have several last-minute additions and Josh would handle those at the front door. At nine-fifty, a sibling group of five arrived, unregistered. By ten-ten, all twenty-one registered children and an additional fifteen were crowded around the tables with more children and parents waiting on the front porch.

"Padre was right." Josh hurried into the art room and grabbed several pieces of poster board. "Andres, can your volunteers stay for an afternoon class? Say, one to three?"

Andres called out, "Hey, can all you volunteers stay for an afternoon session? Every day this week?"

Most of them hollered yes. One of the board members caught Andres by the arm. "We need more chairs. With eight tables and six to a table we could actually handle forty-eight kids each session. We've got enough volunteers for a one to two or three ratio."

"Yup, great idea. Hey, Josh. Call Padre and tell him the pope wants more chairs over here, like a dozen or more." Andres rushed toward the living room. He turned and called back, "Call Fly and Nando, too."

Josh quickly made up a poster board announcing the afternoon session and hung it in the front window. He also revised his enrollment list to forty-eight kids. Damn, that's a lot of kids to pack in here for five days. On the front porch, he handed out the promotional flyers and tried to explain in Spanish and English that they could take a few more kids in the morning session, and were opening up an afternoon one. The mass of parents and children grew noisier, all crowding around him, trying to get his attention.

All at once, he heard a yell from Fly. "People, relax. Form a line. Be polite. QUIET DOWN." Nando repeated it in Spanish. Slowly, a line formed down the sidewalk and the people quieted. Grinning at Josh, Fly said, "Now, Josh, what is it you want to tell them?"

Josh explained that they could accommodate a few more kids in the morning session and were opening up another session. Everyone got excited and started chattering as the questions flew.

"Can my kids attend both sessions?"

"Will they get snacks?"

"Will they get paint on their clothes?"

"My youngest is three, can he come?"

"I have four children and five dollars per child is a lot to pay each day."

Fly grabbed a flyer and raised his hand to get everyone's attention. "People, read this thing. It's in Spanish and English." He let them glance at it. "Now, all your questions are answered on it. Right?" He raised his voice over the commotion. "Quiet down again. See, preschoolers are not accepted. You are supposed to send the kids with an old shirt to wear. The price is five bucks for the week per kid. You are supposed to send them with a snack, but juice will be served." He looked at Josh and whispered, "Only one session each, right?"

Josh nodded.

Fly raised his voice and informed them of that.

When one mother complained, Nando piped up. "This ain't daycare. It's art lessons. What more do you want for a dollar a day?"

Padre An and Father Frank pulled up to the curb with the trunk open, stuffed with folding chairs. While Josh started registering people and collecting their money, Fly and Nando, along with several waiting dads, started unloading the chairs and hurrying them inside.

One of the dads interrupted Josh. "This afternoon, about three, you leave those rusty ones on the porch. I will come by and take them to my shop and sand and spray paint them. They'll be dry by morning. I have an auto-body shop. I think you have enough to deal with. Especially with all these kids and women."

Several other women recognized the priests and asked Padre An what they could do to help. He led them over to Josh and, after a brief discussion, they agreed to bring snacks for all the children for both sessions and provide extra shirts for painting. Most of the crowd dispersed, some to return at one. Several waited on the porch for the morning session to end.

Josh finished the last registrations, sucked in his breath, and entered the living room, expecting chaos. Instead, he found it noisy, but well organized. Kids and volunteers chatting and laughing as they worked on their projects. Andres gave him a thumbs up. "Andres, what about lunches for your volunteers? Now that they're going to be here longer."

"God, that slipped my mind, it's been so chaotic."

Padre An was near the door. He turned toward them. "I'll run by Jorge's Grocery and have them quick make up some tortas. I'm sure Jorge will be glad to bail us out."

Forty-five minutes later, he returned with enough food to feed half the neighborhood, plus a six-pack of Modelo for Josh and Andres. "Jorge says this is for after the kids leave."

After the volunteers cleaned up and prepped for Tuesday's classes, Josh, Andres, Fly and Nando collapsed into the kitchen chairs. Andres passed the Modelos around.

"Wow, Joshy, we had over eighty kids today. Four times what we expected. I'm glad you put a sign on the porch that registration is filled, unless you want to offer evening classes, too."

"No way, Jose," Nando cried. "Hey, Andres. You got some cute volunteers. Think Fly and me can get their numbers?"

"You'll have to ask them yourselves. They'll think you're wimps if you don't." Andres took a sip of beer and winked at them.

"Don't matter, Nando. We're gonna be up on the north side. Too far to chase girls down here." Fly stretched and took a small sip of his beer.

"North side? What's going on?" Josh leaned forward in his chair.

"Didn't you hear? We're going to a group home. It's up in Rogers Park. Three other dudes. Seems like a cool place. Only problem is we gotta change schools in the middle of the semester, but I think we'll be okay." Fly took another small sip.

"Well, technically, we don't have to change schools, but who the heck wants to commute that far, it would take us close to an hour. We'll be okay." Nando sighed.

"This came up awfully fast, didn't it?" Josh leaned back in his chair. "What will you do in the summer?"

"Yup," Fly said. "We been on a list and all at once, things happened. I liked the staff we met and they said we seemed well trained by Mrs. T. We're moving up there Sunday. The Thompsons are taking us after they go to church."

Nando leaned forward after taking a careful sip of his beer. "We're expected to find a summer job and go to summer school if needed. We'll be cool…"

The four talked a bit more before the boys went home.

Josh opened another beer. "I think we need to do something for them, a little party or something. They've helped us out so much. You should have seen those two take control of the crowd on the porch. Like they'd been organizing mobs forever."

"Joshy, it wasn't a mob. It was just a bunch of anxious parents excited to get their kids into a decent, low cost activity." Andres opened his beer. "Hey, did everyone pay their five bucks per kid?"

"Just about. A couple said they'd bring it tomorrow and one asked if she could pay each day. I said fine. I think the board had a good idea to charge a little bit. This way, even though our costs are covered by the grant, the families are invested in the program, too." He scratched his head. "I think you better add some classes for next week when we start our after school and evening programs. I'm still blown away by over eighty kids."

"I know, I know. I'm thinking for regular afterschool and evening classes we'll limit it to thirty kids, max. Spring break is fun and we can do easy projects. Next week, when we start the after school and evening classes, I want to introduce some real art and work on quality instruction, not just keep 'em busy doing stuff. Some of these kids have some talent." He pulled Josh to a stand and hugged him. "This is so exciting."

Josh snuggled into his arms. "Yes, it is. Yes. It really is." He looked toward the dining room and realized it wasn't a dining room. It was an art classroom and would never be a dining room again. He nestled his head into Andres' neck. "The kids were great. So were their parents. Somehow, it feels like we're part of the community, now."

Over forty children attended each of the two daily sessions during spring break. Several parents brought snacks each day and made sure the volunteers were fed a lunch, usually tortas. On Wednesday and Friday, after the afternoon session, two moms came in and washed the paint off all the chairs and tables.

One even brought an eight-pack of toilet paper and cleaned the bathroom. In Spanish, she told Josh, "You can't clean up after all these kids. This is your home. I wouldn't let all these kids in my house." She stepped from the bathroom into the kitchen. "You two are good men. You'll make good fathers someday." When Josh turned away to blow his nose and wipe his eyes, she scurried over and hugged him.

~ * ~

On Saturday morning, Josh and Andres slept in then went to Jorge's for some groceries. "What? You no want more tortas?" Jorge shouted when they checked out. "Everybody's talking about the classes. How many you got signed up for after school?"

"Well, how many are registered? Or how many will show up?" Andres laughed. "We have set some size limits and broken the age groups down more."

Jorge bagged their groceries and stuffed them into their cart. "I will spread the word. They have to register and pay a little bit."

At home, Andres started to prep for pozole while Josh prepared a cake to bake. "Think the boys will be surprised?" He handed a beater to Andres to lick.

"I think so. All they know is they're coming over with the Thompsons for some snacks and cake and ice cream."

When the Thompsons walked in with Fly and Nando, about ten people jumped up and yelled, "Surprise!"

The boys were shocked. Two of their teachers, a guidance counselor, their case manager, and several volunteers they got to know during the week were excited to attend the last-minute get-together.

Fly wiped his eyes. "I never had a surprise party thrown for me. Hardly ever a party. Thank you."

"Me neither," added Nando. He looked around and whispered to Andres, "You even invited the prettiest girls."

Andres nudged him. "Get their numbers. You're not going to be that far away. They live in Pilsen."

That night, Josh and Andres crawled into bed. "I'm exhausted," Josh said. "What a couple of weeks."

"I know. What are you doing tomorrow? Taking it easy?" Andres scrunched around on their bed to lie facing him.

"Doubt it. I've got another grant to work on, plus begin the reports for the next board meeting. How prepared are you for Monday's classes? You know, I won't be home from work in time to register the new kids or help sign them in."

"I know. I'm not too worried. You've set up a great system and one of the volunteers is a grad student who said she'll handle it. Hey, can you pick up something to eat on your way home? I teach high school Monday, too, and may not have time to put something together."

"Sure, no problem. I'll pick up some more tortas from Jorge."

"Oh, God. Are you trying to pay me back for all my quesadillas?"

Chapter Fourteen

Easter Sunday, April 24, 2011

The driveway and the street parking in front of Grandpa Joey's and Grandma Lisa's small frame house were filled. Andres eased the van to the curb in front of the next home, a two-story brick McMansion. "Hope we don't lower their property values." He glanced over at Josh. "Nervous? Is your dad coming?"

"I have no idea." He leaned toward Andres. "Yes, I'm a bit nervous. Maybe a kiss will settle me down."

Andres quickly complied. "What will the neighbors think? Two men kissing in an old van on Easter Sunday. Hurry, let's get in the house before the police get here."

Josh's grandparents' Cape Cod style home, built in 1943, was well maintained and had a white picket fence around the front and back yard. It was meant to be a starter home. Grandpa Joey and Grandma Lisa loved the neighborhood and instead of moving to a larger home, added a sizeable family room with a fireplace, another bathroom, and a laundry room to the back. As a young boy, Josh always loved the house, especially the upstairs bedrooms with their slanted ceilings and the angled closets and crawlspaces. The house was the last remaining Cape Cod on the street, the others were replaced in the '60s and '70's with step ranches or later with McMansions.

"Bout time you two bums got here." Josh's oldest sister, Sara, gave them each a big hug as a swarm of nieces and nephews rushed up. The hugs were followed by more from Lisa and Emily, Josh's twin sisters, his grandparents, plus solid handshakes from his three brothers-in-law.

Marge stuck her head out of the kitchen and waved them over. She hugged Andres first. "I am so excited you two came. This is wonderful."

Josh wrapped his arms around her. "Thanks, Mom." He kissed her cheek. "Is Dad here?" Marge shook her head. "Is he coming?"

"I don't think so. He told me to go on ahead. He wouldn't confirm he was going to follow." Marge half-smiled. "I think he wanted to. I also think he was extremely embarrassed to come and wasn't sure how to act. He's definitely been better about not saying anything critical about you two when I talk about you, or update him on what you're doing." She shrugged her shoulders. "He's the one with the problem. Anyway, let's have a great time."

She pulled Josh and Andres into the family room. "Hey, everyone! Josh and Andres are going to hide the Easter eggs in the back yard, so all you grandkids go to the living room and wait till we call you."

The kids groaned, but rushed out of the family room. Josh and Andres raced around the yard, trying to hide some eggs that would challenge the older kids. The two laughed when Marge counted down to release the kids into the yard. They came off the porch like the start of the Kentucky Derby.

Josh and his sister, Emily, stood in the yard, watching the kids run around, searching for eggs. The youngest grandchild, Little Joey, four, seemed a bit overwhelmed. They watched Andres take him by the hand and help him find eggs the other kids were missing. "He's wonderful with kids, isn't he?" Emily squeezed Josh's arm. "I heard how he is with the kids' art classes you're offering. Grandpa and Grandma loved their visit during spring break."

"I wish they'd stayed longer. Did they get the paint off of them yet?"

Emily laughed as Little Joey pulled Andres up to them. "Hey, Mom. Andres is cool. Is he your brother, too?"

Emily laughed and squatted down in front of him. "No, Josh is my brother. Andres is Josh's partner, his boyfriend, and they live together."

"Oh, are they like you and Daddy?"

Maggie looked at Josh and Andres who were laughing as they waited for her answer. She pulled the little guy into a hug. "No, they're not married like Mommy and Daddy, but they love each other just the same as if they were."

"Oh. So, what do I call Andres?"

"You can call him Uncle, just like you call Josh. You have two uncles that live together, isn't that cool?"

"Yup. C'mon, Uncle Andres and Uncle Josh, you gotta help me find more eggs cuz I'm the littlest cousin."

Josh and Andres made sure Little Joey found the most eggs.

At the dining table, Little Joey sat between his favorite two uncles. Josh looked around at the happy chatter. A stab of pain went through him. How many family gatherings had he missed? How many had he attended and been miserable when his dad made sarcastic comments? He buttered a roll for Little Joey who beamed up at him as Josh placed it on his plate.

Little Joey chewed a big bite of roll and, his mouth still full, yelled, "I like having Josh and Andres here today. I hope they come back every holiday. Hey. When's Christmas?" He poked Josh. "You gotta come see what Santa brings me, okay?"

Josh laughed with everyone else, even as he felt a twang of regret that his father wasn't there. Couldn't he change?

Walentina's Diary

The following Saturday morning, Josh ran his razor over his neck one last time. As he wiped his face with a hand towel, Andres burst into the bathroom. "Josh, I think I found Walentina's papers! Your great-great-grandmother's. The ones no one could find."

"Where the heck were they?"

"They were under the shelf paper in my paint closet. They're in an old brown envelope. I put them in the chest in the office with all the other diaries and photos."

"Can I at least see them? I want to know what they say. This is exciting. What can we learn about my great-great-grandmother?"

Andres ran to get them. He snickered as he handed them to Josh. "Here. Why don't you read them to me?"

Josh slid the pages out of the envelope. "I can't read these. They're in Polish. We have to find an interpreter." He shook his fist at Andres. "Why didn't you just tell me? I got all excited for nothing. I'll call Grandma Lisa to find a translator."

Josh loosely wrapped his towel around himself and started toward their bedroom. Hearing voices, he jerked to a stop. Clutching the envelope in one hand and his towel in the other, he hissed to Andres, "Why are kids here?"

"Oh, crap. We forgot the time. That's the nine-thirty art class and the volunteer texted me just before I found Walentina's papers and said she was running late. Turn around. I'll bring you some clothes."

Goddammit, Josh thought. *I'm still getting used to this schedule of rug rats in our house. Well, enough of the house to be a pain. It's bad enough our living and dining rooms are now filled with folding tables and metal chairs and we watch TV in the bedroom and our office bedroom is stuffed to the gills with supplies, our guest room barely has room for a guest, and we have classes till eight or later four nights a week and most of the day Saturdays. Now, I guess I must fully dress before leaving my bedroom or carry my clothes to the bathroom on Saturday mornings. Life in a fishbowl. We need a place of our own, but where? When should we start looking? It's not that we can't afford a place. When should we move? We sure as heck don't want to spend time commuting to this place and to our jobs.*

Grumpy, and frustrated he couldn't read Walentina's diary in Polish, he dressed in the bathroom and slipped past the chattering children into the overflowing office. He quickly made copies on the office-sized copier they leased, then placed Walentina's diary in the safe and the copies in the chest. He sat down and started going through the mail. They raised enough money to insulate and drywall the second floor and start the third. They received their approval as an historic landmark and were getting good publicity, which was helping with their fundraising efforts. The tax credit process, though extremely complicated, was well underway and looked promising.

By rights, I should be excited, he thought. Yet something was still missing and it was more than their lack of privacy, or where they would move to. Nor were he and Andres unhappy together. If anything, despite

Josh's feelings about losing the house, they were more content together as they focused on the massive project.

He laid the mail down and sighed. The sound of laughter from the children sounded so wonderful. They still hadn't dealt with that. Having children was the elephant in the room. Yet, how could they deal with it while living in this situation? He stuffed the idea to the back of his mind. *How the heck were the dots going to connect? It's hard to trust the process.*

Chapter Fifteen

Eva Arca

Josh tried to focus on the paperwork in front of him, only to be interrupted by a knock on the door. One of the high school volunteers Andres recruited from the high school art club stood, holding the hand of a small brown-skinned girl with huge brown eyes and black hair. She was dressed in blue jeans, a White Sox shirt and wearing a Sox cap with her long dark braid pulled through the back of it.

"This little girl showed up today, but her parents never registered her and classes started weeks ago and she doesn't know her phone number. Can you help deal with it? Andres is filling in for a sick volunteer. I've got the rowdy bunch today and can't leave them unattended."

"Sure. What's your name?" Josh asked the girl.

"It's Eva. Eva Arca." Her eyes stared directly into his, not at all intimidated by her circumstances.

"Where do you live?"

"I don't know my address. I don't know my phone. I live over there." She pointed vaguely toward the street.

"Hmm, what's your parents' name? Who's your mommy?"

"My mommy's name is Selena Arca. You can't call her. She's in jail. She might have killed someone."

How do you reply to that? Josh paused before responding, "Wow. That's kind of sad. Who are you living with now?"

"I don't know her real name. She says just call her Mrs. T."

Josh thought. Oh, Lord. The past few weeks, it's been so quiet over there. I thought the Thompsons quit taking in foster children after Fly and

Nando moved to the group home. Wonder what they're up to.

Josh looked down at Eva. "Do you live with Mr. and Mrs. Thompson? They're our friends who live across the street."

She nodded. "They're my new foster parents. I've had a bunch."

"Why did you come to the art class?"

"Well, I seed the kids coming in and thought maybe I could meet some, so I just followed them in and did what they did until that big girl counted and said I was an extra. Can I go do art now?"

"Does Mrs. T know you're here? Did she give you permission?"

"No. Why's she need to know?"

"Maybe because she's worried about you? Did you think of that?"

"Nah, foster parents don't care. I wanna go make art now."

"Tell you what, I'll let you make art, but I'm going across the street to tell Mrs. T where you are and if she says you have to come home, then you must go home. Understand?"

Eva flashed a smile that said she just won this battle.

Josh led her out to the tables and quietly told the volunteer and Andres he'd be right back. As he opened the front door, Mrs. T sped up the front porch steps. "Have you seen a little girl? 'Bout this high? I was on the toilet, Mr. T is at the grocery, and that little mite wasn't watchin' the TV when I came out, so I started looking around the streets and noticed you all got a bunch of kids over here."

"She's here. She's a cutie. I told her I was going to tell you where she was and ask if it was okay for her to stay and make art. Is it?"

Mrs. T shook her head. "By rights, I shouldn't, just to teach her she needs to talk to me about what she wants to do. She's an independent one, but she's had to be. I thinks we're bout the eighth foster home she's been in since she was three. She's five now, headin' for six. Yes, yes. She can stay. I'll be watchin' for when she comes out. Thank you most kindly."

Josh was shocked. He stepped outside onto the porch, closer to Mrs. T. "Eight foster homes in less than three years?" He heard the door squeak behind him and realized Andres stood in the doorway, watching them. "I can't grasp that. Does she know who her mother is?"

"Yes and no. She's had some visits with her momma, supervised ones. She'll have more if I got anything to say about it. Eva says she remembers her, but some of her foster mothers have asked her to call them 'mom' and that just confuses her, as far as I'm concerned. That's why I ask all my fosters to call us Mrs. T and Mr. T. They don't need to be confused any further if and when they see their real momma." Mrs. T smiled at Andres as he came up to them. "I 'spect, once she's settled in a while, Eva will ask 'bout her real momma. I'll tell her the truth, and that includes the fact her momma loves her. I never tells them their kin folk don't love em and was bad people. They jist did some bad things." She shook her head. "It's jist gonna be a long, long time, if ever, before Eva sees her momma as a free woman."

The three were silent.

Andres cleared his throat. "Hey, I thought maybe you two quit taking care of kids. Two weeks ago, you told us you were out of the business."

"Well, we thought we were finished, too. Told the agency we didn't want any more teens, and to keep our license open and that once in a great while, we'd take an infant on an emergency basis. Just for a few nights, you know. Last week, they called and said they had to get Eva out, her foster parents were tellin' stories on her and they figured out Eva was fine, it was the adults who were the problem and they needed to get her out fast. So, we took her." She pulled her thick glasses off and wiped them with the ever-present lace hanky from her bra. "Told the caseworker we'd give her a week or two to find a good placement. Well, the case manager called and said Eva has a three-year old brother and his foster parents were old and decided they couldn't care for him anymore and gave their thirty-day notice. Then she asked if we could take him as well. That was last night. So, Mr. T and I spoke and decided we was bored and might as well take them both for as long as we can stay healthy." She paused and looked like she didn't believe they were doing this again. "First, I told her, we're older than them other foster parents are, how come you're asking us? And she said, 'You're younger in spirit.' She should know, she was one of our foster kids who got herself educated and now is paying it back by working for the agency that finds the DCFS homes for foster kids. I think she knows us too good."

Josh touched Mrs. Thompson's elbow. "You two are amazing. I'll walk Eva across the street and bring some papers from Andres. You can sign her up for as many classes as you want."

He heard the door close as Andres stepped back inside the house. "Say, how are Nando and Fly doing?"

"Well, you know we like all our fosters, but those two grew kinda special to us. I think it was because we were getting so old and maybe a bit soft in the head." She shook her head and blew her nose. "They're doin real good in their group home. They're with three other boys and the case worker called us and said in just two weeks they became the leaders of the home. We're right proud of them. Nando called a bit ago and was all excited to hear we're takin in young kids again. Said he and Fly might come out and help us if we need it." She marched down the steps and called back, "Thank you very much. Now I gotta get back and start gettin' a toddler's bed ready. Eva's goin to be surprised when her brother shows up tomorrow."

Registration papers from Andres to sign kids up for classes were on the seat of his chair when Josh returned to his office. The sounds of noisy chatter and chairs scraping on the floors signaled the end of morning art classes. Josh picked up the papers and stepped into the dining room, trying not to get bowled over by the surge of young humanity charging for the doors.

Eva glanced up at him, then grabbed a handful of wet paint brushes and ran them out to the kitchen sink where she began rinsing and shaking them out. Watery paint droplets flew against the backsplash and on the counter. "I ain't ready to go yet. I gotta help this big girl clean up."

Josh caught a glimmer of a smile on Andres who stepped toward the art storage room. He laid the papers down, told Eva he'd be in the office and to get him when she was finished.

A few minutes later, Josh noticed Andres barely glance his way as he walked Eva by the office and out the front door. She carried the papers, along with an excited and proud look on her face.

Now that's interesting, Josh thought. *Andres is walking her home. I'm not going to say a word to him. Just wait and see.*

Mrs. T signed Eva up for one class that met after school on Mondays and Wednesdays and one on Saturday mornings. Eva showed up for every class offered each day; except Friday and Sunday, the only days classes weren't offered. She was the first to arrive and the last to leave. She began bringing a peanut butter and jelly sandwich she'd nibble on between classes. Several times, she forgot and, one time, Andres found her making a sandwich on their kitchen counter. Almost as much peanut butter was going on the counter as on the bread. "Ain't you got no strawberry jam? I like crunchy peanut butter best."

Josh noticed Andres began buying strawberry jam and jars of crunchy along with the smooth which Josh liked. One day, Josh heard Andres tell her to wipe up after herself, they didn't have maids to clean up after her. He watched as she stuck her tongue out at him, but she always cleaned up after that.

It didn't matter the age group or the media being taught. If Eva was too young and not yet skilled enough, she became the helper, washing out brushes, sharpening the pencils, unwrapping and stacking the paper in the correct bins, cleaning the paint cups, changing the paper on the tables, sweeping the floors and telling the kids to quiet down when they became too noisy. At times, she became too bossy and was ready to enforce obedience with her little fists. Those times, she sat in a chair in the office or off to the side of the room, holding a rag doll, until she could get her temper under control. Andres found the ancient rag doll with a missing eye somewhere during remodeling. He shook the dust off and told her she could hold it when she was in trouble during art classes.

Eva and the Thompsons arrived at an understanding with the approval of Josh and Andres. If she wasn't home, she was at the art classes and wasn't wandering around or going to other people's homes. One day, she brought her little brother. "This is Spider Man, but we calls him Spidey for short. He'll be good. He listens to me cuz I'm the oldest and he thinks if he's bad, he might have to go live with other people." She paused and gave them her gleaming smile. "Oh yeah, his real name is Salvatore, but he don't like it."

Spidey started coming frequently, even though they weren't offering preschool classes yet. He was usually well-behaved. At the end of classes, if Josh or Andres weren't available, a volunteer walked the two across the street. After a while, Josh gathered that Andres usually walked the kids home, especially when Josh wasn't home from work or was working on board reports or writing grants. One evening in late May, Josh walked Spidey and Eva home. As they opened their door, Josh heard a baby crying. "It's Peanut," cried Eva. "My baby brother came to live with us too. Come meet him. His real name is Pacho. He likes being called Peanut. Well, I like Peanut better, cuz he looks like one."

Mrs. Thompson met them, carrying a tiny fussing baby. "He's seven days old. Eva's mama had him in the jail and she's been convicted to twenty years and bein' sent downstate to Logan. He's a little out of sorts with all the changes he's had this past week. Think we're in for some rough days and nights around here."

Josh stared at the little thing wailing in Mrs. T's arms. Had he ever held a baby that tiny? What would it be like? Would they break if you didn't hold them correctly? He shook his head to clear those thoughts and said, "Well, let us know if there's anything we can do. These next few days, just send Spidey with Eva every time we have classes going on. I'll tell Andres. His volunteers love the little guy." He didn't add that he suspected Andres did as well, but wouldn't admit it.

That night, as they prepared for bed, Josh said, "Did you know Eva has another baby brother the Thompsons' have taken in? Peanut. He's a week old."

"Oh, Lord. I suppose you signed him up for classes, too. That's all we need, a baby crying while Eva makes peanut butter sandwiches all over the kitchen and Spidey needs help peeing in the toilet." Andres threw a pillow at Josh. "Dammit, Josh. I'm not ready to raise kids. I may never be. Just quit pushing it, will ya?"

"Andres, I haven't said anything about raising kids in a long time. What the heck is bugging you? All I did was ask if you knew Eva and Spidey had a baby brother." He tossed the pillow back at Andres. "Besides, you're the one buying crunchy peanut butter and strawberry jam and keeping extra pairs of *Spider Man* underpants hidden in the bathroom."

"Go to sleep, Josh. We're not talking about kids." They were both quiet. Andres rolled over and wrapped his arms around Josh, spooning him.

Bella & Marge

Through all the chaos of their home becoming an art center, Andres and Josh managed to keep one bedroom as a guest room, albeit a crowded guest room. One time, Andres was speaking on the phone with his mother who said she wanted to come spend another weekend with them and watch the children make art. "I won't interfere," Bella told Andres on the phone. "I'll just be a little mouse who might do some cooking in the kitchen. Do you think the kids might like some cookies?"

"Mom, between them washing out paint brushes in the sink, running back and forth to the bathroom and being so excited, I don't know how you could bake cookies. Especially ones that won't have paint bristles in them or some type of paint."

Andres and Josh loved their Friday evenings and Sundays. They were the only days classes weren't being offered. On Friday afternoon, Bella rode the train into the loop, met Josh at his office, and came home with him. The men scheduled a visit for Marge on the following weekend. They were excited to have Bella visit for the weekend and looked forward to Marge coming next week. Andres picked up some pad Thai, spring rolls, green curry and Thai fried rice. They sat around the kitchen table, relaxed and chatting. "Mom, if you want comfortable chairs, we have to move to the basement, or if you want to watch TV, you can join Josh and me on our bed. This place is a zoo." The doorbell rang. "Oh, God, some kid probably thinks they have a class." Andres trotted through the dining and living rooms filled with folding tables and chairs.

"I'm here. I can't wait to watch these kids make art tomorrow." Marge, Josh's mom, gave him a kiss and scurried toward the kitchen. Andres stood there, stunned.

Josh jumped up when his mother trotted in. "Ma, I thought you were coming next weekend." He gave her a hug as Bella jumped up and hugged her, too.

"Next weekend?" She checked her phone calendar. "Oh, my goodness. This is a new phone and I'm trying to keep everything on it. Oh, God. I must have nudged that dial thing with the dates wrong. This is my first smart phone. I'm sorry. Want me to reschedule? Except I already booked something else for next weekend." She laughed.

"Heck, no," Bella said. "You stay and help me make cookies. Hey, you do have to sleep with me. They only have one guest room now with a double bed." She giggled. "We will have a sleepover. Isn't that what little girls call it?"

"A slumber party. That's what big girls call it. Maybe it should be an old lady's pajama party."

"Yes, but we have to watch TV with the boys on their bed. I hope they have some popcorn. I hope we don't spill any between the sheets."

Andres groaned, shrugged and got out another table setting and began filling Marge a plate. "I suppose Josh and I could sleep in the basement, there are two couches down there."

"No, no, no." Marge said. "I haven't had a slumber party since I was sixteen or seventeen. This is going to be cool."

"I never went on one." Bella giggled. "Unless you count the night I got pregnant with Andres. We didn't sleep much that night either."

"Oh, God." Josh snickered. "I knew there was a reason we wanted to keep you two separated."

That Saturday, the classes didn't produce as much art or instruction as normal. They did produce a lot of cookies. Marge and Bella quickly established a system of rotating kids in and out of the kitchen to help mix, bake, cool, sample, and bag. Each child left with their own bag of cookies with instructions to take them home and share them.

After the kids were gone, after the volunteers cleaned the rooms and put away the supplies, sampled some cookies, and departed, Andres brought up four bottles of homebrew from the basement. Marge quickly made some bologna sandwiches and set them on the table with a bag of chips. "Whew," she said. "I'm tired. That was almost more work than my grandkids when they come over."

"Mom, you're tired from staying up all night, giggling and gabbing with Bella." Josh bit into his sandwich and sipped his beer.

Bella pointed her bottle at Marge. "Tonight. Tonight, we be good girls and sleep." She took a sip. "This stuff is strong. I might need a nap before I start cooking." She looked at Marge. "Those kids were so cute, I just loved them. And you," she looked at Andres, "are so wonderful with them. You are so much different than your father and grandfather."

Andres startled, then looked out the window. They finished eating in silence.

Chapter Sixteen

Andres and Meg

Andres taught art all day at the high school on Mondays and Wednesdays. He arranged for the high school art club to meet immediately after school from two o'clock to three-thirty, then rushed home to begin the community art classes at four which lasted until eight. The younger kids came at four, the junior high and high school came at six. Several of his high school art club students volunteered for him and usually rode from school to the house with him. Frequently, he ended up driving them home after the community art lessons. Those days were long and tight.

Tuesday and Thursdays, during the day, he tried to squeeze in several hours to make his own art, but that was difficult because he also had to make sure the supplies for the community art program were available and the volunteers had lesson plans to follow.

Fridays, he tried to focus strictly on his own art until Josh returned from his job.

Saturdays were busy with community art classes until two, then he collapsed for several hours. Saturday evenings and Sunday afternoons he tried to keep open for him and Josh to spend time together, but occasionally he had to attend the showings of his art at the galleries who represented him. Josh was just as busy. Andres knew he worked at least forty-five hours a week at the legal firm, then came home to write grants, pay bills, organize board reports and help him coordinate the contractors.

Tuesday morning, after their moms visited, Andres was trying to catch up on making some personal art to sell. He couldn't focus. His mind kept wandering to Eva, Spidey and Peanut. His mother's words floated through his mind about him being good with kids. He knew that. Knew he had an affinity for children and how to teach them, how to assess their inner spirit. He recalled those were old Josef Sawicki's words, Josh's great-great grandfather who wrote about teaching children in the first diary. He smiled that those words came to mind, assessing a child's inner spirit. It was so appropriate and he realized he unconsciously worked with kids that way. So, why wouldn't he consider raising children with Josh? Maybe I do need to speak with someone, but who?

After thinking a moment, he knew who, or at least where to start. Could he bring himself to call her? What was the worst thing that could happen if he did? He recalled reading parts of *The Book of Maybe: Finding Hope and Possibility In Your Life* by Allison Carmen. Josh loved it, but he would, he was always reading self-improvement books for tips on becoming a better manager and person. In the book, Allison Carmen asked the questions: What's the worst thing that can happen if I take this action? And what are the alternatives that could happen?

Andres realized he needed to do something. He rarely had difficulty making decisions or understanding his own motives. The idea of children and his negative reaction to it was confusing to him. Why? What was blocking him? He googled area funeral homes and called the one who handled Uncle Manny's burial.

"Kaminski and Smith Funeral Services, this is Meg, how may I help you?"

"Uh, Meg, this is Andres Rodriquez, you helped bury my uncle, Manny Rodriquez. Remember?"

"Of course, I remember you, Andres. How are you? How can I help you?"

"Well, Josh told me about your conversation. I, well, I would like to talk to you or someone about that topic. Alone. At least for now, alone."

He felt a little odd, asking a person from a funeral home to talk with him about having children, even if she was gay. Then he remembered her mentioning she was a psychotherapist before she took over the funeral home.

They set a time to meet at the rooming house for noon, Thursday. Meg said she would bring sandwiches.

Andres was nervous as he opened the door and led her through the living and dining room class areas with art mounted on the bulletin boards and the walls.

"Um, this place doesn't look like it did the last time I was here. Josh mentioned you planned to start programs in the future. I had no idea you were turning your home into temporary classrooms." She paused to study several of the art pieces. "From the quality of some of this work, it looks like you are doing a great job. This is impressive."

"It is. We're thrilled with our students, and it has changed our living arrangements a little." He wasn't sure what to say next, but decided to dive in. "Which makes the idea of having kids seem almost ludicrous when we don't have any place to actually put them." He led the way into the kitchen, nervously poured two glasses of water and set them on the kitchen table, spilling several drops. He abruptly turned and started some coffee brewing.

"Andres, I know it took some guts to call me. I am honored you did, now relax. I won't bite and I'm confident that, should you decide to have children, your housing situation will work out. Life is funny that way." She sipped her water, then used a napkin to wipe up the drops on the table. "Let's sit down and you tell me why you called me."

Andres took a big breath. "I'm not sure where to start. I know, hell, everyone knows, I love kids, yet when I think about raising them, being responsible for their entire lives and how they turn out, well, my mind shuts down. I can't see it happening." Meg nodded. "When I make art, I usually see it, or part of it, in my mind, and go with it. And though I have an idea I want to convey, the piece may come out much different than what I thought at the beginning. Somehow it still conveys my original idea." He stood up and began to pace around the room. "Sorry, it's hard for me to stay seated, I'm always on the go. Anyway, when it comes to children, not only do I not see an end idea of them, I feel this great fear."

"Can you tell me more how that fear feels? What do you see? You're an artist, any colors?"

Andres paced and thought. "I think I see red, like anger. I don't use a lot of red in my work, only to highlight or emphasize. I feel…" He paced some more. "This is hard. I always stop when I try to think about what I truly feel. I think I feel disappointment or failure. I hate those feelings." He smacked his right fist into his left palm, then froze. He slowly sat down, shaking his head.

"Andres, what just happened?"

"I realized I just did the same thing my father always did when he was upset with me or wanted to make a point. I can't believe I did the same thing. I just realized I do that when I'm frustrated with someone or about something, not often. It never occurred to me it's the same thing my father did when he was upset."

"Was your father upset a lot of the time?"

"Most of the time, Dad ignored Mom and me. He was very distant, lived in the same house, but lived his own life, including bringing other women home to his bedroom. Once in a while, he decided to play father and would want to go play in the back yard, foot a soccer ball around, play catch, shoot hoops. He rarely asked about my life, though occasionally, he did ask about the soccer team I was on till I went to high school. He chatted about his dental business, how he couldn't wait till I was old enough to begin helping in the offices, learning the tools, the equipment, taking science classes and going to dental school someday." He stood up and began pacing again. "On the rare occasions he asked me what I wanted to do for fun, I usually replied I wanted to go downtown to the Art Institute of Chicago. He'd do what I just did and say, 'Art is for pansies. You're not a pansy.' He stormed off and didn't speak to me for weeks at a time."

"Andres, did he ever abuse you? Physically or sexually?"

"No, he never did. I rarely remember him touching me, like holding me or cuddling me. If he came to one of my soccer games and I did well, he might give me a high five after the game. I remember seeing him hit his fist into his hand a few times when I missed a pass or a goal. Some of those times, he hollered, 'That was a pansy shot.'" Andres stopped pacing and poured their coffee, setting out milk and sugar. He sipped from his mug. "Most of the time, it was like he barely existed. My mom and I got along great. She refused to baby me, demanded I be responsible, encouraged me in whatever interested me and learned about my interests along with me. She could be strict, never mean or violent. I think she did swat my butt a few times when I was overly belligerent as a preschooler, but that was about it. She set high expectations and those didn't change when I told her I was gay. I came out when I graduated high school. I told her when I was fifteen."

"When did you tell your father?"

"I think Dad knew for years and that was why he got so frustrated with me. Especially once I hit high school and my art took off. By my sophomore year, I think he realized I wasn't interested in dentistry and was deeply disappointed. I didn't officially tell him I was gay until my eighteenth birthday in May. That was the day he told me they were moving to Plainfield. That I could attend Joliet Junior College out there and transfer to the University of Illinois or UI-Chicago for pre dental and he would pay for it."

"Were you surprised about the move? About the college plans?"

"Not really. I suspected he wanted to move when he set up two offices in that area and started complaining about the commute. That day was the first he told Mom about moving, too. I already knew he was not interested in supporting my artistic schooling. Anyway, I told him I wasn't moving with them, I would declare myself legally independent from them so I could seek my own financial aid, I would find my own housing, and I would enroll at UI-Chicago as an art major and fund it myself, plus get some state grants. And by the way, I was gay. And he needed to deal with it. I was calm, cool and collected." Andres smiled.

Meg stood, stretched and poured them each more coffee, then sat down. "Wow. That was a lot. What did your father do? How did he react? What did he say?"

Andres twitched. His face grimaced. He sat down, grabbed a napkin and wiped his eyes and blew his nose. "He smacked his hand in his fist, turned and walked out the front door. The day after my graduation, they moved."

"That's a lot of change for a just-turned eighteen-year old. What did your mother say? How did you deal with it? How did you feel?"

"On the day I told them all that, she cried after he left. She pulled me into a big hug and said, 'Now you know why I raised you to be independent. You will be fine. Your life won't always be easy, but you will not only survive, you will succeed. You are ready to leave the nest. I'm proud of you." Andres wiped his eyes again. "What did I do? I bought a

162

big old van to haul my art supplies around in, bought some ladders and began painting houses, inside and out, and mostly lived in my van till Josh and I moved in together. I was so busy, I didn't have time not to be fine. Mom always told me to bloom wherever my seed landed. So, I did."

He stood up and began pacing again. "How did I feel? I tried to keep too busy to feel. Partly because that's just how my dad was and…and maybe I didn't want to acknowledge those feelings of a father being disappointed in his son who was an artist and was gay and could never measure up to his own wishes. In so many areas, Dad is exemplary. He's honest with his clients and businesses, can be generous, has different rates for people without insurance; lets them pay over time, even if it's two dollars a week. Yet at home, he was immoral. Can you imagine bringing women home to screw while you have a wife and child around?" He stopped pacing. "Don't even ask me why Mom and I stayed. It was easier to live with him than try to make it on our own. She wasn't a legal citizen till I was in college. So, don't even ask. We're not going there." He stopped pacing and took a deep breath. "Sorry, I guess I have some anger issues with my dad."

"Andres, your story is amazing and you should have some issues with your father. That's normal. The question is, how do you want to deal with them? How are they affecting you in wanting or not wanting children? After your upbringing, which I can tell your mother did an incredible job, you don't have to want children. Either way is fine with me. You and Josh can work together on not having children, on how you can both support each other in that decision and still meet both your needs. Obviously, the question is important to you or you wouldn't have called me. I don't think you can answer it until you address the reasons holding you back. The blockages." She paused then quietly asked, "What was that motion when you swiped your hand across your shoulder? Did you realize you did that?"

Andres sat down again, hard, and stared at her. "No, I didn't. Josh told me I did that recently in front of him and several guests when I was upset about something. I smacked my fist then, too." Tears came to his eyes and he shook his head to clear them. He didn't speak for several minutes. "Josh asked me the same thing and I don't remember doing it. When I think about it, well, sometimes I feel like my father is sitting on my shoulder, smacking his fist, telling me that was a pansy thing to do, that pansy artists never amount to much. And-and I guess I was trying to swipe him away. It's like I had several friends in high school and college who were super religious, one Catholic, two evangelicals. I swear they ran around with God or Jesus or Mary or somebody sitting on their shoulders, judging every move they made. I had to back off from the friendships because they judged me too." He stopped talking and put his head into his hands. "I think the blockage might be the image of my father smacking his fist and yelling…"

"Yelling what?" Meg asked softly.

Andres stood and slowly walked around the room. "That day I told him I was gay. He yelled that fucking homos are worthless to themselves and to society. He said thank God I wouldn't have kids so he didn't have to worry about fucked-up grandkids. That being gay, at least no woman would have me so I couldn't pass being a faggot on to my kids and fuck them up too. That I'd probably die of AIDS anyway." Andres sat down again, tilted his head back, and began crying. "I'm sorry," he whispered. "I'm sorry I didn't keep better control."

Meg slid over to him and put an arm around him. "Don't be sorry. Don't apologize for unplugging something painful like I think you just did. Don't you?"

Andres nodded.

Meg's phone beeped. She pulled it from her pants pocket. "Looks like we got a new client coming in. The staff went to pick him up from the hospital." She stood. "I need to use your bathroom and will have only a few more minutes. You think about what your next step should be. Whether it's meeting with me again, meeting with just Josh, the three of us meeting together, or just you absorbing this for a while before deciding what you want to do. No matter what you decide, I will be supportive of you and Josh. You two are terrific."

When Meg returned from the bathroom, Andres was sitting at the table, pouring himself more coffee. Tears were still on his cheeks as he half-smiled. "I think I better understand what was blocking me, but I'd like some time to think it through. I'm glad you mentioned I have the freedom to decide either way for myself. Give me some time to think about my next step. And, given the condition of our living arrangements, it's not something I need to deal with tomorrow. Although it's definitely not something I want to push to the back of my psyche and ignore." He stood and grinned. "Is psyche a good word? Did I sound like a therapist?"

Meg laughed. "It sounded fine to me and I'm not sure anymore what a therapist is supposed to sound like. Here, I thought you were going to ask about *my* blockages to wanting kids. I'm glad you jumped in, that means you're serious about figuring yourself out."

Andres walked her to the front door, shook her hand, then they hugged. He walked back to the kitchen. Aunt Jemimah said two-forty-five. Wow, classes began at four. He wandered into his studio and began sketching a stream with an old dam made of rock and torn open in the middle. He glanced at his watch, stood, then sat back down and added several figures, small ones with fishing poles. He started to get up, sat back and lightly added two adult ones, then a tent.

He flipped a clean sheet over the page.

Arca Children Need a Family

Several weeks later, a woman came in at the end of Thursday night classes. Eva waved at her. The woman asked to speak with Josh and Andres. "I'm Parashayla White, I'm the Arca children's case manager from Metropolitan Services. Can we talk for a few minutes?"

"Sure, is there a problem?" Josh looked anxiously at Andres and checked to see that Eva and Spidey were still at a table, drawing.

"No, it's not a problem, but it could be. See, I just realized how much time the kids were spending over here. Mama T, I mean Mrs. Thompson, speaks highly of you two and how much you mean to the kids. The facts are, you have a number of high school students and other adults coming and going. Have you had background checks done on yourselves and are you doing them on the volunteers?" She must have noticed the blank looks, then the fear on their faces. She smiled. "Don't get worried or upset. This is not an official visit, but I think it's something you should consider, especially if you plan to expand the children's programs whenever you get this place finished."

"It makes sense," Andres said. "Actually, I have been fingerprinted and a background check done in order for me to work at the high school. It's been so long ago, I forgot about it. What do we have to do?"

"It would make a lot of sense, especially for liability issues with the kids you're working with. It would only take one complaint from a kid, saying he was touched inappropriately, and you could be in trouble. So would your insurer." She paused. "You are insured, aren't you? I don't mean just building insurance, but for program liability."

"Judas Priest," muttered Josh. "What else don't we know?"

Parashayla laughed. "I'll be glad to work with you on policies and procedures. I suggest you contact an insurance agent tomorrow." She looked to see how Eva and Spidey were doing, then around the room, as if to see if anyone else remained who might be listening. "Can we sit down?"

Josh and Andres moved some art supplies out of the way so the three of them could sit down. "Would you like some coffee or tea?" asked Andres. "I have both ready and not too old. The coffee is decaf."

"Tea would be nice." She waited till Andres came back with cups, the tea and coffee. "I'm going to surprise you even more and what I will say has nothing to do with your insurance and background checks, though I hope you move on that quickly." She took a sip of tea. "Good old Lipton, it's still my favorite." She studied them carefully. "So, this is confidential, something I've been thinking about for some time. The Thompsons are not getting younger. Mrs. is seventy-three and Mr. eighty-four. They are still amazing, but I am worried about the long-term future for Eva and her brothers. Mr. T had a pacemaker put in several years ago, and though he won't admit it, I think he's having some angina or other problems now. An infant, toddler and six-year old are a lot for their ages." She took a big breath, held it a moment, then said, "I want to find a stable foster care placement for the kids to stay together. More than that, someone who would consider adopting them."

Josh's mouth dropped open as Andres shrunk back in his chair. They looked at each other in stunned silence. Finally, Andres asked, "And you think we might be interested in doing such a thing? With an infant? Why?"

At least he didn't leave the room, or tell her no, Josh thought.

Parashayla responded, "I didn't know, but wanted to throw it out

166

there. I am extremely attached to these kids and don't want to see them split up again. Plus, I'm extremely attached to the Thompsons. You know they were my foster parents, too. I was a rough teenager headed in the wrong direction and they did wonders with me. I know they will not be able to keep doing this forever and I want to be thinking ahead, rather than having to react in a crisis. All I can do is ask you to consider it. I'm not looking for an answer tonight." She slid her chair back as if to stand. "Oh, one other thing. The Thompsons suggested you two. Last week, she told me, 'Those two boys across the street would make wonderful parents.' I asked her why she said that, and she replied, 'I got this feeling we're not going to be able to raise these youngsters till they grow up and I want to see them in a good home. Those two boys would make great parents. All that Eva and Spidey talk about is Andres and Josh.' So, now that I've ruined a good night's sleep, I'm leaving. Here's my card. Call me anytime with questions about anything. I'll drop off information for you to get started on background checks for you and your volunteers." She turned as if to leave, then paused. "Oh yes, Mrs. T thinks you both are dying to hold Peanut, yet too scared to ask. Better face your fears." She laughed as she walked toward the front door.

Andres waited by the living room window until he saw Parashayla take Eva and Spidey into the Thompson's home. "Did you set her up? Huh, Josh? Did you talk to the Thompsons behind my back? Why did she just show up tonight and start talking about us taking the kids?" He stepped toward Josh and started to slap his fist into his palm, but stopped himself. "Did you know I talked with Meg?"

Josh shook his head and held his arms out in surprise. "No, and I won't ask what you spoke about. Tell me when you're ready."

Andres looked at Josh with a slight expression of chagrin. "I didn't mean to snap. I'm trying to change, be more open, but I'm not ready to talk more about it. Just ignore what I said. I do love those kids."

"Thank you, Andres. I did nothing behind your back. I know you're reluctant to think about children of our own. I know you love them and you love teaching high school. You love working with the neighborhood kids. You're like the pied piper with them. Thanks for apologizing. Someday, we can talk rationally about it." He walked into the kitchen and pulled a bottle of red wine from the pantry. Pouring two glasses, he handed one to Andres. "I'm not trying to push you into parenthood. I know we both come from somewhat dysfunctional homes with distant fathers. However, that doesn't mean we will parent the same way. I'm not rushing you or trying to manipulate you, though I'm not going to stay in the closet about my interest in someday raising children. Maybe, after honest discussion, I might change my mind. I sure as hell am not going to take on kids without you besides me."

"Thanks. I am thinking more about it." Andres sipped his wine, sat down at the kitchen table, jumped up, grabbed the dish rag and began wiping paint off the surface. "We overbooked tonight's class and used the kitchen table for overflow." He sat back down. "Josh, I'm sorry. I know you're not pushing me and it was unfair to accuse you. I just need some time to think. I do love kids. I don't want to turn out..."

Josh almost said, 'Like your dad,' but didn't. *He's got to figure this out by himself,* he thought. *If I try to help, he'll think I'm being manipulative. The last thing I want to do is raise kids without one-hundred percent support from both of us. Besides, where the heck could we raise them? Certainly not in this fish bowl. We're back to breathing paint fumes again.* He refilled Andres' wine glass and ruffled his wavy black hair. "Andres, take your time. I'm glad you spoke with Meg, she's wonderful. Hey, I've never changed a diaper anyway."

Parashayla was correct. They did not get much sleep that night. Neither man spoke after kissing good night, but neither seemed to sleep much. Josh felt some frustration over the two of them not being on the same page regarding children. We couldn't do anything about it right now anyway, he reasoned. We're most likely going to move from this place and we can't raise kids until we have a permanent home.

He let his mind wander. Family. He thought of all they were learning about family from the diaries they read. Good grief, the huge Sawicki family. Ten kids. I sure as hell don't want ten, and it's more than numbers and DNA. Family is sometimes who you choose and who chooses you. Many of his gay friends learned that after being rejected by their parents. He thought of Aunt Kate being thrown out of her home for being pregnant by someone who looked like Andres. And Hank's diary with the letters about Arnaud. Orphaned, shipped off, being taken in and adopted by his aunt. Manny being taken in at age eighteen, dangly arm, the first Mexican in the neighborhood. What were the photos of those people who looked like holocaust people about? How did they relate to Uncle Manny and this place? Were they part of a non-DNA family too?

He tossed and turned and realized Andres did also. *I'd love to hear his thoughts. Are they similar to mine or is he dreaming up a new piece of art? I bet he's thinking about his dad, kids and his fears. I also bet he's thinking about his mother. How she made a home and raised him in a difficult situation. God, I love that man. I hope we come together on this.* Josh finally faded off to sleep, only to wake to the sound of loud jazz from the radio alarm. For once, he was glad Andres set the sound level so high.

Chapter Seventeen

Summer 2011

It was Sunday. Andres was at an art exhibition. Josh was home alone. He heard kids chattering outside the kitchen window and turned to watch Eva and Spidey and several neighborhood kids, all in their swimsuits, pull a sprinkler on a long hose away from the rooming house. Where did that come from? He remembered Andres saying he'd purchased a hose to water some of the old beds of day lilies and roses, but not about a sprinkler like the one attached. The kind that arcs a spray. The kind that kids run through on hot summer days. Which was happening now.

He stepped out the side door to watch the kids shrieking and laughing as they ran through the chilly spray. His immediate thought was to wonder if this was a liability. An accident in the making that could bring a law suit. They were more than just homeowners now. They were an organization. He was sure liability issues weren't something Andres would have thought of when he told the kids they could play with the sprinkler. He decided to not interfere with the fun. After all, wasn't this simply being neighborly?

Mrs. T walked over, carrying Peanut with a diaper bag slung over her shoulder. Josh kept looking at the baby, now three months old, wiggling, smiling and cooing. "Man, he's grown."

"Yup, and he's a live wire, too. Just like his big sister and brother. He watches every move they make and don't care none when they wrestle him around like he's a bag of feed."

They chatted a few minutes until a shriek curdled the air. Spidey was running too fast and slipped face first into the big elm tree. His nose and chin were bloody. Mrs. T flipped the baby into Josh's arms, dropped the diaper bag from her shoulder, trotted over and picked up Spidey. "Josh, watch the baby. I got to clean this wild one up. Hope he don't need stiches. Mr. T is at the store." She turned to the kids. "Slow down. No racin' and you mind Josh." She carried the squalling Spidey across the street. She turned and hollered, "Quit holdin' him way out from you. Hold him closer. He ain't gonna break. Just support his head a bit."

Joshua cautiously shifted the baby into the crook of his left arm and tried to relax. Was this going to be a liability issue? Peanut smiled up at him as he tried to get his fist to his mouth, then waved it around. Josh forgot about liability issues for the moment. The Thompsons weren't going to be bothered over it. He decided to stay in the yard as long as the kids were present.

He began rocking Peanut and felt himself relaxing. He even took several steps to make sure he had his balance. *Peanut really is a peanut,* he thought. Little, but then he had no ideas what size a three-month old baby should be. The baby wriggled and kicked. Josh was surprised how strong the pintsized guy was. He watched the kids running through the sprinkler and shifted his body so the baby could watch, too. *This isn't too bad,* he thought.

Eva ran up to them. She thrust her wet face into the baby's and gave him a wet kiss on the cheek. Peanut jerked, but didn't cry. Eva put her pinky finger into his tiny fist and he grabbed tight. "Can I take him through the sprinkler? Please? I'll help change his wet clothes."

"No. You are not taking Peanut through the sprinkler. What if you slipped and fell? Now go back and play. Us two are doing fine."

Mr. T suddenly drove down the street. He whipped his black shiny Buick up to the curb, a cell phone to his ear. Mrs. T scurried down their steps, holding Spidey. "We're goin to that quick care place over on Halsted. His chin might need a stitch or a better Band-Aid than what I got. There's milk and diapers in the bag." Mr. T flashed his big grin, stuck his hand out the open window, waved and hollered as he sped off, "Eva, you best be good. We be back soon."

Eva waved and did a cartwheel through the spray.

Like they're going to an outing to Navy Pier, not for stitches, thought Josh. He realized with all the children they raised over the years, this was part of childhood and nothing to sweat over. He carefully shifted Peanut to his shoulder, supporting his head. He was amazed at how strong the baby's neck was when the tiny guy started twisting his head around, trying to see Josh and the kids playing.

A few minutes later, Eva ran up, shivering. "I wanna dry off. Can we go in your house? You got a towel?" She turned to the other kids. "I'm going inside with Josh now. You can go home." She ran over and turned the spigot off. Josh wasn't sure the other kids were ready to quit, they didn't look cold, but they shrugged and trotted off toward their home two doors down. At least Eva made the decision to send them home so that he didn't have to. He picked up the diaper bag without dislodging the baby and followed her up the stairs.

Eva ran to the bathroom and emerged with a large towel wrapped around her. She carried a small hand towel and began wiping up her wet steps through the kitchen. Peanut began fussing and thrashing around. "He's hungry," Eva yelled. "That's his hungry cry. You know how to work his bottle?" Before Josh could answer, she opened the bag and pulled the bottle out. She twisted the lid off, reversed the nipple, checked for leaks and handed it to Josh. "Go sit in the rocker. You need to rock him. I'll tell ya when to burp him."

She followed him into the guest room where they kept the rocker and hovered over them as he sat down. The baby latched onto the bottle and sucked lustily, making little piggy noises. Josh couldn't believe how noisy he was or how hard he sucked on the bottle. Eva kept checking the level of formula in the bottle. "Okay. You gotta burp him now." She grabbed a burp-cloth out of the bag and put it on Josh's shoulder. "Now put him up high on your shoulder and pat his back or rub it hard."

"How will I know when he's burped?" Josh patted at the baby's back, afraid he might injure him.

"Harder. Them's baby pats. You can't hurt him."

Josh patted harder.

Eva grabbed his hand and made him pat harder yet.

Josh jumped when the little guy let out a huge belch.

"Now tell him that's a good boy and pat him awhile to see if he has another. Then you can feed him again. Then you gotta burp him again. I'm going to the table and draw him a picture."

The baby fell asleep as he drained the bottle. Josh burped him again and sat rocking him, the baby dead to the world up on his shoulder. *What is there about holding a sleeping baby*, he wondered. This is addictive. The baby stirred, so Josh lowered him to his left arm again, slipped his right hand under the baby's butt and gently patted. Eva drew and sang quietly to herself. Josh felt like he was rocking himself to sleep. The baby stretched, twisted and let out an explosion. Josh felt the diaper fill. Oh my God, now what?

Eva was right there. "You know how to change him? He just pooped his pants and the sooner you change him, the sooner he'll go back to sleep. He gets crabby if he has to sleep in poopy diapers." She whipped out a diaper and wipes and a changing pad. "Here, put him on the bed. You ain't got a changing table." Josh started to lay the baby on the bed. "No, Josh. Lay him on his back." She watched Josh pull the little White Sox sweat pants off and stare at the next layer of clothing. "That's a onesie. Now you gotta unsnap him and if he's leaked through, then you gotta take everything off him."

Under Eva's directions, Josh unsnapped the onesie, it was still clean, and figured out how to undo the diaper. "Whew. Does it always smell this bad?" Tears came to his eyes and he choked a bit.

"He always smells. Ya just gotta get used to it. Want me to do it? Huh? I thought big people like you knew how to change dirty diapers."

"No, no. I didn't, but I can do it." He lifted the little guy's legs and pulled out several wipes. *My God*, he thought, *how many cracks and crevices does a baby have?* He wiped away, just when he thought he had a clean baby, he discovered another spot he missed. Peanut kept fussing at the inconvenience. At last, Josh stuffed the wipes and rolled the dirty diaper up. He set it aside, and leaned over to unfold the fresh one just as Peanut sprayed him, full force, soaking his T-shirt. "Whoa, I didn't expect that." He laughed with Eva.

"He likes to do that. That's why you gotta learn to unfold the fresh diaper first and have it ready."

At last, Peanut was changed and back to sleep in Eva's arms on the bed while Josh changed his shirt and washed his hands. He couldn't wait to tell Andres and hoped Andres would laugh about his baptism by baby pee.

The Thompsons scurried into the room. Spidey had a bruise on his forehead, his nose was scraped and two Steri-Strips crossed his chin. He proudly licked a large purple sucker and handed a red one to Eva.

Mrs. T picked up Peanut while Mr. T grabbed the diaper bag. "Didn't need no stitches, jist them strip Band-Aids what I didn't have." Mrs. T looked quizzically at Josh's fresh shirt. "What happened, Eva drag you into the sprinkle machine?"

Josh shook his head. "Umm, no. Peanut did."

"Didn't you know to lay a clean diaper over him when you're changing the old one?"

"I do now. That was my first time and Eva coached me through it. She's a real helper."

Eva waved her sucker at Josh.

Mrs. T laughed. "I ain't supposed to tell you this, but he did the same thing to Andres the other day while you was at work. Now you both been baptized by Peanut." She winked and hustled her little brood out the door and across the street.

I'll be damned, thought Josh. *I'm not going to ask. I'll wait to hear about this when Andres tells me. Makes me wonder what he and Meg talked about.*

Chapter Eighteen

Mr. T's Stroke—September 2011

Josh and Andres were deep in sleep when Josh's cell phone began vibrating on the dresser. Josh vaguely grew aware of it, then it stopped. Next, it seemed like some light was flashing. He groaned, opened his eyes, glanced at the clock which said one-forty-two, and realized the multi-line office phone they installed for the Gallery to handle their class registrations and business was flashing. He sat up and groggily answered it.

"One of you boys needs to get over here right now. Mr. T is actin queerly and I called nine eleven and they should be pullin' up any second." The line went dead as Josh heard a siren round the corner and stop across the street.

He nudged Andres. "I'm going over to the Thompsons. Something's wrong with Mister and the emergency squad is there." Josh jumped into his clothes and ran across the street in time to see the paramedics load Mr. T into the ambulance.

Mrs. T was pulling on her jacket and searching her purse for the car keys. "I'll call you when I find out more. He got up to pee and said his leg felt tingly and he seemed to slur his words. I gave him an aspirin and called emergency. Peanut will wake up about six-thirty, change and feed him and he might go back to sleep. Eva and Spidey need to get up at seven-thirty and go to school. They know the way, but Mr. usually walks them. They gotta be there at eight-thirty and Spidey has to be picked up at eleven-thirty and Eva at three-thirty. Now turn your dang phone on so it rings." She snatched up her purse and pulled a five-dollar bill out. "Here, I usually make Eva's lunch. She'll be thrilled to buy it." She marched out the back door toward the garage.

Andres slumped in, dressed in his night wear, basketball shorts, a sleeveless White Sox t-shirt with lots of paint stains and orange flip-flops. "The ambulance just took off. Who was in it? I couldn't grasp what you said, I was sleeping so hard."

"It's Mr. T. Sounds like a stroke to me. Are you teaching today? What day is it anyway?"

"It's Tuesday, so no, I'm off. I can cover if you want to go to work." He yawned, grabbed an afghan and collapsed in the recliner. "I hope the old guy is okay. Get some sleep, Joshy. The *terroristas* will be awake before we know it."

"Thanks, I have a slow day today, so can go in a bit later." Josh found another afghan and stretched out on the couch. "Thank goodness art classes don't start till next week."

At six-twenty, Peanut made his needs known. "Andres, wake up and go fix a bottle." Josh jumped up, ran to the boy's room and, in the darkness, managed to find and pull Peanut out of the crib, hoping to not wake Spidey. He fumbled around at the changing table, then noticed a small night lamp over it. In the dim light, he figured out all the pajama snaps, changed Peanut without another spraying, picked him up, patted the baby who quickly quieted down, turned off the light and hurried toward the door with him tight in his arms. In the dark, he banged his knee against Spidey's bed. Banged it so hard, he jerked in pain and almost lost his balance, which scared Peanut into wailing at the top of his lungs, which woke up Spidey who added to the din with even more decibels. Andres rushed in, handed the bottle to Josh and told him to go rock him in the living room.

~ * ~

Andres knelt down by the youth bed and tried to pick up Spidey, who began flailing his little fists, arching his back and screaming. "I no want you. Why you here? I want Missus T. Where is she?"

"Sh, sh, sh. Mr. T is sick and Mrs. T asked Josh and me to watch you kids for a while. It's okay." He tried to rub Spidey's back.

"Don't touch me." Spidey pummeled Andres with his little fists.

Andres remembered hearing that babies like to be wrapped tight. He used both hands to move Spidey closer, then sat on the bed and pulled him into a tight hug. Spidey screeched louder and thrashed about even harder.

God, for four years old, this little guy is strong, Andres thought. He held on, trying to not let Spidey go, to pat him and soothe him all at the same time. He began rocking back and forth, hoping the movement might calm the little guy. It didn't.

Spidey fought and struggled even harder, all the time screaming for Mrs. T. "I hate you. I hate you." He managed to free one little fist and caught Andres on the nose. Andres jumped as tears came to his eyes.

He managed to get the hand under control. "Ouch. That hurt me. What do you want, little man? What will make you stop this? Mrs. T is coming back in a while." He tried to rock harder.

Josh appeared at the door and turned the light on which startled Spidey. Josh glanced at Andres. "Got your hands full? My kid is fine and sleeping on the floor. I was afraid to leave him on the couch. I think he's rolling over now." He squatted down by Andres and Spidey whose efforts were slightly diminished. "Spidey, everything is going to be okay. Mrs. T will be back soon. Would you like a cheese stick?" He held out a string-cheese stick.

Spidey quit crying and reached for it. He fumbled with the cellophane wrapping. "It's wrapped." He started to wail again.

Andres grabbed it, opened it and handed it back. "Is that better? Can you say thank you?"

Spidey bit a bite off and shook his head, still glaring at Andres. He took another bite, his mouth filling up like a chipmunk. He chewed and tried to swallow, then managed to say, "I need a dwink."

Josh ran off and came back with a small glass of water. He started to hand it to Spidey, but Andres stopped him. "I'd really like Spidey to say thank you for getting him a drink."

Spidey chewed and swallowed several times while glaring at Andres. Finally, he took a big swallow and muttered, "Tank you." He gulped down the water and took a final big bite of the cheese stick. He sighed. His eyes drooped.

Andres cuddled him close and slowly rocked him as he relaxed. "Were you scared when you woke up and found us here and Mrs. T gone?" Spidey slowly nodded. "Are you okay now? I think you should go back to sleep and we'll get you up for school in a little while. Okay?" Spidey closed his eyes. Andres waited a few minutes, then slipped him under his covers and put his spider doll next to him.

Josh retrieved Peanut, put him back in his crib and turned out the lights. As they went back to the living room, he glanced at Andres. "Are those blood drops on your nose?"

"Probably. His fists are tiny, but powerful, just like his sister's. Say, why are you limping?"

Josh glanced at the clock. "Good grief. Less than five hours of night time childcare and we both look like the walking wounded. How are we going to make it through breakfast?"

"Don't know. Let's nap a few minutes. I might make them pancakes and bacon if I can find the stuff."

"Oh, Andres. Let's keep it simple. They usually eat toast and cereal, I think. Let's not make a big production. Besides, we may need to make pancakes for dinner tonight if Mrs. T can't get home. That would be quick and easy and a treat, I bet." He paused. "My God, we've been so busy, I wonder how Mr. T is doing. At his age, anything could happen." Both men were quiet as the implications for Mr. T's future sunk in.

Andres nudged Josh. "Hey, how did you know to bring Spidey something to eat when he was so upset?"

Josh rubbed his eyes. "Not sure. Maybe because I've been around my mom and sisters when my nieces and nephews have been upset. Sometimes, when they're preschoolers and were really upset, I've seen them just let them scream it out."

"Yeah, I can see it now. Me trying to wrap him up with all my loving feelings made him worse. I wonder if he got my message about manners?"

Josh grinned at him. "I doubt it. I'm not sure meltdowns are the time to teach manners."

Eva stumbled out, rubbing her eyes. "Why are you here? Where's Mr. and Mrs. T? What was all that screaming a while ago?"

Josh patted the couch and motioned for Eva to come sit between them. "Eva, Mr. T got sick in the night and had to go to the hospital. Mrs. T is with him. Andres and I will get you off to school and take care of you guys all day or until she comes back. Okay?"

"Is he gonna die?" She started to tear up. "He's awful old, but he's the bestest foster dad I ever had."

Andres put his arm around her. "We don't think so, but we will tell you everything we know when you get home from school. Okay? Guess what?" She looked up at him, tears still brimming in her large brown eyes. "I'm going to walk you and Spidey to school, pick you two up, watch Peanut and maybe we could have my famous pancakes for dinner tonight. What do you think?" She snuggled into his embrace. "One more thing, Mrs. T gave us money for you to buy your lunch at school today so you don't have to take one of my liver and onion sandwiches. They're the only kind I know how to make."

Eva giggled. "That's great. Hey, you know how to make peanut butter sandwiches, too." She stood, yawned and stretched. "What's liver? It sounds gross."

"It is," said Josh. "He was just kidding, I hope. Now, what's your morning routine?"

She looked at him with a questioning expression.

"What do you do after you get up? Go to the bathroom, change your clothes, brush your hair, eat, brush your teeth, check your school bag. All those things are called a routine because you do the same things every day, probably in the same order."

"Oh, ya. I do all that stuff. We just call it things I gotta do in the morning." She meandered toward the bathroom. "Hey," she called back. "Ya better get Spidey on his morning routine. Just watch it, sometimes he's grumpy."

"Okay," Andres said. "Say, what do you guys eat for breakfast?" He stood and moved toward the hallway.

"There's four cereals. We get to pick two and mix them if we want. Juice too, and peanut butter toast. And hot cocoa when it's cold. Is it cold yet?"

"Nope. Sorry, it's still warm out." Andres opened Spidey's door and softly called, "Spidey, hey, Spidey, it's time to get up and go to school." He turned on the light to see Peanut wriggling and smiling at him. "Spidey, it's time to wake up. Your brother's already awake."

Spidey stretched and yawned. "No. I tired. I stay home. Take Peanut to school."

Andres laughed and sat down on the edge of the bed and began lightly stroking Spidey's back. "Peanut's not old enough for school, but I'm going to walk you and Eva there."

Spidey bolted up. "Why you walkin' us? Where's Mr. T? He walks us."

"Mr. T is sick and Mrs. T is with him at the doctors. It's okay. Josh and I will take good care of you today. C'mon, little man, let's get you to the bathroom and into your school clothes." It appeared Spidey had no recollection of his early morning outburst. Andres undressed him then took him to the bathroom where he washed him up and helped him dress. On his way to the kitchen, he picked up Peanut.

In the kitchen, Eva was giving directions to Josh on where to find things, which cartoon dishes each child used, and trying to talk Josh into making hot chocolate. She grabbed Peanut from Andres, hugged him and lifted him up to her face. She took a sniff. "Phew. He stinks like pee. Didn't you change him?" She tossed him back to Andres.

"So that's his routine?" Andres asked with a wink.

"He pees all the time. That's his routine cuz he's a baby. Don't you know nothing? Hey, after I eat, I need help brushing my hair. Today, I want a braid."

Josh poured some juice for her. "Um, I might be able to handle some brushing, but not braiding. I haven't learned that yet."

She glared at him. "I said I want a braid today."

Andres turned toward her. "Eva. Is that how you talk to Mr. and Mrs. T? In that tone of voice? No saying please? Josh and I haven't raised kids before. Mr. T is sick and Mrs. T must be with him. You need to help us by not being demanding. Do you understand?"

Her face tightened into a frown, her eyes squinted and she looked like she might throw a fit. Andres continued to look calmly into her eyes. Finally, she looked away. "Okay. Could you or Josh please help me brush my hair?" She drank her juice and began shoveling her mix of Honey Nut Cheerios and Rice Krispies into her mouth. After eating, she brushed her teeth and brought a brush to Josh. "Please?"

Josh wiped the baby's mouth, sat down, took the brush and began brushing her long dark hair. "Your hair is beautiful. Once in a while, when I was younger, my older sisters would have me brush their hair. Yours is longer and thicker."

"Was theirs pretty, too?"

"Yes, but shorter and not as thick and more blond, kind of like mine." He held the back of her hair up so he could brush from the underside. "Wow. So far, no snarls."

"Nope. I ain't been chewing bubble gum when I fall to sleep. Mrs. T uses peanut butter or just cuts them out and then she yells at me for sneaking gum to my room."

"Eva," Josh said. "I can't do a braid, but I think I can do a decent ponytail. Would you like one?"

"Really? There's some stretchy thingies on top of the fridge. Thank you." Eva beamed.

"Josh, you gotta hurry." Andres pulled Peanut out of his highchair. "Spidey is ready and waiting by the door. I'm going to change the baby, put him in his crib, then I'll walk Eva and Spidey to school." He rushed for the boys' room.

Josh stood up and called back. "We're done here. I'm going to shower. I'll see you later."

From the boys' bedroom, Andres heard a door close. The bathroom door was closed when Andres hurried from the bedroom toward the front door. He called, "Okay, Eva, grab your book bag and let's go. Spidey and I will be on the front porch."

Eva joined them and they set off down the steps. Eva looked around. "Where's Peanut? He always goes with us so Mrs. T can get stuff done."

"Peanut's in his crib, Josh is showering, then he'll go to work when I get back from walking you two."

"Josh went to YOUR house to shower."

"But the bathroom door is closed, he's in there."

"No, I closed the bathroom door. Josh went out the front door.

Don't you understand nothing?"

Andres tore back into the house, cursing inwardly at himself and Josh. While he got Peanut from his crib, Eva manhandled the stroller through the front door and down the steps. They took off at a fast pace, till Spidey complained and Andres placed him in the jump seat of the stroller. They arrived at the school just as the last children and parents were going in the doors.

"I go in that door, first grade, that's my teacher. You have to check me in," Eva instructed. "Spidey goes inside to pre-K, but I don't know the room number yet."

Eva's teacher looked him over with a sense of distaste as she asked Andres his name. "Are you certain you're on the approved list to bring and pick up these children?" She didn't give him time to answer. "You need to go register at the office, right now. Be prepared to wait so they can call the Thompsons. This is highly unusual."

"Mr. T got sick and had to go to the hospital in the night," Eva stated loudly. "This is Andres. Him and Josh are our best neighbors. I make art over there all the time."

The teacher softened her expression, but still looked skeptical. "Just go in the main entrance, buzz the office and tell them the circumstances. I'm sure there'll be no problems." She patted Spidey's head as she looked Andres up and down again.

Andres waited in a long line of parents discussing sick children, picking up homework assignments and trying to set up meetings to discuss their children's behaviors. He felt like he was entering Cook County Jail, though he'd never been there. At last a woman stepped out from an office and saw him with Spidey. She motioned him over. "Hi, Spidey. Who's that with you and why?"

Andres started to explain.

"Come over here and I'll help you." She gave him an odd look and led them to another spot on the counter away from the line. She picked up a clipboard. "So, now who are you? Why are you with this child? Please show me your driver's license or an ID."

Andres panicked. He was still in the same clothes he wore when he rushed over in the middle of the night, baggy basketball shorts, no underwear, flip-flops and a scuzzy, sleeveless paint-streaked t-shirt. Hey, they were clean, but no one would notice. "Um, as you can see, I'm not wearing much. It was an emergency situation. Mr. Thompson got sick in the middle of the night and we had to rush over there to watch the kids and they're not back yet and we don't know how Mr. T is doing. And, well, my wallet is still home. I can run home and get it."

The woman tapped her pen on the counter. "Sir, please slow down. Now, what is your name?" She emphasized each word as if he was a primary student.

"Oh, I'm sorry. It's Andres Rodriguez, I live at 4822 South Justine and I work at Benito Juarez High School in Pilsen. Part-time, I'm not teaching today. I teach art. We're good friends with the Thompsons. Real good friends."

He'd never felt this nervous before. Of course, he'd never taken other people's kids to school and been half-dressed with no ID. What if this warden-like lady asked him for info on the kids, like their birthdays?

A man walked out of one of the offices and strode up to the counter. He glanced at a note in his hand. "Who are you?"

Andres told him.

The man smiled. "Good. I'm the assistant principal, it's nice to meet you. I just spoke with Mrs. Thompson who was concerned because she hadn't put you on the approved contact list for the children."

"He doesn't have any ID on him. This is unusual. Especially because these kids are wards," the woman snipped.

"Well, he looks and is dressed like Mrs. Thompson just told me he probably would be, and I'm sure by the time he picks up this little man at eleven-thirty, he can find his wallet and we'll make a copy of his ID then. I'll bet he even changes his clothes. Now, take Spidey to his class. It's room 115. Go left from our door and down the first hall to the right. His teacher anxiously awaits him." He started to leave, but turned back. "Oh, yes. Mrs. T said Mr. T will be all right. He will need some therapy. It appears his stroke was mild. I'm sure she'll update you when she can reach you." He winked at Andres and left.

Andres pushed Peanut in his stroller back to the old rooming house, found some crackers to keep him occupied, and kept him in the stroller in the bathroom while he showered. *This kid is never leaving my sight, and neither is my wallet,* he thought, still slightly flustered and embarrassed over the miscommunication with Josh, and the experience of being half-dressed at the school. He gave Peanut a bottle on their way to pick up Spidey at eleven-thirty. The baby fell asleep by the time they arrived.

The warden-like lady was much friendlier when he gave her is driver's license to copy. "I know where you live. Aren't you the ones doing art classes for kids?" Andres nodded. "Well, I'm glad to see that old place being used for something good. Back some time ago, there were some nasty people staying there."

Andres had no idea what she meant. He handed her some flyers about the art classes. "Well, I know nothing about the past there, but this is what we're doing now, and in about a year, we hope to have it converted into a community art center."

Mrs. T phoned him as he walked back to the Thompsons with Spidey and a sleeping Peanut. "I don't text so will call ya when I can. Right now, I ain't got much time, their movin' him to a room and goin to keep him for the night and get his therapy set up. It was a mild stroke. He's goin to limp a bit. His mouth doesn't full-on work, but not so you notice much and he can still talk fine. Once he's settled, I'm runnin' home to shower and come back here to be with him. If you boys can handle it, I might stay the night. Think about it and let me know."

"I will," Andres replied cautiously. "Hey, do you want a list of all the mistakes we're making?"

"Nope, as long as there's no blood or wounds on them. You gotta learn sometime, now don't ya? Just figure this is good practice for the real thing someday. All right?"

Andres was quiet a moment. "Yes. Thank you. I think you're right." He cleared his throat. "Mrs. T, there's no problem with us spending another night, we'd love to. Now, you take care of yourself and Mr. T."

He grasped Spidey's hand more snugly. Spidey squeezed his hand back and grinned up at him. Andres thought, *Holy cow. I just agreed that this is good practice for the real thing.*

Spidey chattered about school as Peanut slept.

A half-block before the Thompson's home, Josh called. Andres couldn't resist answering, "Hey, Josh, why did you leave Peanut home alone in his crib?"

Josh gasped. "Me? I told you I was going to take a shower. I assumed you were taking him with you and the kids so I could go to work. My God. Andres, how long was that baby alone? Oh, my God. We could be arrested for abandonment. Andres, how long was that baby alone? Did you go straight home and start a project after taking Eva and Spidey to school? I thought you knew I was going home. I said I was going to take a shower. Didn't you realize that meant at home? How long, Andres? How long? Andres, where is the baby right now?"

"Well, I just picked him up from the police station and you and I have a warrant to appear in court next week. We may have to post bond. Mrs. T said she's never speaking to us again and we should never try to have kids." Andres couldn't help giggling.

"God damn you, Andres. Tell me the truth. Did you forget the baby and for how long?"

"Yes. I thought you were staying with him until I got back from taking the kids to school. For some reason, I thought you meant you would take a shower at the Thompsons while I was gone. That's why I left him in the crib. Which, now that I think about it, makes no sense, but it did at the time. We were a little rushed and new at all this. Anyway, we owe bossy Eva a prize. She figured it out as we stepped off the last step from the porch. So, ninety seconds, two minutes at the most. Peanut was still slobbering on his teething biscuit like no tomorrow. He never missed us."

"Damn you, anyway. You just took ten years off my life. I'm going to kill you. What will the Thompsons say? We have to tell them."

"Umm, we actually don't, although I think they will get a kick out of it anyway."

"Why don't we need to tell them? You're not making any sense."

"I just got off the phone with Mrs. T. Mister had a mild stroke, will need therapy, probably have a limp and his mouth is slightly affected, but not his speech. She wants to spend the night with him and asked if we could stay over again. I said yes. I asked her if she wanted a list of our mistakes and she said as long as there's no blood or marks, we should consider it good practice."

"Andres, this is crazy talk. What did she mean, good practice? Practice for what?"

"Practice for raising our own kids, someday."

Josh was silent. Andres could hear him clearing his throat and swallowing before whispering, "How did you answer?"

Andres cleared his own throat to whisper, "I told her I agreed, whole-heartedly." He paused. "Joshy, did you see me swipe at my shoulder or hit my fist into my hand when Spidey was so out of control?"

"No, you seemed very calm, why?"

"Well, I realized I didn't have my dad sitting on my shoulder. I didn't have to brush him off. I heard my mother encouraging me instead. I think my blockage is pretty well over." He heard a sniffle from Josh.

"Damn you, Andres. What a time to tell me. In thirty seconds, I walk into a high-powered meeting. What will I do with these tears in my eyes?"

"Tell them you have fall allergies. Hey, hurry home, we're having super-duper pancakes, eggs and sausages for dinner tonight. Unless you want quesadillas."

"Pancakes, you sweet nut."

Andres whispered, "I love you, too."

~ * ~

On Saturday morning, after art classes, Josh walked Eva and Spidey home. He'd been working when Mr. T was brought home and hadn't seen him yet. Mr. T was in his recliner, holding Peanut, as Mrs. T fixed lunch. Josh knew Mr. T might look different, but he was surprised to see how much the old man aged in the five days since he last saw him. His mouth drooped to the left, not as severely as Josh saw in other stroke victims, but it was noticeable.

Peanut held out his arms and started squealing for Josh to pick him up. "Guess ya made yerself a good friend," Mr. T said as he tried to raise Peanut in the air. "Whoops, guess my left arm ain't like it used to be."

Josh took the baby and tossed him gently in the air. Mr. T's voice was weaker, though still jovial. His pronunciation was slightly slurred, his eyes still held their brightness and glitter.

Mr. T watched Josh with Peanut, his grin was a little crooked, and no less cheerful. "Guess I can't do that anymore either, but I can still hold him and bottle him, so life ain't that bad. Thanks for helpin' out. You two are good menfolk and the kids love ya."

"We had a good time and learned a lot. Any time you need us, just call." Josh slid the baby back into Mr. T's lap and went into the kitchen.

"You two spoiled these young uns that night you fixed them supper." Mrs. T shook her fist at him. "Mickey Mouse pancakes, sausages, eggs, peanut butter toast with jelly and hot chocolate. All in the same meal? Now I gots to do some retraining." She laughed as she told Eva and Spidey to go wash their hands for lunch. When they were out of the room, she pointed toward Mr. T in the living room. "You two would be good parents for these kids. I think we're at the beginnin' of the end for that old man in there. Ain't gonna happen tomorrow, but it's gonna happen and I don't want to be raising kids by myself. Unh-uh. Not this old lady. You best start thinkin' real serious. You've got some time, and you already got some good practice in, didn't ya?"

Josh grinned. He wasn't sure how to respond. What with watching the children, working, plus the art classes, he and Andres hadn't had the time to talk about anything since Mr. T returned home from the hospital on Thursday.

Mrs. T gave him a hug. "Besides, you both been baptized by the Peanut and lived through one of Spidey's tantrums." She laughed when Josh looked surprised. "Ain't you figured it out? There ain't no secrets around here. Not with Miss Eva." She gave him a gentle push. "Go home and gets some rest. I knows you two usually take a nap Saturday afternoons. You two need it, especially after this week."

At home in their kitchen, Andres handed him a home brew. "Let's go downstairs, listen to some music and sit on a couch. I can't stand to sit on our bed to watch TV, or at the kitchen table and have to look at the classrooms, even if I am proud of the kid's artwork."

They sat on the couch, half turned toward the other, and slowly sipped their beers. Andres broke the silence. "How did the Thompsons seem?"

"Mr. T acts like nothing happened, but he's definitely limited with his left arm. Mrs. T, well…" his voice trailed off. *Should I share my conversation with Mrs. T? Andres said his blockage about kids was over.* He took a big breath. "Andres, you said your blockage with having kids is over or nearly over. I have some questions. Okay?"

Andres grinned at him and waved his homebrew to continue.

"Mrs. T just told me we need to get serious about whether we're interested in parenting the Arca kids. She doesn't think Mr. T will live a lot longer. She said it's the beginning of the end for him. So, I have three questions. One, are we interested in having children? Two, fostering or adopting? Three, do we want the Arca kids or should we look at other options like surrogacy, older kids or just one child?"

Andres stood and began pacing. "You know I spoke with Meg, right?" Josh nodded. "She implied the same questions." He scratched his head and looked around the room. "For me, it's clear now. Though it wasn't before. After those days with the kids, I'm totally focused." He turned toward Josh, then knelt in front of him. "Josh, I want to take the Arca kids. I think we should get licensed as foster parents and begin a transition." He raised his hand to stop Josh from responding. "I know we don't have a place yet, but I think our dots will connect in the future like they have in the past. It's time. I'm ready. Let's start the process." He leaned in and kissed Josh.

"Whew," Josh said. "For a minute, I thought you were kneeling to propose marriage. I agree about the kids, let's call Parashayla and find out when we can start the classes. She can help us talk with the Thompsons, who, I bet, won't be surprised."

Andres laughed and kissed him again. "It's not legal for us to marry yet. I guess I was proposing almost the same thing. Let's start a family."

Josh kissed him again and pulled him onto the couch. "Let's snuggle. We haven't made out on a couch in a long time."

Chapter Nineteen

Thanksgiving and Christmas 2011

It was pure bedlam. Tables and chairs were being hauled out of the living and dining room classrooms and up the stairs. More people carried things up and down, stomping, laughing and talking loudly up on the third floor. All Josh and Andres wanted to do was sleep in, make love, fix some pancakes and eggs, watch a DVD, and later, join the Thompson clan upstairs for a Thanksgiving dinner.

Mr. T's mild stroke in September didn't slow him down much. It did give him a limp necessitating a cane, limited the use of his left hand, and gave him a crooked smile. He still drove. Whether he should or not was a matter of discussion.

Early in October, Parashayla approached Josh and Andres with the idea of using the third-floor space for a Thanksgiving dinner with as many of the former foster kids and families that could be contacted. "We know the place isn't finished, but the third floor is better than the second right now. We'll dust and mop and set everything up in the morning and take it down when we finish. We'd love to have a big celebration while he's still around."

"There's no bathrooms up there yet, or heat," Andres replied.

"Hmm, we can bring several space heaters and I guess they'll have to come back across the street to the old folks' place when they have to pee. Or…Say, you do know you two are invited…"

"So that means our bathrooms will be available? Like a quid pro quo?" Josh laughed. "Are you inviting us just to have convenient facilities?"

"No, but that's a good idea. I knew you'd let us." Parashayla grinned at them conspiratorially. "I heard through the DCFS grapevine that you start foster parent training next week. Is that right?" Before they could reply, she said, "I also heard a rumor you two have changed Peanut's diapers. Is that so?"

"Yup," said Andres. "And Eva has been our chief instructor and inspector. She says we passed." They all laughed. "So, when Mr. T had his stroke, we decided to get moving. We're not ready to sign on the dotted line, but we are seriously interested in being ready for Eva and her brothers in case anything happens, and changing diapers is no big deal. We think it's good that adoptive parents have to be licensed foster parents in order to adopt wards of the state. We're learning a lot."

Parashayla hugged them. "I'm glad. Their biological mother has at least twenty years in prison. She indicated she will sign away her parental rights and is glad to have them in a stable environment and supportive of you two taking them some day. Their father is dead and most of their relatives are in Mexico or Texas and have never met them. God, I hope this can work out!"

Parashayla never specified what time, 'in the morning' meant, and the men didn't ask. Thanksgiving morning, they were awakened by their doorbell at six-fifty-one. After each ensuing interruption, someone righteously declared, "Sorry, we promise not to bother you anymore." Except someone else did, and the commotion hadn't stopped.

Just before the start of the activities, as the number of people stomping up the stairs increased, Josh and Andres heard Mr. T yelling, slightly slurred, "Get your hands off me. I ain't gonna be carried. I can makes the stairs me self." Both men laughed when they heard him say, "Besides, my missus is carryin' an empty jar for me to pee in case I drink too much lemonade. Now, get away from me." The sounds of his steps were slow and steady with the thump of one foot, the cane, and the next foot. Just like *The Little Engine That Could*, thought Josh.

That night, exhausted after eating and laughing and getting to know the diverse families that showed up to honor Mr. and Mrs. Thompson, Josh asked, "How the heck many people do you think showed up?"

"At least a hundred, not all at once, maybe more. I can't get over the mix. Not only racially, but economically. It was great seeing Nando and Fly. They are so mature now. Say, did you see the homeless man who showed up and the Thompsons remembered fostering him thirty years ago?"

"That was amazing." Josh took a slow breath. "It's a shame so many homeless are former foster children. I heard the man keeps in touch with an agency and that's how Parashayla got word out to invite him."

"Did you know one of the other foster sons took him downstairs to the studio bathroom and got him all showered, shaved and dressed in clean clothes? Nando and Fly even helped some." Andres looked away, as if trying to hide a grin.

"Where? Andres, just where did the clean clothes come from?"

Andres couldn't contain his laughter. "Some were yours and some were mine. I think that's where Nando and Fly helped. I heard they were the ones who said they would find the man some clothes as long as no one asked any questions. The homeless man was very thankful. So was the foster brother."

"I thought that flannel shirt looked familiar. No wonder Nando and Fly kept looking at me and smirking. Oh, my God, are we going to become a branch of the Salvation Army next? An art gallery, a family history center, and a clothing shop for the destitute? Now, turn your phone off, I'm cutting the wires to the doorbell and tomorrow, we're sleeping in and doing everything we were going to do this morning. Good night."

Both slipped into a deep sleep, only to awaken at one a.m. to the shrill of the fire alarm. Andres glanced at the alarm system display pad on the wall and yelled it was on the third floor. Josh followed Andres who grabbed their fire extinguisher. They could smell smoke as they pushed open the third-floor fireproof door recently installed. Both saw the flames attacking one wall of the efficiency where the food had been served. The space was awaiting completion, along with the new addition behind it.

"It's near the space heater," Andres hollered. "Take that broom and while I spray, you see if you can get it unplugged."

Josh grabbed the wide, industrial-sized push broom, stepped as close as he could without getting burned and swung the wide end toward the outlet. The plug came loose on his second swing. Andres hollered the fire still wasn't out and to get the other extinguisher near the stairway. They heard sirens and Josh remembered, thankfully, the new alarm system was connected to the fire department several blocks away. As they finished using up the second extinguisher, three responders clomped up the stairs and into the room, carrying additional extinguishers and quickly extinguished the fire.

"I think we got it. It's a damn good thing your contractor was smart enough to hook up this system before you were finished and that all the side walls and stairwells were rehabbed to meet fire code."

Josh and Andres, sweating and still scared, nodded.

"Don't worry," another firefighter said. "We're not leaving until we know all the heat and possible sparks are out of those studs. You shouldn't use them damn little heaters, but I bet you ain't got the furnaces set up yet, right?"

Josh and Andres nodded again. Josh explained what the party was for.

"I know who them Thompsons are," said one. "They're good people. Still, I wouldn't go lettin' folks have any more parties up here if they gonna need space heaters."

"Don't worry. We won't, and if there's a next time, we'll check the place a lot closer when they leave." Josh heard the front doorbell ring. Trotting down the stairs, he opened it to find Mrs. T breathing hard. She wore her winter coat over her nightclothes.

"Is you all rights over here? What happened? Did we leave somethin' still plugged and it caught on fire?"

Josh thought quickly. The last thing he wanted was for the Thompsons to think they caused the fire. "No, no, Mrs. T. This had nothing to do with the party. It appears there was a short in one of the boxes on the second floor and it triggered the alarm. The department is checking every floor and outlet now and will soon be leaving. Now, just get back to bed."

Mrs. T hugged him and hurried home.

The firemen spent an hour making sure no heat remained in the studs and that the wiring and outlets were good, plus they checked each floor and the basement.

After they left, Andres said, "God, I feel so guilty. This could have been much worse. As it is, it only ruined several studs that can come out anyway."

Josh hugged him. "We were both so tired last night. When Parashayla said everything was cleaned up and turned off, I felt like we could double check in the morning. You're not the only one who feels guilty." He paused. "Damnit. I love this place, but how long are we going to keep living in a freaking community center? What are we going to do? I don't know how much more of this I can take. My hands feel tied. We started foster parenting classes, we want to have kids, we're falling in love with the Arca kids, yet we have no place to put them!" He stopped himself before escalating further. Yelling and screaming wouldn't solve anything.

"I know. I feel the same way and I'm worried how we could take in the kids and raise them here in some semblance of normalcy. Besides, not to add to the dilemma, but I'm not sure our place will meet DCFS licensing standards anyway." He pushed Josh toward the bedroom. "We need sleep. Something will work out. I still feel it. Somehow, we'll make all this work, the Art Center and our lives."

Josh relaxed. "I know, I know. Let the dots connect. Just hold me in bed for a while."

Christmas Eve

Around ten-thirty on Christmas Eve, Josh and Andres slipped into the Thompson's home. A small, sparsely decorated artificial Christmas tree stood on an end table, with a glass of milk and plate of cookies in front of it.

"I told the kids we don't do Christmas up big around here, but Santa most definitely was a comin'," Mrs. T said. "I don't think these little ones never had a real Christmas, so that's why I asked you to help us surprise them. I can't wait to see the looks on their little faces when they see this. Now, Andres, you go get the bikes you two bought them and the big things outs of the garage and Josh, you get along with him and bring in the tree."

By midnight, a fresh tree was up, decorated to the hilt. Stockings stuffed with trinkets, candy and fruit hung from the buffet. Two boy's bikes, one red, one blue, rested in front of the tree, plus wrapped presents, new clothes, and books crammed the area. There was hardly room to walk through the living room. "That little Eva made sure Santa heard her say she wanted a red boy's bike and no darn girl's one. She's got a baseball mitt comin' in one of them boxes. She sure is a tomboy. Least she ain't fightin' as much at school. Don't know if it's because Mr. T told her Santa didn't come for children who fight or if she's feelin' more secure round here."

Mrs. T handed each of them a gift-wrapped box. Andres started to shake it. He stopped at the look Mrs. T gave him. "It isn't much, but there's a whole lot of meanin' baked in them. You can eat them at home." She paused. "You know, it just don't seem right for you two not to see the looks on these kids' faces in the morning. That recliner over there sleeps real good and so does that couch. I'll gets you some blankets and you just makes yourselves comfortable."

Mr. T told them he had to get his beauty sleep and limped off toward their bedroom. Mrs. T bustled back with blankets and pillows. "When Mr. T's off to bed, I got his bottle of Jack hid cause he ain't supposed to be drinkin' on his medicines. Just a minute, and we'll have us a little toast."

A raspy voice came from the hallway. "Old woman, I know exactly where you keep my Jack and I'm comin' out for a sip. You know you can't hide anythin' from me. Who knows, a sip of Jack may make me even more bootiful."

Josh slept on the couch and was first to hear whispering from the kitchen. He poked Andres and they looked across the dining room to see three sets of huge brown eyes glistening in the dim light from the kitchen stove. Josh turned on the tree lights and the eyes got even larger. Josh and Andres walked across the dining room and knelt by the kids who snuggled against them, still speechless. Peanut, who surprisingly looked wide awake, was in Eva's arms until Andres took him.

"Let's wait a few more minutes so Mr. T and Mrs. T can sleep, okay?" Josh asked.

The kids waited, or tried to. Soon, Peanut started to wriggle and squeal, wanting to get down and crawl.

"Eva, why don't you walk quietly to their bedroom and wake up the Thompsons. Just be quiet, all right?"

Andres snickered and gave Josh a skeptical look as Eva and Spidey tore toward the bedroom, screaming, "Santa came. He's real, he came and so did Josh and Andres."

Josh and Andres spent the day with the Thompsons and kids. That night, getting ready for bed, Andres said, "I think that was one of the best days of my life. Short of meeting you, of course."

"I feel the same way. I can't wait to finish the foster parent training and begin the licensing process. I think the kids are beginning to realize we're going to be close to them for a long time."

"Someday, I want to be called Papa, that's Spanish for Daddy."

"I'll settle for Dad."

There was silence as they climbed into bed, kissed good night, turned off the light and drifted into their own thoughts and dreams of the prospect of parenthood. The only fly in the ointment Josh knew of was that their housing situation might not meet the requirements for a DCFS foster home. Might not? It couldn't, unless they turned it back into a full apartment, which made no sense. Let's just make a decision to rent someplace, he thought. That raised other issues. *How big a place? Where? Locally or further out? West, north or south? The suburbs?* He hated that thought; both he and Andres were city boys. *Was the art center secure enough to move out of? Who would watch it?* It was a circle of issues, all solvable, but how and when?

Chapter Twenty

Community Crisis

Someone was banging on the side door. Andres, who had just returned from running errands and was working in his studio, opened it to find a workman. "Mister," the man spoke rapidly in Spanish. "Mister, somebody was just here looking for you and they are very upset. They have been here twice last week and no one was home."

"What did they want?" Andres was perplexed.

"They say a big meeting is being held at the community center tomorrow night. He said something about old faggots and AIDS and not in their community."

"What the hell. Did you say anything?"

"I told them I don't know what is going on here. I'm just a laborer helping pour the footings for the addition while we got a break in the weather. I don't know what is going to happen here. No one told me. I just go wherever I'm told and pour foundations. These two people were very upset. Here, they gave me this paper." He handed Andres a flyer written in Spanish and English.

NOT IN OUR COMMUNITY!
We heard 4822 South Justine is to become a nursing home and medical center for old
GAY MEN WITH AIDS!
NOT IN OUR COMMUNITY!
NOT AGAIN!
JOIN US AT THE COMMUNITY CENTER MEETING ROOM!

OUR VOICES WILL BE HEARD
Wednesday, January 12 at 6:30 p.m.
Organized by the: Back of the Yards Neighborhood Group

Andres started laughing. "This is absurd. What are they talking about? Gay men with AIDS and not again?"

"Mister, I tell you, they are very upset and carried a big stack of these flyers and said they were going door to door and all over the area. What is this place, anyway?"

"We're converting an old rooming house into a community arts center. We won't be housing anybody."

"Well, all I got to say is these people acted like rabid dogs. So, good luck." He turned and went back to his work.

Andres took the flyer inside, poured himself a coffee, and debated what to do next. He knew Josh hated receiving calls on his cell at work because he was always so busy and frequently on conference calls or in meetings. Andres called the main number and asked to speak to Josh's assistant, Lon. He asked Lon to have Josh call him as soon as it was convenient. Forty-five minutes later, Josh called. Andres gave him a quick run-down of his conversation with the worker and read him the flyer.

"I'm flabbergasted," Josh replied. "Where the heck did that come from? What do they mean, a nursing home for old gay men? AIDS? What the hell?" He was silent a while as Andres waited. "I don't get it. Haven't they seen the kids coming and going every night and Saturdays?"

"I don't get it either. And not again? What's that all about? When would old gay men with AIDS have lived here? I'll walk over and talk with Jorge. He hears everything. In the meantime, why don't you call Denny for his advice?"

"Good idea. I'll do it right now."

The moment Andres walked into the grocery, Jorge rushed over to meet him, waving a flyer. "Andres, these people just left. They wanted to post this on our bulletin board and front window and have us put one in each bag. I told them no. They are *loco*. What's going on?"

"I don't know what's going on. I was hoping you might have heard some rumblings. I have no idea what they are referring to, especially when they talk about AIDS and again."

Jorge reread the flyer. "Ahh, *un momento*. Let me ask my mother-in-law. She hears all the gossip, even more than me. Besides, she lived around here longer than me." He scurried off to the deli area and chatted with her. Returning, with her following him, he said, "She has heard just a little. There is no official Back of the Yards Neighborhood Group. There is an Association which has been around for years and these people are not them. She said several people were talking about this. Seems it is started by some longtime residents, mostly white, who were upset back in the '80's and '90's when Manny took in AIDS patients."

"He what!" The images of the gaunt-looking people in one of the albums flashed through Andres' mind. "I knew nothing about that. Is that even true?" He turned to Jorge's mother-in-law.

She nodded. "*Si*. I heard that before, many years ago. He apparently did it because they had nowhere else to go. They were undocumented and their families would not take them in. He did it for a long time. No one in the neighborhood got that disease from any of them, including Manny. I don't know why these people are still afraid. I think Manny was an angel and should be nominated for sainthood." She tenderly patted Andres' arm and left.

Andres was stunned. On his walk back home, he dialed Josh's cell and filled him in on everything he learned.

"That explains those photos. The dates on the pictures match the crisis. Listen, my first thought was to ignore it, but Denny got all excited. He said it was a great opportunity to tell our story to the community. That we haven't made a public announcement or really informed the community about what we're doing. We were planning to do so, just later, when more funding was secure. He said, *carpe diem*, seize the moment, call the paper, ask them to cover the event and, if possible, help promote the meeting."

"Really? It's an opportunity? Only Denny would think that." He paused. "Well, as usual, Denny is probably right. So, what next? We don't have much time."

Josh laughed. "That was my first reaction, too. How can we accomplish anything on such short notice? Denny told me to call the local media and get it out on Facebook, apparently, there're several local groups

I should join and post on. So, I did. Listen, I just got off the phone with Rob Gutierrez, the editor of the local weekly paper that's printed and posted online in Spanish and English. He heard rumors of the art center and was excited about the idea and was wondering when we would announce it. He just heard about the meeting tomorrow and agreed to cover it. Get this."

"What? Get what?" Andres' head was spinning.

"I called him ten minutes before their deadline. They publish tomorrow and he's going to do a quick story about the conflict, plus his conversation with me about what's really happening. He already interviewed the leaders for their story of Manny taking in AIDS patients and why they think it's going to happen again. He doesn't have time for us to tell the real story, which I couldn't confirm anyway. He encouraged us to find out more and be prepared to describe what we are actually doing at the meeting and what actually happened with Manny and AIDS patients."

"Um, okay. I'm just walking into the house. I'll skim through Manny's diary to see if he mentions anything and dig out that photo album. Jesus, does the excitement never end?" Both laughed, then sighed.

When Josh arrived home, the men held a quick conference call with the board's executive committee. Most members said they could attend the community meeting. Synoma hurried over and they quickly developed a flyer in Spanish and English that outlined the goals of the Art Center and the progress they were making. By then, Andres was able to confirm that Manny did take in AIDS patients for over a decade and they included a paragraph of the history of the building, including the noble efforts of Manny to help those who no one else would help.

About fifty persons showed up at the meeting. Mrs. T came with the children. The office woman from the Arca kid's school was there. She smiled and waved at Andres as she sat down on a bleacher seat. Six elderly people introduced themselves as the head of the Neighborhood Group and seemed frustrated that Jorge insisted on interpreting for them. They launched into a diatribe about the rooming house taking in AIDS victims years ago and now planned to do it again. For proof, they showed pictures of the building with new windows and the footings for the addition on the back. Josh noticed smirks on many of the audience and realized some of them were the parents of children taking art classes. The leaders of the group quickly ran out of steam and asked for questions. Several community members rose to their feet.

"So, have you spoken to the two men who now own the building?" a young mother asked.

"No. They avoided us. Every time we went there, they wouldn't answer the door."

"So, how many times did you go there? What times? Most people work during the day. Did you contact them in writing, leave a note? Who else confirmed this was going to be a medical place for elderly gay men with AIDS? Did you go over there in the evening? If you had, you would know what's going on there."

Josh and Andres stepped forward as Synoma and several board members handed out their flyers. Josh spoke first. "Thank you for coming out tonight. I am Josh Sawicki, my great-great-grandparents built the rooming house. This is Andres Rodriguez, my life partner. His uncle, Manny Rodriguez, inherited the place from my great-grandmother and he left it to us." He paused till the crowd quit reading their flyers and their attention focused on him. "We owe you an apology." He nodded at the Neighborhood Group organizers who looked a little bewildered as if they realized they no longer controlled the meeting. "We should have done a better job of publicly informing the community of our long-range plans with the old place. We planned to do so, but at a later date. So, I apologize to these group leaders and I also thank them for giving us the opportunity to let you know what's going on." He motioned at Andres.

Andres stood. "Jorge, can you translate Spanish to English?"

"*Si, si,* maybe not too good. What I don't understand, I will make up."

Everyone laughed.

"Wait, wait!" One of the organizers stepped forward, shaking with anger. "That Mr. Manny snuck this kind of people in years ago. He didn't ask permission from anybody. He quit taking in healthy people. How do we know these guys aren't going to do the same? They're related to Manny and they're gay, too. How do we know they won't just say it's an art place on the first floor, but upstairs have these sick men who could pass AIDS on to the kids? Huh? How do we know?"

There were murmurs from several older folks in the audience.

Jorge stared at the old man. "Listen, did anyone in the neighborhood get AIDS from the people Manny took care of?" He looked around the room.

No one raised their hands or said anything. Most glared at the old man. "Did anyone in your neighborhood group stop in my store and talk with me about these two young men?" He pointed at the man who complained. "Did you?" The older man shook his head. "That's too bad. I would have told you what they are doing with that old place and told you what good men these two are. Besides, I could have sold you a torta or a taco. Heck, I'd even make a peanut butter sandwich with good jelly for you."

That brought a laugh and seemed to break some of the tension. Jorge nodded at Andres to begin.

"This committee is correct," Andres began in Spanish. "My uncle, Manny Rodriguez, did take in AIDS patients." He paused as several flashes from cameras went off and the audience focused on him in silent anticipation. "For twelve years, he cared for a number of mostly young men, men my age, younger, and into their middle-thirties. Do you know why he cared for them?" He waited as some people looked confused and a slow look of recognition spread across other faces. Raising his voice, he stated, "Because they had no place to go. No place! Most were undocumented, nearly all had been disowned by their families because they were gay, or some couldn't go home for fear of telling their families they were gay and had AIDS." He looked at the committee, his eyes bright. "So, yes, you were correct. AIDS patients used to live there. Guess what, no one in the community, including my uncle, ever caught the disease. Neither will the kids attending our classes." He shook his head. "I need a drink."

One of the mothers in the group hustled up with a bottle of water. Andres thanked her. Everyone was quiet as he took several long drinks and wiped his mouth.

"Now, let me move on to what we are all about. These are our people from the community, board members, who are helping us with the plans and leadership of The Rooming House Gallery." He introduced the board members present and quickly gave an outline of the plans, their current funding, anticipated opening date, and all of the classes they were currently offering. "We currently have over one-hundred-fifty different children a week, taking classes." He looked at the crowd, most appeared surprised. "I know, that's a lot of kids. I run the program and it surprises me when I total up our attendance records. Just think what we can do when we can open classes for adults, seniors, the disabled and, get this, and show off their work in a gallery!"

The crowd broke into excited chatter.

Synoma raised her hand to get attention. "Before we leave, I want to thank this group for setting up this meeting. On the one hand, they should have done more due diligence in truly finding out what we are doing. However, rather than be angry or hold ill will, I want to publicly thank them for getting us off our butts in promoting the Gallery." She nodded at the group leaders. Several looked chagrined, several still angry." And I invite them to come visit one evening to see the classes in operation and some of the incredible artwork our children are making." She motioned toward the reporter. "You too, Rob. We're sorry we didn't bring you in on this sooner."

The grumpy old man hollered, "Just you wait till your kids get sick. We told you so."

Mrs. Thompson walked over to him. "Mister, you don't know what you is talkin' about. Sometime, you come by my house right across the street. I'll sweeten you up with some cookies and coffee and tell you what's really goin on there." She waved her finger in front of his face. "I means it. I won't bite, and my coffee is good, too." She patted him on the shoulder like he was a child. He pulled away from her with a grunt and stalked out of the building.

As they walked out of the meeting after being nearly mobbed by parents asking questions, Synoma said to Josh and Andres, "Can you handle more kids signing up? I think we stirred something up tonight."

Andres nudged Synoma's arm. "Can the board handle getting this building finished sooner?"

Chapter Twenty-one

Decisions—February 2012

The executive committee of the board squeezed around a small table in Andres' studio as volunteers worked out in the dining and living room areas with noisy kids on art projects and lessons. Synoma was now the board president and ran a tight, efficient meeting with the goal of being well prepared for the full board meeting held the third Tuesday of each month in the local Savings and Loan meeting room. Both meetings included Arnaud and/or his cohorts on Skype. Organizational things came together quickly and all felt the excitement of anticipating a fall opening.

The committee updates, plus board reports, were sent one week in advance to be read by the members who were expected to be prepared, ready to discuss the items and to take action if needed. Tonight's meeting involved mostly reports, including the recent community meeting and unexpected positive publicity. The part-time grants writer and development person, Julie, reported the tax credits were expected to bring in approximately seventy-five thousand, and she excitedly confirmed that three gifts of fifty-thousand were received to match Annaud's Apple stock challenge. One of those gifts was to remain anonymous for the time being. Josh suspected that Grandpa Joey, Kate, Krys, Tim and other family members might be behind the anonymous gift, but wasn't sure. Julie also shared a donor made a gift of one-hundred-thousand dollars and had the naming rights for a floor or the new addition. She added the donor asked to remain anonymous until announcements of the opening were made. Denny conference-called in to report the new addition would be completed by June, plus the small gravel parking lot behind the building would be ready by July and paved if funds came in. Julie and Josh informed the group that enough small grants and donations were coming in to run the programs they were currently operating. They reviewed a report which projected how much income would be needed when the building opened. The last item on the agenda simply stated, 'Arnaud's comments,' and no report was included.

"People, I want to commend you," Arnaud's voice crackled over the Skype connection, his polished-stone string tie clasp glinting as his two fellow gray-haired consultants smiled and nodded. "Rarely have we seen a group advance as quickly as yours." He paused as everyone clapped. "There is more business. My cohorts and I feel you need to make another transition. I don't know about you, but projections for full operation were a little scary to me and not realistic. Your emphasis has been on getting the building up and ready. Now you need to switch gears and start figuring out how the heck you're going to keep it running." He paused as a look of accomplishment on their faces turned to one of, 'oh no, we have more challenges.' Still, no one looked shocked. "I know you've been planning on finding a full-time executive director and halftime program director which I'm guessing everyone assumes will be Josh and Andres. That somehow, each of them can do this while maintaining their other challenging jobs, just like they've been doing for nearly three years now." He paused again to look at their faces. "I think I just lassoed your attention."

Josh looked at Andres. Just how did this old guy a thousand miles away read his mind? Andres looked at him as if thinking the same thing. Getting the building to where it was kidnapped all their extra time. It was like having a second full time job. They had not taken a weekend camping or kayaking trip since inheriting the place, spent a night away, or done anything that could be considered relaxing and a break. How much longer could they keep doing this? Did he want to? Josh thought about what started as inheriting an old building that would make a nice home and a cool little art gallery for Andres and other evolving artists became something far bigger. In ten years, did he want to be living in a bedroom, using the kitchen with thirty kids packed around him, no dining room, no privacy? That was assuming the funds didn't come in to remodel the first floor into classroom space and offices. If they did, where were they going to live? Also, what about the Arca children? His heart and mind somehow knew they would become part of their lives. How and when, he didn't yet know, but both he and Andres were on the same wave length. What about Andres? Between teaching two days a week, the high school art club, plus his hours at the center, he had little time to do what he liked to do—make art. The man needed time and space to do it. He startled. Everyone was looking at him.

"Josh, did you catch what I just said?" Arnaud asked.

"Um, no. Sorry, my mind was wandering. Please repeat it."

"I said I'm guessing what I think you were thinking about and that is, do you really want to be the executive director and CFO of this organization for a long time? Andres, do you truly want to be the program director for a long time? You need not answer right now, this is about this group expanding their assumptions and looking at other possibilities, though your reaction would be helpful."

"I can go first," Andres said. "I would love to be a half-time art director, but I can't do that plus teach part-time, which I love, plus do my own work, which is dropping off because of my lack of time. I can do two of the three things well and one of those things must be making art. I couldn't make a decision right now about which I prefer, teaching high school or the center. I love both so much, but that's where I'm at. Plus, not to sound selfish, there's no way Josh and I can live here much longer like we are now. Not paying rent is wonderful. However, for our personal life and some of our future interests, well, this is starting to suck."

Several of the committee members looked surprised.

Josh wanted to jump up and pull Andres into a hug. The guy was so gutsy and honest. "I have been thinking," he said slowly, "maybe not as concisely as Arnaud or Andres. Sitting here, right now, I realized I do not want to be the executive director and that this group needs to think in terms of new, professional leadership. Like Andres, I want a life outside of this place, but still close to it. It's hard to think about not being a part of it, my DNA comes from this place and I want to remain involved in some manner. This past week, I received a promotion at the firm. I am now not only the office manager, but also the paralegal manager. It's a great boost in salary and responsibility." He took a deep breath. "My point is, I can't keep this pace up and expect to have any personal or family life." He felt his cheeks turn pink. He and Andres had not spoken with anyone present about their thoughts on a family. Did he inadvertently announce something? No one else seemed to catch the significance of his words. Andres grinned and winked at him. Why that kind of wink? Josh forced himself to listen to Arnaud.

"So, people," Arnaud said. "I don't think I need to say more. I wouldn't bring this up to the full board next week. Let's meet in two weeks as the executive committee and talk about it some more. That will give everyone a chance to digest and think about what leadership the organization truly needs. Think about this: do you truly need an executive director? A full-time program director? A development director? A volunteer coordinator? It's hard to get all those in one person or a person and a half and it's going to be touch and go finding the money to pay staff for your first year or two. So, think outside of the corral a bit more."

He cut his computer connection as the members of the executive committee looked at Josh and Andres, some in surprise, several in understanding.

After the board members left and the volunteers cleaned up the art areas and departed, Josh collapsed into the old recliner they still kept in the kitchen. Andres opened the fridge. "Let's have something stronger, how about a Moscow Mule?"

"Good idea, do we have a lime?"

"When does a Mexican not have a lime?" Andres quickly mixed vodka with ginger beer, ice, and a nice wedge of lime. "Here, you get the only copper cup we own, I'll use a glass and no, this glass doesn't hold any more than that cup.

Andres sat in the old rocking chair. Mae's. Actually Walentina's. He re-glued it and made new pads from material he discovered in one of the closets. It was a prized possession of both of theirs and something they didn't want to store in the basement with the other furniture. "You look shocked. I feel shocked. Most of the board will be as well."

"I know. Believe me, I surprised myself when those words came out of my mouth. I feel totally at peace." Josh sipped his Mule. "This is good." He looked out the window into the dark, gathering his thoughts. "It was like my entire life floated, actually sped, in front of me after I heard

Arnaud's words. It became so clear, all in an instant. I have a wonderful career and a job I love. I am not a trained or learned nonprofit director, though, I could now teach a class on starting one up." He looked closely at Andres to see any reaction. Andres' smile was warm and encouraging. "I'm still adjusting to my decision and it may take a bit of time, but I'm convinced it's the right one for me. It's not that I don't love this place. Even after overcoming my concerns for giving it up and realizing it will never be our home, I still feel right about what we did. Also, it just hit me that, unless I am totally committed to lead this organization into the next phase and find the funding to keep it going, I could actually be a handicap." He took another sip and pushed the chair back a notch so his feet were partially elevated. He waved his copper cup at Andres as if telling him it was his turn to speak.

"I think that's wise thinking, but I may need a bit of time to adjust also. Not being fully committed…I think that is super wise thinking. It's helping me realize this place can run without us. That's a hard thought. Don't you agree?"

"I do. I think that's also life. What are your thoughts? Do you want to pull out now, too? I see you being more necessary to this place than me, yet I don't want to lay a trip on you."

"You're not, trust me, you're not. My biggest conflict right now is between two loves of my life, I mean, other than you." He flashed his grin and winked. The same wink as earlier, the one that usually meant he wanted to get naked together. "Don't worry, we need to finish our heavy discussion before I get amorous." Andres licked lime from the edge of his glass. "See, I can go either way. I could devote half my time here for a very long time, be part of the community, the kids, the artists and so on. Or I could devote half my life to teaching at the high school. Either way would be fulfilling for me. I know that sounds strange after all the sweat, time and money I've sunk into this place, but that's the way it is. I just can't do both, once this place opens, and still think of getting back to making art." He took another sip, then tilted the glass and drained it. "I have time to make up my mind. I'll know this spring if my contract with the school will be renewed. So, I'm going to punt and wait to make a decision. Besides, who knows what else will happen in our lives by the time this place opens in the fall." He pointed to a paper hanging on the fridge with the finger-paint handprints of Eva, Spidey and Peanut.

He pulled Josh from the chair, kissed him and led him toward their bedroom. Along the way, he picked up the copy of Manny's journal and the photo album with the people who looked like survivors from concentration camps but they now knew were AIDS patients. "For afterward. I'll start reading from the beginning. We know the ending," he whispered.

"Does that mean you're getting too old to make love all night?"

"Hmm, don't think so. I do know I've been dying to start reading this last journal and to learn more about my uncle. Just don't fall asleep."

"While you're making love to me? Or after, when you're reading to me?"

Chapter Twenty-two

Civil Union and A Family

Sunday afternoon, February 12, 2012, Mr. T was not feeling well and the kids were spending the afternoon and evening with Josh and Andres. Spidey tore by on his tricycle. Eva flew around on her two-wheeled scooter like she was practicing for a circus performance. One leg out to the side, then back, then jumping to switch feet, sashaying her little behind. Peanut rolled and skootched with a toy in each hand to wherever he thought the action was, or his bottle. Josh and Andres sat in beanbag chairs they hauled to the second floor which was nearly finished and provided a great space for the kids to run off their energy on a damp cold gray Chicago day.

Parashayla came into the room. "I'm here. The pizzas are downstairs in the kitchen. Who's ready?"

Eva and Spidey tore down the stairs as Josh picked up Peanut. "Good timing. We're hungry and you arrived at just the right time." He tossed the little guy into the air, making him squeal, and followed the gang down the stairs and into their kitchen.

After a half glass of orange pop was spilled by Spidey, cleaned up by Josh, and the first couple of pieces of pizza addressed their hunger pangs, the adults began to talk.

"I have some news that may be of interest to you two guys," Parashayla said with a coy smile.

"I'm still too hungry to ask mystery questions, just tell us." Andres handed a pizza crust to Peanut to gnaw on and grabbed another piece for himself.

"I am now a licensed officiant for the state of Illinois. That means I can legally preside at weddings, funerals, and civil unions. Want to set a date?" She winked at them as she forked a piece of pizza into her mouth.

Josh felt his cheeks warm as he looked at Andres who started blushing. "I don't know what to say other than congratulations."

"Well," Andres drew out the word. "I can't say Josh and I haven't talked about something like this. We do want to be ready to take these hooligans if needed and it would be nice to be a legal couple." He cleared his throat, reached in his pocket and pulled out his iPhone. "How about May fifth? Upstairs. Something simple."

Josh stared at him, then slowly said, "I guess the dots are connecting." He was quiet a moment. "It's fine by me." He slid a piece of pizza onto Spidey's plate and cut it up. *This seems so calm,* he thought. *No stress, no hassle, we're going to be legal partners. We're going to have the same rights as married hetero folks.* He bit into another piece of pizza and looked at Andres. Andres picked up another piece and quickly took a bite, his eyes never leaving Josh's. They chewed in unison then, simultaneously, they each lifted their hands and gave a thumbs up.

"Are we talking of a funeral or a civil union?" Parashayla sounded innocent. Her eyes said otherwise.

"They ain't dead. What's a civil union?" yelled Eva.

"It's the same thing as a wedding, but for gay people. Men and women get married, men and men or women and women who love each other have a civil union. Isn't that wonderful?" Parashayla patted Eva's arm.

Eva nodded, but Josh thought she looked like her wheels were turning.

After helping clean up, Parashayla said, "I have to leave. I'm so excited for you two and you're both so busy. Is it okay if I take the lead on planning this?"

Andres looked at Josh. Both beamed. "You're in charge, just tell us what to do," Andres said.

Josh hugged Parashayla. "Thank you. This seems like such a logical next step."

"It's about love, Josh. Love and logic." Parashayla kissed him on the cheek and left.

The kids followed her to the door to hug and kiss her. After Parashayla left, Eva stopped suddenly in the dining room class area. She looked at Josh and Andres. "Wait a minute. You can't just get married. You gotta get engaged first. One of you got to ask the other to marry him."

"Well, okay. I guess that's the way it's usually done." Josh looked at Andres. "Why don't you ask me?"

"I think you should ask me," Andres said. "You're older. Age before beauty."

"You two are disgusting. Just wait." Eva ran to a storage cabinet and returned with two straws and a pair of scissors. "I know how to do this. Now quit acting funny. This is serious and you can't be joking around." She turned her back to them. "Okay, I'm almost ready. Spidey get over here. Bring Peanut. We're going to be the ones who watch them and make it legal."

"Like witnesses?" Andres asked.

"Yes, that's the word." She turned toward them and held out her hand. "The longest has to ask the other. I'm counting to three, then you both pull the straw out and compare them. One. Two. Three. Pull."

Josh and Andres pulled out the straws and compared them. They were equal length.

"I did that on purpose. You both gotta ask the other. Now get on your knees and face each other and, at the same time say, 'I love you. Will you marry me?' You can't joke around." She watched as Josh and Andres dropped to their knees. She quickly scooted Spidey and Peanut next to her to watch them. All of them in a little circle amidst the folding tables and chairs, the smells of paint, and a variety of kid's artwork on the walls.

Josh was serious as he knelt. Andres looked the same, as if the impact of what they were doing suddenly hit both of them. They took each other's hands. Their eyes moist. They nodded their heads in unison and began together, "I love you. Will you…?"

At that instant, Peanut let out an explosion so loud they all jumped and began laughing. When they stopped to catch their breath, Eva giggled. "Ya still gotta say yes to each other."

"Yes," shouted Josh and Andres together.

"Eva, now that we're officially engaged, can you recut the straws so we can see who changes Peanut? That was a real blow-out." Andres picked up Peanut and held him away from his body. "He's even leaking through."

"Ya both have to. He's going to be a mess." Eva giggled and ran off, taking the straws with her.

Saturday, March 10, 2012

Andres took a big breath, slowly let it out and opened the side door into the garage workshop of JJ Sawicki, Josh's father. Loud, sports-talk radio hit him. JJ stood at a workbench, partially turned away from the door, intensely focused on gluing pieces of wood together. Walnut and oak pieces, Andres noted, that were meticulously cut, planed and sanded to the same precise sizes. Andres noted the well-kept shop, everything in its place, the painted swept floor. *I see where Josh gets his neat freak,* he thought. He stepped further into the shop, but JJ appeared to be concentrating so heavily, he didn't hear or notice.

Andres took another deep breath. *Carpe Diem.* He reached up and shut the radio off.

JJ jerked and stared at him. "What the...? Why are you here? Is something wrong with Joshy?"

"Josh is well." Andres stuck out his hand.

He held it there till JJ cautiously reached out his meaty hand and gave a limp squeeze. Before JJ could withdraw his hand, Andres squeezed harder. Even harder, until JJ returned a firmer grasp. Almost like a contest, both men intensified their grips. Both still silent.

JJ let go first. "Why are you here? Where's Joshy?" His voice was husky, weak, he sounded insecure.

Andres tried to keep his voice calm, yet strong. "Your girly office manager son is in the house, probably having coffee with his mother. His flaky faggot artist boyfriend has a question for you."

JJ blanched, stepped back and looked around. He pulled two stools out and nodded for Andres to sit as he thumped his stocky body down. Andres could see why his physical build helped him play football in high school. "What is the question?" The words were soft, fearful.

"I came to ask for your son's hand in marriage."

JJ shook his head. He choked. Looking around, he unsteadily stood to reach his coffee thermos and took a big swallow.

"Oh," Andres continued, "I know the technical legal term is Civil Union, but it's as close to marriage as two men in love can get right now."

JJ gulped another slug of coffee. Beads of sweat started to form on his forehead.

"You don't have to answer right now, and, to tell you the truth, it doesn't matter if you approve or not. You see, Josh and I are tired of both of our fathers' bullshit, your rudeness, your insulting language, your attitudes when you encounter us. You've had several people try to get through to you within the last year. Right?" JJ cautiously nodded, his eyes looking at the floor. "Well, we're not sure that worked, so we decided to confront you. Each father, separately. Today. We're not making any threats. We're not demanding you change, but we would like to feel you're a part of our family and to truly feel we're a part of yours. You know, just basic human stuff."

JJ took another long slug of coffee. *Good thing that stuff isn't hot,* Andres thought.

"I-I don't know what to say," JJ muttered.

Andres stood and picked up the last bowl in a line on a shelf. It appeared to be the most recently turned bowl from a line of bowls JJ made. "I didn't realize you were an artist. These are getting pretty good. Have you always been artistic or worked with your hands?"

JJ jumped off the stool. "I'm not an artist." His face showed shock at such an idea. "I've always liked messing around with wood. Now that I'm getting closer to retirement, I decided to focus more on something I've always been interested in, woodworking and turning." He stepped over to his lathe. "I bought this six months ago. It's a beauty. Here on the wall above the bench, are all my tools. See, this is a spindle roughing gouge, this is a gouge, and here's a parting tool." His face grew animated. "See, I can turn wood where I fasten it at each end on the lathe, or for bowls, I screw this faceplate on the end of the wood piece and mount it here. Then I work on the bowl and when I'm finished, I cut the tail off and smooth and sand

213

the bottom. That's how you get the flat bottoms on wooden bowls. I tell you, it's not as easy as it looks." He pointed to several misshapen and lopsided bowls sitting in a row that ended with several fine ones. "This was my first attempt. This is my latest."

"You've made tremendous progress. These are almost as good as what I see in art galleries or weekend art fairs. Have you considered what you're eventually going to do with them?"

"Oh, heck. I was just doing it for fun. You know, something to keep me out of Marge's hair and off the streets and out of the bars when I retired. Figured I'd start giving my better ones to family, never thought about after that." He ran his fingers through his hair, as if excited at the thought of doing more with his handiwork.

"Well." Andres smiled. "Even with the size of your family, you're going to run out of people to give them to or who truly want a dozen of them. Maybe you should get one of those pop-up awning tents and check out all the craft and art fairs."

JJ sucked in his breath and stretched, a smile on his face. His expression changed to one of uncertainty as he let his breath out and looked down at the floor. His voice soft and shaky, he asked, "Andres, do I have to answer your question right now?"

"You never have to answer it. Words don't always matter. We'll know by your actions." Andres turned and stepped briskly toward the door. "Take care of yourself, JJ, and keep up that good work."

JJ rushed past him, almost bumping into him, and opened the door. "Maybe. Maybe we should go inside, see if Joshy and his mother have any coffee left."

~ * ~

Josh stayed quiet in the van as Andres eased it onto I-80 West toward Joliet. Finally, he couldn't stand it any longer. "What went on out there? At least you came into the house with all your digits and no stab wounds. Dad seemed the most relaxed around us than he's ever been."

Andres slowed as a semi passed them, spewing slush from the overnight March snow.

"Mom is dying to know. She wants me to call her after I meet with your dad."

Andres remained silent for several more miles. "I think I sounded calmer than I felt. Winning a handshake squeeze-off didn't hurt." He laughed. "Maybe you should think about that with my dad."

"So, you had a handshake squeeze-off contest. Was that it? Did you talk?"

Andres replayed the conversation and how JJ didn't know how to respond until the topic changed to woodworking. "I think he was surprised, well, shocked, when I referred to his work as art. He'd never thought in those terms and now his son's flaky faggot artist boyfriend was talking to him like another artist." He laughed. "Your dad's expression when he realized his work is art was priceless. We should have had a secret camera." He glanced over at Josh. "Are you nervous? We're about five minutes away."

"Yes. I think dental tools can do damage quicker than wood-turning tools."

"You'll do fine. The shock value is tremendous. This was a fantastic idea, if I do say so myself." Andres patted his chest.

Josh laughed. "Just what brought this to your constantly spinning mind?"

"So far, nothing else seems to have broken through to them. Actually, I think figuring out my blockage over children gave me the confidence to at least try to make a break-through with our dads. What's the worst that can happen? They disown us? Not speak to us or call us names? Stab us with their tools?" He pulled into a Washington Street parking lot on the east side of Joliet. It was between an older brick office building and a large Mexican grocery store. "I'm going in there." He pointed to the grocery store. "Mom said they have great produce and meat. I'll do some shopping. Text me if you die or when you come out. I love you."

Josh nervously looked at the clock on the wall as he entered the small, plain reception room. His timing should be accurate. Bella confirmed Art Junior's schedule and if all went as planned, Andres' father should be with his last patient of the morning.

The receptionist smiled up at him. "Do you want to make an appointment? Our hours are over for today."

Josh swallowed. "No, I need to speak with Dr. Rodriguez personally. I only need a few moments and can wait till he's finished."

The receptionist didn't seem surprised. She pointed at the waiting area. After answering a phone call, she left her desk and returned in a few moments.

A woman with a middle-school aged child came through the clinic door, the child cautiously licking his lips as if trying to sense them. A few moments later, Dr. Arthur Rodriguez, Jr. walked out. "Yes, someone wanted to have a word with me?" He startled when Josh stood up and stuck out his hand. "Oh, it's you. Is something wrong with Andres?" Josh shook his head. "Come back. Come back to my office." He led the way into his small neat office and closed the door.

Josh noticed several newspaper clippings about Andres framed and hanging on the wall along with all of the dental certifications. He stuck his hand out again. Why not? If it worked for Andres-the-pansy, maybe a squeeze-off would work for a girly office manager. Reluctantly, Art Jr. took his hand. Josh squeezed firmly until the doctor responded, but the doctor quickly released and moved behind his desk. He motioned for Josh to sit. "Why are you here?" His voice was brusque.

"I have a big question to ask of you. We just came from my home where Andres asked the same question of my father." Art Junior's eyes squinted in confusion. "I came to ask for the hand of your son in marriage, actually a Civil Union. We plan on holding the ceremony in May."

Art Junior shook his head as if to clear the cobwebs. His eyes glared. "What the hell. You don't need my permission. Do what you want to do. I don't give a damn."

"Really? You truly don't give a damn about your only child? I don't believe that." Josh stood, feeling his confidence and some anger grow. "If you don't give a damn, then why do you have these on your walls?" He lifted one of the framed articles off the wall and waved it. "I know we don't need your permission to marry. However, it's a big deal to us and it should be to you. See, both you and my father have treated us like crap since we came out as gay. We are both successful. We are transforming an old house

216

into a community art center. We love each other, and neither of us has brought shame to our families." He paused, reminding himself to stay calm and focused. To buy time, he rehung the article. Glancing at Art Junior, he realized he certainly had his attention. Taking in a big breath, he purposefully raised his voice. "I have another question of you. Don't answer out loud yet. Actually, several more questions. Ready?"

Reluctantly, the dentist looked up at him and said yes.

"How did you like your relationship with your father? Was it satisfying? Life is short, especially at your age now. Just how long do you want to keep the same type of relationship with your son? As a father, is this one satisfying?"

Dead silence ensued. Art Junior slumped in his seat. He started to sit up, his mouth opening like a gasping fish. Instead, he clasped his hand over it as if to stop what he might say.

Josh remembered Andres' words about action. He placed his hands on the desk and leaned over till his face was close to Art Junior's. "You don't have to reply. Your son says actions speak louder than words. Goodbye. Have a nice day." He strode confidently out of the office and through the reception room. Outside, around the corner, he sucked in a huge breath, leaned against the building and texted Andres; 'On my way to help shop, bleeding all the way. Need beer.' Josh found Andres inside the grocery store, and updated him on his experience with *El Doctor*.

Andres said, "I think your dad, JJ, showed the most change. Hopefully, my dad will someday."

"I agree, but my dad was also softened up a bit from my mother leaving him, and from when my grandfather told him he wasn't welcome at Easter dinner until he changed." He placed several avocados in the basket. "Give your dad some time." He poked around in the shopping cart. "No quesadilla shells?"

"We're not to that aisle yet."

~ * ~

Two weeks later, after the Saturday classes ended, Andres and Josh sat on their bed, looking through the responses they were receiving through

217

the mail and electronically to their upcoming civil union invite. The date for it was May 5, 2012. They titled their invitation, 'The No-Shotgun Rooming House Civil Union.' Some of the notes on the responses were laugh-worthy.

No shotgun must mean no pregnancy. What's the excitement without a gun and a kid on the way?

It's about time! Who asked whom?

Polish and Mexican? This I gotta see. Just what are you serving?

Andres' phone rang. "It's Mom. I'll put it on speaker."

"Are you both home? I want to talk with both of you. It's about Andres' father."

"Mom, is he okay? Did something happen?"

Bella laughed. "Yes, he's all right, just not normal. What did Josh do to him? Give him a shot of something?" She laughed harder. "Wait till you hear all this."

"Mom, just tell us."

Andres looked at Josh. "What did you really do to him when you were in his office two weeks ago?"

"I'm not telling." Josh laughed. "Be quiet and let her talk. I can't wait to hear this."

"Your dad, *El Doctor,* has never acted this way toward me since he was trying to seduce me back when I was sixteen. He's been coming home from work to eat dinner with me, and complimenting me on my cooking. A week ago, he even washed the dishes. Of course, he had no clue where to put them. One evening, he asked me to go for a walk around the little lake in the park. He even laughed good-naturedly when I told him it was too slushy out. I mean, it is March."

"Wow, Mom. I'm glad we're sitting down. That's amazing." Andres grinned at Josh who gave him the thumbs up.

"Now, get this. He was on the phone with another dentist. They cover for each other sometimes. He told him about the latest art show you are in, Andres. Told him the name of the gallery and the address. The other guy must have asked something, because the next thing he said was, 'Yes, I have a son who's a marvelous artist. You should buy some of his art.' There was another pause and he said, 'No, he doesn't have children, but he is going to marry his boyfriend in a civil union.' Andres and Josh, I nearly collapsed. I sat down and put my head in my hands like I was going to pass out."

"Bella, Mom, that was incredible. Maybe I should have slapped him around more." Josh took Andres' hand.

"Boys, there's more. He came back into the room and saw me with my head in my hands. 'Are you all right? Can I get you anything?' He sounded all concerned. He reached down and touched my head. That man has not touched me in three decades. I was so shocked, I had to look up at him, and he was for real. He wasn't being sarcastic or mean."

"Mom, what did you say? How did you react? That's awesome." Andres squeezed Josh's hand.

Bella was quiet a moment. "Well, I decided the least I could do was meet him halfway. I told him thank you for talking about *our* son. Next, I asked him if he needed me to rent him a tuxedo for the wedding. He looked at me funny, kind of shuffled around on his feet, then said, 'Yeah. I guess so.'" She giggled. "So, I stood up, patted his hand and told him that was a good answer."

Excited, Josh stuck his face close to the phone. "Bella, what did he do?"

"Josh, you don't have to shout. He patted my hand back, smiled and said he was going online to order some of Andres' art from the gallery for the house and his offices."

"Mom, thanks for telling us all this. I guess it's my turn to shift my attitude and meet him halfway, too. You were right when you told me to not rule out the possibility of him changing. Thank you."

"Thanks, son." She giggled, then teased, "Maybe if *El Doctor* buys enough art, you will have enough money to pay for your wedding."

Josh giggled. "Or at least a better van."

Andres swatted him.

Chapter Twenty-three

The Ceremony—May 2012

The newly refinished floors shone, the soft light filtered through the windows of the second-floor gallery which was nearly finished. The portable walls were covered in children's art and placed to form a backdrop at the east end of the room. Twinkling lights and tulle draped their tops. The guests sat in draped, rented folding chairs. Fly and Nando were the ushers. They stood proudly on each side of the main aisle as Josh and Andres walked down, holding hands. Father Frank and Padre sat in the second row, not wearing their collars, unable to officiate at same sex ceremonies. Parashayla waited in front. Andres' hand twitched. Josh was nervous too and gripped Andres' hand tighter. Both sets of parents walked behind them and took their seats in the front row alongside Josh's grandparents.

Andres and Josh wore matching black tuxedos and lavender shirts with dark contrasting ties. There was no music, just the simple elegance of silence.

Josh and Andres turned to face each other. Eva and Spidey solemnly walked up. Eva stood by Andres, Spidey by Josh. From Mrs. T's lap, Peanut let out a squeal of frustration that he wasn't with them. Eva ran back to the second row, grabbed him, and lugged the just-turned one-year old to the men. She stood him next to Andres. Peanut jabbered and wiped his drooly chin on Andres' pant leg, then sat down and sucked on his pacifier, seemingly satisfied that he was included.

Andres reached down and patted the tyke on the head. Taking Josh's hands, he inhaled deeply, let it out slowly, and softly said, "Josh, you go first."

Josh startled with a look of surprise. He whispered, "No, I thought you were going first."

"Guess we didn't decide this, did we?" Andres smiled out at the waiting guests as if nothing was wrong.

Parashayla covered her mouth to keep from laughing.

The kids looked up as if wondering what was taking them so long.

Josh pulled Andres closer and whispered loudly. "You decide. I don't think people want to wait through an argument."

Andres nodded, took a big breath, let it out, and said, "Josh, I commit myself to be a faithful partner, to love and care for you during good times and bad. I love you and want to spend the rest of my life with you." He paused as if it was Josh's turn to speak, then quickly added, "I also promise to only make quesadillas once a week and to never inherit another rooming house."

When the laughter died down, Josh cleared his throat. "Andres, I too commit to faithfully spend the rest of my life with you. I love you and will care for you in good times and bad." He paused and glanced at the people who were beginning to smile in anticipation of what else he might say. "Andres, I can eat your quesadillas occasionally more than once a week, and I won't care too much if we inherit another rooming house, but I would like you to promise we will never have to live in your old van."

The two men embraced tightly and kissed as everyone clapped.

Parashayla waited till the joyful sounds quieted. "By the power invested in me by the state of Illinois, I declare you partners in a legal civil union. You now have the same rights as married spouses." She raised her hand to get everyone's attention. "This is an exciting day and a wonderful cause for celebration. Thank you for being here to share this joy and occasion. However, before we celebrate with these two wonderful men, before we eat and drink in our happiness for them, I ask for a moment of silence to commemorate all of the LGBTQ folks who have fought for this day, who died before seeing civil unions legalized, and now in several states other than Illinois, marriage legalized too. Plus, for those who endured and experienced so much hate and discrimination of any type."

As the crowd quieted, a loud, "Amen!" was heard from Mr. T sitting in his wheelchair.

After the short ceremony, while the music played, the kids ran around and rode the elevator and the snacks were being eaten, Josh and Andres signed the forms Parashayla would turn into the county clerk's office. Grandpa Joey approached her. "I heard rumors you're responsible for this shindig today."

Parashayla laughed as she signed and folded the forms, slid them into the envelope and slipped it into her purse. "Yes. Guess you can blame me. I became a licensed officiant and wanted to try out my new license." She took a sip of wine and filled him in on the details.

Andres raised his cup to her.

Parashayla gave him a light shove. "They both blushed, so I knew they already talked about a union."

Josh nodded with a big smile.

Andres shrugged, with a look of faux innocence.

"Who spoke next? I wish I could have seen the looks on their faces." Grandpa Joey chuckled, winking at the men.

"Well, Josh was quiet, but Andres said they had been thinking of it, especially because it seemed they might be taking the children soon and they liked the idea of being legally permanent. Damn, I wish this country would hurry and legalize marriage for gays nationwide. Anyway, Andres pulled his phone out, checked the calendar, and said let's do it May fifth. I assumed he meant a union and not their funerals, so I got busy." She smiled at Andres.

"Thank you for giving us a nudge." Andres lightly chucked her arm. "We had been thinking about it. I can't tell you why we were waiting so long. Especially since Governor Quin signed the new law to let civil unions begin June first, last year. Of course, it's not like we've been busy."

Josh took a cup of punch from a volunteer carrying a tray. "Parashayla, after you left that evening, we realized neither of us proposed to the other. We only talked about getting hitched."

Parashayla's eyes glistened. "What did you do?"

Andres laughed. "We couldn't decide who should ask the other, so we asked Eva to cut two drinking straws behind our backs. We told her one should be short and one long, but they should look the same when she held them out to us."

Eva had been listening behind the men. She jumped into the middle of them, holding Peanut. "I knowed what they was doing, so I cut them the same. After they pulled them out, I told them they both had to get on their knees and ask each other, then they had to kiss nice and they couldn't laugh, cuz this was supposed to be serious."

"Did we?" asked Andres, trying to keep a straight face.

"You tried, but Peanut pooped his pants real loud and we all fell over, laughing. It was fun."

"That was one romantic engagement scene." Laughing, Grandpa Joey pulled Parashayla into a fatherly hug. "I think you've been responsible for several things in their lives." He turned his head toward the men's fathers. "That spurred Josh and Andres into some other actions." He pulled a sticky Peanut from Eva's arms. "This little guy has more punch on him than in him."

"He keeps dribbling when I give him a drink outa them fancy cups," Eva yelled.

Grandpa Joey laughed. Looking at the men, he asked, "Are you boys going to take a few days off? Maybe go somewhere?"

Eva jumped up and grabbed Peanut out of his hands. Before she ran off, she hollered, "They don't have time. They're taking us to Lincoln Park Zoo tomorrow, then coming back to clean the upstairs apartment in my house. I think they're moving up there, so we don't have to cross the street to see them anymore."

"I think that answers your question." With that, Andres took Josh's hand and pulled him toward their parents.

A Family

3 weeks later

Andres and Josh raised Mr. T out of the minivan and into a wheelchair and pushed him up the temporary ramp that Andres and a neighbor had installed while Mr. T was in the hospital. They lifted him into the hospital bed in the living room while Mrs. T scurried around, locating a urinal, bedpan and a little bell. The old man snorted when he saw the bell and tried to laugh at Mrs. T. She kissed him. Another stroke five days after Josh and Andres' marriage left him incapable of feeding himself, walking, even speaking. It was sad, especially for the kids, especially for everyone.

The weekend following Mr. T's major stroke, Josh and Andres moved the kids' beds to the Thompson's upper flat, plus their own furniture and personal goods. Andres moved his art supplies to the Thompson's basement. Mr. T's health started to deteriorate before their wedding and the two men began helping more with the children. Their foster parent license came in late April. Now, the flat was their legal home, leaving the Thompsons the first floor to themselves.

Shortly after their civil union ceremony, Andres also received word that his high school contract to teach art would not be renewed due to financial cutbacks, so he officially became the half-time art director for The Rooming House Gallery. Josh submitted his resignation as the executive director subject to when his replacement could be hired. The board decided to seek a director of development rather than an executive director because the board was now strong enough to function effectively. The board began the search process to replace Josh.

On May eighteenth, the two men received their official confirmation from DCFS that they could begin the adoption process. They decided to wait to tell the children. Today, May twenty-fifth, they were packing their new/used minivan to attend a Memorial Day weekend family camp at YMCA Camp Pinewood near Muskegon, Michigan. Several local families were going to caravan with them. For Josh and Andres, it was their first weekend away since moving into the rooming house. With Chicago rush hour traffic, it turned into a five-hour drive, but they were prepared with snacks and a video player and a stop at the Michigan Visitor Center rest stop and playground.

On Saturday afternoon, they took the kids on a hike around Lake Echo. They stopped to sit on 'crooked tree.' Camp legend said it was the work of Native Americans who bent it over a century ago. A tree came out of the ground about three feet, then bent ninety-degrees to form a long seat, then bent vertical again. Campers and families had visited and sat on it for decades. "Kids," Josh began, "as you know, we are now your legal foster parents." He paused as they looked at him. Before they could speak, he continued, "Plus, we just got the papers that say, in a year, we should be able to legally adopt you. What do you think about that?"

"For real?" Eva gasped. She jumped down and began leaping and shrieking. "A real family? A forever family?"

Spidey jumped off and began running in circles. "You my dads? My real true dads?"

Peanut jabbered and slobbered on his cookie.

Eva slowed down, walked back to the men. "Wait a minute. What about the Thompsons? They took us in. What's gonna happen to them?"

"Good question," Andres said. "What would you think about us buying their house? You kids and Josh and I could live on both levels and build an addition on the back for the Thompsons. That way, they would still be part of the family."

Eva was quiet. She pulled both men off the log and hugged them. "I like that. We can be one big family." She started spinning in circles, waving her arms and yelling, "We're a family. A new family." She dropped to the ground, dizzy. Pointing at Andres, she continued, "Can I call you Papa?" Pointing at Josh, "And you Dad or Daddy?"

"Yeah," Spidey shouted. "Daddy and Papa. Daddy and Papa. Daddy and Papa."

Peanut sat on the ground, throwing sand and grasses into the air, squealing and jabbering 'da da da da' as Spidey raced around him. At thirteen months, Peanut had difficulty toddling in the sandy soil and on the rough trails.

The family started down the trail again. Eva became pensive. She slipped her hand into Andres' and looked up at him, her eyes filling with tears. "Will I ever see my real mommy again? The one in prison? I'm s'pose to see her every month."

Andres waved at Josh to stop walking. He squatted so his face was level with Eva's. "Of course, you will see her again. Just because we're adopting you doesn't mean you still don't have a real mommy. We want you to see her as much as possible. We love your mommy. She didn't have to say you could be adopted by us. That was very unselfish of her, don't you think?" He pulled Eva into a hug.

She nodded, hugged him back, then gave him enough of a shove so he lost his balance and sprawled onto the trail. She raced down the trail, hollering, "We're a family with Mr. and Mrs. T and I still got a real mommy."

Andres climbed to his feet in time to see Josh wiping his eyes as Peanut rode on his shoulders. He grabbed Spidey's hand and ran after Eva.

Every time they came close to the lake's edge, Eva and Spidey shouted across the water, "We...Are...A...Family." They waited for their words to echo back.

When they returned from their hike, Echo Lake lived up to its name. The entire camp knew they were a family. That evening, at dinner in the dining hall, the cook surprised them with a freshly decorated cake that read, 'A New Family!'

On June first, the men and the Thompsons signed a contract for Josh and Andres to purchase the entire two flat. Denny James began drafting plans to remodel the place into a single-family home with an in-law addition on the back for Mrs. T. Their first step would be to tear down the Thompson's old garage and build a large one with an airy studio upstairs for Andres.

Mr. T was fading and not expected to live more than a few months. Hospice started regular visits to bathe him and check on his condition.

Chapter Twenty-four

Connecting the Dots

Friday, September 14, 2012

Josh and Andres sat around their kitchen table, the same one they moved from the old rooming house, the red and chrome one Hank and Mae bought back in the fifties. The Aunt Jemima clock hung on the wall, loudly ticking. It was nearly midnight, but they were too excited to go to bed. The Rooming House Gallery open house for funders, board members, donors, community leaders, artists and close family ended about ten that evening. They were still hyped, talking about the event and the wonderful reception from the attendees.

"Lea Ming said her piece will be out tomorrow afternoon in Sunday's Trib early edition. The space was being held for her to write it up tonight. The photographer was out and shot the building, art, and us on Wednesday. Leah seemed extremely excited and I can't wait to read it." Andres sipped his beer.

"I can't get over how many people came. I was worried…"

"Hell, Josh, you're always worried."

"I know. I was worried some of the city leaders wouldn't attend, but the deputy mayor even came." He waited, then reached over and nudged Andres' arm. "I'm thankful our dads came. Aren't you?"

"Thankful, yet not too surprised. I mean, they did come to our wedding. Oh, Josh, that was priceless. Tonight, both sets of parents came in the '56 Ford and parked it right out front. I think they're becoming good friends. Our mothers have loved each other since they met, now their two homophobic husbands have found fellowship. Well, former homophobes, their actions are showing significant changes. Manny would have loved it. He was like your great grandparents, always trying to bring people together."

"You know," Josh said, "after reading all the diaries, a few of the fathers were nonexistent, others failed at times, and some were even horrible persons, yet look how well almost all the kids turned out. Somehow, the generations developed strength and character. Does it seem that way to you?"

"Are you speaking for us, as well?"

"Maybe. Maybe I am. The other thing that struck me was redemption. In most cases, things worked out well. I guess that's redemption of some sort. That's starting to be true for us and our fathers. I remember when your mother told us to not give up hope about our dads. I think grandkids might have inspired some interest, even though we didn't use that as a bribe when we each talked with them." Josh yawned and stretched. "Let's go to bed."

Newspaper Article

The Tribune
Sunday, September 16, 2012
(Front Page, 4 columns, below fold with before and after photos of the building)

New Community Art Gallery With A Twist of History
By: Lea Ming, Arts & Culture Editor

In 2009, when domestic partners Andres Rodriguez and Josh Sawicki inherited a three-story rooming house built in 1887 with nearly thirty rooms, they knew exactly what they wanted to do with it. "Convert it to an art gallery," said Rodriguez. "A gallery for Chicago up-and-coming artists. Along the way, it evolved into a community art center with classes for youth and people of all ages in a diverse neighborhood." The building is also listed on the National Register of Historic Places and is the only former rooming house in the

Chicago area to be listed.

A private opening and tour for funders, artists, community leaders, the board of directors and other guests was held this past Friday evening at The Rooming House Gallery at 4822 S. Justine and I was fortunate to attend. The public grand opening for the gallery will be this coming Saturday, September 23, from twelve till five p.m.

Our tour began in front of the building guided by Rodriguez and Denny James, the renovation architect. From the street, the building looks much like it did when originally built, with freshly painted gray wooden siding and white trimmed windows. The sidewalk diverges into two. One goes straight to the covered front porch and the original wooden entry door with leaded glass. The other walk curves around the building to the left and passes through flower beds with benches conveniently located to rest or enjoy the landscaping. "Eventually, we plan on adding outdoor sculpture and more pathways," Rodriguez explained.

The original building is twenty feet wide by eighty feet long. A sixteen by twenty-four-foot addition now extends and widens the back of the building. The side walkway curves around to the large entrance located at the rear of the addition. The addition is built of elegant dark gray cement block and ties in nicely with the old home. Across the back of the addition is an expanse of glass three stories high, designed to let additional light into all three levels. All three floors are accessible from the front or rear of the building, though the elevator and handicapped parking are at the rear entrance. The addition includes emergency exits from the second and third floors. "The entire building meets stringent fire code requirements," James said.

In the original four-bedroom home on the first floor are spaces for art instruction, a small meeting room, and an accessible bathroom. Several walls are covered with cork to display students' artwork. It is almost another gallery in itself. From the quality of the art hanging there, I think the gallery will have a long future of good exhibitions of local art. The back apartment of the original building now contains two administrative offices, and a registration area that opens into the new addition. The first floor of the addition includes the elevator and space for receptions or small events.

The second floor is the gallery sponsored by the law firm of Guiseman Whitley & Chan and holds art from Rodriguez and up and coming area artists. It makes unique use of the windows through the installation of floor to ceiling screens that filter and redirect the light. Plus, the light from the new addition's large window provides a focused source. Portable walls set at various angles break up the long narrow space to give the gallery an expansive feel. On this floor, the new addition contains bathrooms and a small kitchen for caterers.

The third floor, whose layout is similar to the second, will rotate monthly with shows from community artists, school art competitions, occasional big name Chicago artists, and related special exhibitions. It also holds the Sawicki-Rodriguez Rooming House Historical Center with the hundreds of photos, copies of original diaries and secrets of the old place, all discovered during construction. "Originally, we planned to leave the old walls of an efficiency apartment in place and use that for the historical center, but a small fire during construction altered those plans and we ended up removing all the studs and expanding into the addition, which gave us more flexibility," said Rodriguez.

Throughout the three years of rehabbing the building, Rodriguez, an artist and educator, and Sawicki, a paralegal supervisor for an international law firm, discovered diaries, letters and correspondence of ten people who resided here over the years, along with photographs dating back to the 1890's. When asked if they found any unique stories, both men laughed. "Unique is putting it mildly," said Sawicki. "Almost every person who recorded something had a secret. Those secrets ranged from being one hundred percent Jewish instead of Polish, to having an unknown French love child conceived in World War I show up at age fourteen, to a teenage male prostitute running the streets of Tijuana, Mexico, to the place operating as an underground hospice for undocumented

AIDS patients during the '80's and '90's."

"The bottom line is, though," said Josh Sawicki, "this place will be a fine art gallery, and a vibrant community art center as we integrate ourselves further into the Back of the Yards community. Plus, we will be able to share one-hundred forty-five years of unique history in a very personal way." When asked about if there was any dissension from the community regarding the center, Josh replied, "Several older members of the community remembered when Andres' uncle, Manny Rodriguez, took care of AIDS patients and were afraid we would do the same. Once our mission was publicly articulated, we have had nothing but tremendous community support."

Turn to today's Art Section for photos and a full review of the art by Rodriguez and area artists. It's a rich, diverse collection of contemporary, sculpture, photography, mixed-media and other styles.

The Rooming House Art Gallery promises to be an asset to Chicago. Just be sure to allow time for the family history center when you visit. You will want to come back again and again because of all the changing exhibitions, plus the many stories and photos in the history center could keep one occupied for weeks, if not months.

The Rooming House Gallery, 4822 S. Justine St, Chicago, IL, www.trhg.org.

Wednesday, September 19, 2012

Josh thought Andres was kidding when he answered his office phone early that afternoon and heard, "Hey, domestic partner, I need your help. Take a cab." He started to laugh, but stopped when Andres snapped, "Where the hell is your cell? I'm serious. I picked up Spidey from kindergarten an hour ago. He's still puking. Peanut has diarrhea and the school called to pick up Eva. She's been fighting. Now take a cab straight to school."

"Sorry about my cell, it's in my suit coat and I left it in…Oh, never mind. I'm on my way."

Now, Josh sat across from the principal in his office along with Eva and the social worker whom he assumed was partially there because Eva was still a ward and had been in fights before. Eva was red-faced. She kept clenching and unclenching her small fists with several bruises starting to show around her knuckles. Josh wondered what the other kids looked like as he tried to pick her up to set her on his lap.

She pushed him away and wailed, "Don't touch me. I don't want nobody touching me 'cept Mr. T, and he can't even wiggle his fingers anymore. He just lies there. He's the best dad I could ever have and now he's dying."

Josh felt his gut clench. Would he and Andres ever warrant such a response? How long would it take to feel equal to Mr. T? He recalled his mother's advice about words spoken in the heat of emotion. He forced a calming smile at Eva and patted her arm. She seemed to relax a bit.

Two days earlier, Mr. T slipped into a coma and the hospice staff began visiting several times daily to care for him. Over the past few weeks, Josh and Andres tried to limit the kids' exposure to the old man, but now he could see that might have been a mistake. "Were you fighting over Mr. T? Did someone say something about him you didn't like?"

"No. I was fighting because Salvi and Eric were teasing me when I said I was going to have two dads. Two real dads. They started saying you must be homos and fags, cept they said the F words too. They said I'm gonna get all messed up, growing up without having a mommy." She started to sob and ducked away from the social worker who was attempting to wipe her eyes and nose with tissues.

"Are you upset about having two dads and not a real mommy?" the principal asked, sounding a little surprised at the idea himself.

Josh wanted to slug him. What ice age did they find this guy in?

"No, of course not," Eva shot back, glaring at him. "I love my two dads. One is Dad, and the other one we call Papa, cause he's Mexican like us. I didn't like them saying I'd be messed up without a mommy 'cause I won't be and using the F words and calling my dads' homos and fags. Them are bad words and nobody should call anybody them words." She allowed Josh to pull her onto his lap to wipe her eyes and nose.

The social worker inched her chair closer and patted Eva's arm and shoulder. "So, Eva. It sounds like you are upset about Mr. T dying. You're going to miss him very much and when the boys teased you and said bad things about having two dads, you couldn't control yourself and struck out at them. Does that sound like what's going on with you?"

Eva nodded and wriggled tighter into Josh's embrace.

"My goodness," said the social worker. "You do have a lot going on in your young life."

Josh squeezed Eva and asked, "I think we need to focus on what is bothering you the most. Is it because you know Mr. T is going to die soon and you're afraid of that? Is it that we're going to remodel the house so Mrs. T will have her special space after Mr. T dies? Is it that you're afraid the adoption won't go through with Papa and me?" He was quiet a moment, then gave her a gentle poke. "Is it because you don't want to go home where one brother has been pooping all day and the other is puking?"

"Daddy," she said, sitting up straighter, "you know that ain't true. I can help with them. I can help take care of Mr. T too. You have to let me be around him. I been around him since they took us in and now you and Papa been telling us not to bother him."

"I think that's part of the issues here," the social worker said. "Eva, you do have a lot going on right now, but how is fighting going to help? Did slugging Salvi and Eric help you take care of Mr. T? Is it going to stop your brothers from being sick?"

Eva shook her head and whispered, "No. I'm sorry."

"Eva," the principal said, "would you be willing to meet with Salvi and Eric? I've already met with them and I think they're sorry they said bad things to you."

Eva looked at Josh as if she wanted to say something. Josh nodded for her to speak. "I guess I can. I shouldn't have fighted them. I should have just told them I wouldn't play ball with them. They like me on their team, cause I'm good."

As they left the school, Eva slipped her small hand into Josh's. Both were quiet on their walk home. *Wow,* Josh thought. *Things keep happening faster and faster. One day, we're two carefree guys. Now, we're civil partners and licensed foster parents, driving a minivan with car seats and have an almost eight-year old foster daughter who knows how to use her fists, plus her two brothers are puking and pooping all over the place today. Andres and I can't wait to officially adopt them.*

~ * ~

So much happened so quickly, he couldn't remember when the knot in his gut eased up about not having a forever home to live in. In fact, he never had time to even think about finding a future home. It just happened. No stress, no worry, just like Andres said it would. The dots connected. Some days, he regretted all the wasted energy he spent worrying about a permanent home. Like when he was a teenager worrying about never meeting someone and all at once, he met Andres. Maybe his fears dropped when Andres realized what was blocking him over having children. Is that a symbiotic relationship? Now, that would be an interesting psychological study. Still, he hoped he wouldn't worry about the kids growing up. A smile crossed his face as he thought he shouldn't bet on it.

Josh smiled again as they walked past The Rooming House Gallery. The big public opening was this Saturday. He was now the treasurer for the board, which was plenty enough responsibility. Today, three people at work handed Josh clippings from The Tribune about the festivities, and Quianna called to tell him her phone was ringing off the hook with people wanting to volunteer and send contributions. Early in the summer, she resigned from the board to apply for the position of Development Director. There were several well-qualified applicants, but her standing in the community and unique abilities won the selection committee over. She gladly resigned her bank position to accept the position, even though it was less salary. Josh was relieved to turn over the leadership to her. He knew she was better qualified than him. There was no way he could have continued, worked his real job and become a parent, too.

"Hey, Dad, what's those words say on the porch wall?" Eva asked as they crossed the street. "Papa was working on something when we left for school. He wouldn't tell us, just said, 'Wait and see.'"

The words were etched and fired onto artistic ceramic tiles with a trail of dots leading from tile to tile. They were displayed in an oak frame that was mounted above the mailboxes. Going up the steps, they slowly sounded out the words together, "The—Roo—ming—House—An—nex."

Eva looked up at him, a questioning look on her face.

"Annex means a building close by. I think that means we're continuing the tradition of the old rooming house."

She still looked confused.

"Well, all kinds of people found love and a family in the old rooming house. It looks like the same thing is happening over here. Don't you think?"

Eva jumped into his arms and wrapped her arms around his neck.

Late that evening, Eva slept soundly, her arms wrapped around her ball glove and the old, still musty-smelling, homemade cloth doll Andres discovered somewhere in the rooming house during the renovation. Eventually, after reading a copy of Kate's diary, Josh thought to text a picture of it to Krys, who confirmed it was Henrietta May, the doll her mother made from scraps while they were broke and living in the efficiency apartment. Somehow, it disappeared when they moved all those years ago. "Wonderful. Eva can keep her. It's still in our family! Try to get it away from her and wash it." So far, they hadn't time to wash it, but it was on a growing to-do list.

By bedtime, Peanut's diarrhea seemed to have run its course, as did Spidey's upset stomach. Downstairs, Mr. T's oxygen pumped softly as he lay comatose. Mrs. T slept on the couch. She refused to leave his side. "I gotta be by him to the end of his time," she kept saying.

Since slipping into a coma, the hospice staff spoke in terms of anytime soon, and wouldn't speculate on the number of days. It seemed a waiting game, sad, yet realistic. That afternoon, immediately after coming home from school, Eva climbed onto the bed and snuggled against Mr. T, patting him, telling him she loved him. She did the same shortly before going to bed. Josh thought she seemed more at peace and ready for the ordeal to end, like he, Andres and Mrs. T.

~ * ~

The windows in the upper flat were open for the breeze and any sounds of distress from the children. On the front porch, Josh and Andres sat in the swing. The same swing that hung across the street for decades, maybe over a century.

In July, the board of directors held a surprise party to thank Josh and Andres for their many efforts in getting the gallery established and off the ground, plus their financial contributions that helped start the process. The swing was their gift. Denny James had it repaired and refinished until it gleamed like a work of art. "Seeing as you got nothing to do now, at least you can do it sitting down," he yelled when making the presentation. He hugged each of them individually and whispered, "See, I'm making progress with this hugging men thing."

The large, end-of-summer moon surged out of the clouds, magically illuminating the normally mundane-looking street and homes. Andres scooted closer, lifted Josh's arm and snugged it around him. "Have we ever been so busy? I thought getting the gallery going was the busiest I've ever been, and I'm high energy. But three kids? Wow." He snuggled closer. "I'm not saying I want anything to change. I don't. This is like heaven and is only going to get better. I mean, how good will life be without runny diapers? Puking? Car seats? Fights?" He waited a moment, then chuckled. "Oh, that's right, someday, they're going to be teenagers."

Josh laughed quietly and squeezed him in agreement. "I never dreamed things would turn out like this or could turn out like this. It's wonderful, and to think it all started on a bicycle."

They were silent, each in their own thoughts as both looked across the street to the old house which held their sweat, worries, their dots, and DNA. Tonight, the place shimmered in the moonlight as if something new, yet still with the lives of many memorialized within it, and the future for many more memories to be told through art.

Standing, Josh pulled Andres up. Kissing him on the cheek, he pointed across the street and circled his arm and hand back to include the tile sign over the mailbox. He squeezed him as he whispered, "Time for bed, old man. These roomers wake up early and they expect to be fed."

A shaft of moonlight broke through the leaves, striking the Rooming House Annex sign. Both men paused to slide their fingers over its tiles, following the dots that floated in and around the words, their lives, those behind them—and the ones still ahead.

Acknowledgements

This novel is dedicated to Rick Dexter. I couldn't write without his support, advise and patience with the spacey interactions I have with all the characters running around in my mind. This is my third novel with Kathie Giorgio as writing coach and chief cheerleader. Thank you! (https://www.allwritersworkshop.com). Carol Schmidt and Marci Yoseph read parts of this book in the early and more lengthy draft of The Rooming House Diaries. Jerry Peterson and the members of Beloit Public Library's Stateline Night Writers group have patiently read, listened to or critiqued nearly everything I've written over the past three years. It's a pleasure to again work with Arlo and Christine Young of Rogue Phoenix Press, Genene of Web and Graphic Designs by Ms. G for the cover art, and Sherry Derr-Wille manuscript editor.

About the Author

Bill Mathis grew up in Clarksville, Michigan, a tiny town filled with big families. He directed YMCA camps and worked in foster care. Upon retirement, he moved to Beloit, Wisconsin and began writing. This is Bill's third novel. His fourth, *Revenge is Necessary* a psychological mystery and crime book set in farm country, will publish in December 2020. Bill enjoys writing, reading, photography and traveling with his partner.

Coming by the Author

at

Rogue Phoenix Press

December 2020

Revenge is Necessary

Chapter One

Junior: Shaw Philip Skogman, Jr., age 17

Saturday, March 26, 2011
Midville, Minnesota

Junior ran faster, his bare feet churning, sinking into the dirt drive, already muddy from three days of rain and now topped with three inches of heavy, wet, late-March snow. The grainy flakes whirled around him, pelting his skin, nearly blinding him. He didn't feel the cold yet. Where was he headed? Where could he go in his Fruit-of-the-Loom white t-shirt and tighty-whiteys at seven on a Saturday morning? His dad might come after him if he headed toward his boyfriend Beany's house.

The image of his father with the double-barrel shotgun bursting in on him and Beany in Junior's bed pulsed with every heartbeat. Beany's words as Junior raced toward the door still echoed. "Run, Forrest! Run!" The same words his mother screamed at his track meets. She loved the movie Forrest Gump. He knew Beany escaped down the back stairs as Junior flew down the front ones. Beany would be well on his way home.

He was a fast runner, too. At least he had a place to run to.

Damn Beany. Sneaking into Junior's bedroom in the early morning, or middle of the night, still dressed, crawling into Junior's bed, ignoring the twin guest bed in the room. The bed his mother moved in over ten years ago when Beany started showing up in the middle of the night, coming in the unlocked back door, slipping up the narrow back stairway and into Junior's room without making a sound.

What caused his father to lose his marbles? Completely lose them. It's not like Beany never slept over before.

"Right, Junior. Duck right." His mother's scream, sounding from the front porch, broke his thoughts. Made his heart thump harder. How could he be thinking about his bedroom and Beany when his father, at this very second, must have the shotgun aimed at him?

He dodged right, closer to the overgrown shrubs that lined the quarter-mile driveway. He heard the shotgun bellow and felt sharp stings on his left buttock, along the back of his upper leg. He ran faster, tried to crouch lower. Birdshot. At least it was birdshot. It smarted, but he was far enough away to realize it couldn't go deep. Must have caught the edge of the pattern. He dodged into the middle of the drive and quickly back to the right. Did that several times. Why? He wasn't sure. Maybe zig-zagging would make it harder for his dad to focus on a moving target. He knew what was in the other barrel of the gun. A slug. That would more than sting if it hit him. It would kill him. His dad was a good shot.

His mother's scream again tore through the wet, thick air. No words. It was followed by the shotgun blasting again and his dad bellowing. Was he in pain? Did he still have the gun? Did he have more shells? Junior threw himself into the ditch and lay in the cold sloppy mud and snow. Hearing nothing, no sound of a thud or a slug whistling by, he stood, turned and took several cautious steps toward the house. His mother's voice floated toward him through the heavy swirling snow. It was less shrill, but still urgent, her don't mess with me voice. "You're safe for now. Keep running. Don't come home."

What the hell did that mean? You're safe, keep running, but don't come home. He turned, lengthened his stride and settled into the 800 meter pace he ran for track. He sensed the front of his soaked t-shirt invading his nighttime warmth, but still, he didn't feel the cold. He stayed to the right of the drive, on the edge, the grass slippery beneath the snow. At 127th Street, he wanted to turn left, run one quarter mile to Milliken and go left a half mile to Beany's house. However, he figured if his dad was still capable, he might jump into his truck and head toward Beany's house down their Milliken Road driveway. If he shot at him once, wouldn't he shoot again? Junior remembered his father's words in the bedroom as he aimed the shotgun at him, "You're not my son." What did that mean?

Junior turned right, onto 127th Street. A half mile further was the small Lutheran church and cemetery where someone might be around and let him in. Why didn't he hear his dad's diesel pickup starting up? His dad must have ignored Beany who was probably home by now. Would he or his mom call nine-one-one? Would his dad show up at Beany's looking for him?

His feet began to sense the cold and the occasional small stone. He was glad the road was mostly dirt, not all gravel. How long did it take to get frostbite? He was approaching the fence of the cemetery when he heard a vehicle slowly splashing behind him. He glanced back. It wasn't his dad's pickup. Junior slowed to a walk as the old pickup eased to a stop beside him. He glanced in and saw Jens Hanson, motioning for him to climb in. There was a tarp covering something in the backend. It was shaped like a casket. Junior opened the door and slid into the warmth. He grabbed the blanket on the seat and pulled it around him like it was the last one on earth.

The Rooming House Diaries
Life, Love & Secrets

Six fascinating and touching diaries are discovered in an old rooming house that detail the lives of the owners and tenants spanning over a century of change in Chicago's Back-of-the-Yards neighborhood. An unwed pregnant teen shows up; a teen from Paris, France appears, the result of a relationship during World War I; the first Mexican in the neighborhood is given a room and eventually inherits the place, his diary describes his young life running the streets in Tijuana, Mexico and how the rooming house served undocumented AIDS clients. The matriarch leaves a long-hidden diary that details her undisclosed life of brothels. Filled with love, life and family secrets, The Rooming House Diaries prove DNA does not always make a complete family.

Prologue

4822 South Justine, Back-of-the-Yards Neighborhood, Chicago, IL

Wednesday, June 10, 2009

Five people were present for the funeral and interment of sixty-nine-year-old Manuel (Manny) Rodriguez. Two of them, Manny's nephew, Andres Rodriquez, and Andres' partner, Josh Sawicki, shared their sparse memories of the man. Two priests read scriptures and prayed over the urn. The fifth person was the female undertaker. The service was over in nineteen minutes.

After the ceremony at Oakwood Cemetery, Josh and Andres returned to the old rooming house that was now theirs. Both felt sad over the passing of someone they barely knew, yet excited over the fact they now jointly owned a three-story building with plenty of space for Andres to make art. The building was narrow, but deep. The first floor held a spacious four-bedroom apartment, behind it a small one-bedroom unit. Each of the two upper floors held fifteen rooms, long unused.

They sat down at the kitchen table in the large apartment. The table was fifties-style, chrome with gray faux marble. A red Aunt Jemima clock ticked on the wall. Josh shifted a tangled pile of keys and pulled a handwritten note across the table. He edged his chair closer to Andres so they both could read it.

Josh and Andres,

Just a few notes.

These are all the other keys Manny gave me. Good luck figuring them out! Father Frank and I got to know Manny better the last few months of his life, to the point we assisted with all the paperwork turning this place over to you two. During his last few days, Manny frequently spoke of diaries and secrets. He said four diaries are contained in the numbered ledgers on top of the buffet. They're mixed in throughout the records of the tenants who used to reside here. He thought there might be two other diaries, but was vague about their possible locations.

The diaries seemed very important to him and he so much wanted you to know about them and read them. Manny frequently spoke of this place and how some of the occupants became his family. We were surprised to discover that both of you have ties to the place. He said you'd both learn a lot about your DNA and non-DNA families. In fact, he wrote the last diary. He strongly expressed his desire you not sell the house. He wants you to live here. He said the place is in better shape than it looks, and it would make a stable home for you, plus space for Andres to make art and possibly display it.

Please keep Father Frank and myself informed as to your plans. We live close by, in the rectory at Saint Bobola's. We will be glad to assist you in any way possible. I hope you two decide to keep the building and live in this community. We always need energetic, young folk establishing roots. Keep in touch, we're extremely interested in hearing what you learn from the diaries, especially the secrets, and what you do with the place. How exciting.

God Bless You!
Father An

Diary 1

Josef Sawicki

Born November 3, 1858, Olsztyn, Poland (East Prussia)
Died April 19, 1936, Chicago

Diary found in Ledger One and translated from Polish to English with occasional comments by Mae Sawicki, Josef's daughter-in-law.

Chapter One

Yesterday, I noticed several flecks of blood in my spittle. I don't feel sick or any worse. To be truthful, I am old and don't intend to live forever. I can't wait to be with Walentina again, God rest her soul. So, today, February 10, 1934, is the day I shall write my story down so my progeny may refer to it and know the many wonderful things I have accomplished, as well as all the truth about me. Not that I'm a dishonest man, but there were times, not many, where I left out a few details. First, I must take a piss, being old has affected such things. I used to have a bladder like a horse, now it's like a puppy.

Now I continue my writing, even after being rudely yelled at by Henryk. I refuse to call my son Hank, like the rest of the world. I named him Henryk, it's a good Polish name. He yelled at me for carrying coal up to the hall stoves on the second and third floors. He said I should at least get dressed first, that limping around in my dead wife's nightgown was not proper and I looked godawful. He says that a lot when I don't dress and stay in her nightgowns, "You look godawful." He doesn't understand sleeping alone is lonely and her old flannel nightgowns make her feel closer to me. I miss her so much. He says fifteen years should be enough.

See, I've been wearing them since the night she died. Except for around the shoulders, they fit me. She always sewed them extra big. She didn't like anything tight around her when she slept. Of course, they tore out around my arm pits so I sewed some longer threads on to connect the sleeves. Mae finally added some material and made the arm holes bigger. "Crazy old man, I don't want you shutting the circulation off to your arms," she said.

He's right. Back when I did it, I figured he'd eventually lose the need to sleep in them. Now, I hope they hold together till he dies. They're getting hard to keep fixed, but he can't live without them. Mae

I've been through some bad things, but losing my wife was the worst. That first night I kept crying and tossing all over the bed. I grabbed Walentina's pillow to hug and felt her nighty under it. It still smelled of her. I hugged it, kept wiping my tears with it, covering my face with it. Without thinking, I got naked and pulled it on over my shoulders and down around my body. Since then, only when I'm in her nighty can I sleep. We'd never slept apart and that was the best I could do.

Just wait till Hank's all alone forever and misses Mae's warm body every night. I know he will, because he sure gets his sausage in her enough, they have seven kids and who knows when they'll start another one. Soon, I bet. Plus, they are not quiet when they couple. Of course, neither were we.

My Young Life

I was born November 3, 1868 in Olsztyn, East Prussia.

Aha! The truth. The old man always said he was born in 1866. Ouch. This baby just kicked me hard. Lord, let it come quickly, I'm huge. Mae, May 1, 1934.

I grew up speaking Polish and German. I'd spit at that word, German, but Mae took the spittoon away, said my old friends would have to spit outside, she was tired of cleaning out the vessel and around the floor where they always missed.

My father was a gem of a man. He was a teacher, a writer, and a dreamer. He was also a Patriot. A true, brave Polish Patriot who hated the Germans for partitioning our part of Poland. He hated the Russians even worse, and wasn't fond of the Austrians, either. He was tall, about five-ten, wide-shouldered with blue eyes that were set so close together, some wondered if he was cross-eyed. From him, I inherited his eyes, the mole on my left cheek, and my wide shoulders and brains. Plus, his bravery.

My mother was small, tiny, maybe five-foot-one. She was also very smart, and spirited, very spirited. From her, I inherited more brains and my spirited voice. *He meant his big mouth! Mae.* Also, my bravery. She too was very brave and strong. They were not peasants, thank God, not like many of the Polish coming over here like lemmings who could barely read or write, if at all. Couldn't figure, only knew Polish.

My father owned a small, private school where well-off people sent their kids. Several rooms were attached that were our home, and everything sat on three hectares of land where vegetables, fruit, sheep and a cow were raised. My mother taught writing, music and art. She also supervised the girl's dorm.   Father taught history, languages, science, math, and supervised the boys.

My father became more and more involved in the resistance and started to neglect his educator duties. When I was eight, he was killed, **Assassinated**, by them goddamn East Prussians for what they said was treason. Treason! He was a Patriot trying to keep the Polish culture alive. Those bastards!

My mother tried to keep the school running, but it was too far in debt so she sold it, paid off the liens and we moved near Posen where she soon met a man and married him. He was a widower, about forty-five, almost fifteen years older than my mother. He was not a peasant either, but he was not educated. He owned one hectare with a small home, one room with a loft, where I was sent to sleep after they saw me, awakened by their moans, observing them couple.

My stepfather raised a few sheep to sell wool and mutton, he was a skilled leatherworker and he had a blacksmith business. He also owned a male donkey and a female horse that he would breed every other year and sell the mules that were born. The mare usually birthed twins. He also rented out the donkey's services as a sire. In fact, that became one of my first duties. Leading or riding the donkey to wherever the peasant or person needed a horse or another donkey bred. Sometimes, I would leave him there, especially when the female wasn't receptive, but when she was ripe, I would stay all day. I watched till they coupled at least three times and were worn out. I could then lead him home. After almost getting kicked, I learned to wait till he was tired out before trying to take him home.

My stepfather was a man who used his words sparingly, like he might not have enough to last a lifetime. Silent Cal, you could say, after our former president, Calvin Coolidge. I think Stepfather was also quiet because he didn't feel as smart as my mother and didn't want to make a fool of himself. He also couldn't figure. Shortly after we moved in, I noticed Mother always showing up when it was time for a customer to make right with my stepfather. I knew how to figure, read, write, and could find most known countries on an atlas. I loved globes and we had one, something few people had in their homes at that time, especially in Poland. I rarely call it Eastern Prussia. That is an insult!

One day, Mother was not feeling well from another early pregnancy and asked me to run down and help Stepfather figure a customer's bill. When I got there, I noticed he was having problems and was ready to undercharge the customer so I turned in front of him and whispered, "Stepfather, you forgot to carry the numbers. It's double that amount." So, he told the man the correct cost. The man seemed surprised, I think he was used to getting undercharged.

After the man left with his leather repairs, Stepfather shook my hand like an adult. He said, "Thank you, Josef. I am not good adding numbers. I am a proud man, but think my pride has kept me nearly destitute. I will make sure either your mother or you are here when it's time to settle accounts."

I felt very proud. First, because he shook my hand. Second, he actually smiled a little and seemed warm and human instead of like a cold forge.

My mother said she got pregnant easily, but couldn't carry a child for long. She was cursed, she'd say. I didn't know what she meant until a neighbor's mare aborted early in her pregnancy. I was ten or eleven. My stepfather and I went to help bury it and I realized it was a partially formed colt. I told Mother how sad it was and she said, "Yes, I know. The same thing happens to me, a lot. I don't know why I'm cursed."

My new life, with no children around, was a big change from being a school teacher's child living with other students constantly around in an atmosphere of learning, fun learning. My parents had different ideas on how children should learn. It wasn't the strict, smack your hands if you get the wrong answer like the nuns used on my children and still do on my grandchildren over at St. Bobola's School. I told my wife, and later, Mae, how I do not want to hear about the kids getting smacked for stupid reasons. It upsets me too much and I want to go set them idiot teachers straight. If my progeny gets in trouble because of their behavior, I want to know and will also discipline them, but not for other dumb reasons. About a year after my daughter started school, I was not welcome because I disagreed with their teaching methods. I had no problem telling those withered-up, crabby, self-righteous old nuns and priests exactly why they didn't know how to teach and how they should teach to each child's inner spirit. Finally, my sweet, but spicy wife, God rest her soul, told me she would tell me when she needed my help, otherwise stay the hell away from the school. So, I did, and from the church, too. That's one of the reasons I rarely go near the place. There are more reasons you may discover.

Mother informed my stepfather she would school me one to two hours a day. After that, he should teach me as much as he could about his work. So, he did. He didn't use many words, mostly demonstrated what he was doing, then watched as I tried to repeat it. I was a quick learner, I always have been, though I had to learn to do things differently as I'm left-handed. I wasn't as interested in blacksmithing, but I did learn the basics. I loved building things. Stepfather also did some rough carpentry and occasional finish work. That was my favorite. Measuring, figuring out the supplies needed, and how things fit together. Building was all post and beam construction with wooden pegs, no nails and screws in the old country. I learned how to dig and install foundations, though I was a little small for moving the big rocks into place.

I also learned how to deliver baby sheep. Sometimes, they are such a helpless animal, dumber than a rock. Late winter, our six ewes started delivering. When I was eleven, Stepfather woke me one night and said he wanted me to see lambs being born. I'd seen puppies born, so figured this would be similar. It kinda was, till Stepfather said this ewe was having trouble. "Over an hour of labor and only a small bag of water showed and broke. She's in trouble. Come here," he said, "I want you to learn how to do this. Rinse your hands off in that bucket of water I had you carry."

Wow! Why did I need to do this? I didn't say that, this sounded urgent.

"Okay, now put your thumb against your fingers and slightly cup them. Now, slide one hand into the ewe and tell me what you feel."

Well, I looked at him like he was crazy. He wanted me to put my hand inside the rear end of a moaning, heaving sheep? I knew it wasn't her shithole, but still.

"Look, Josef, this lamb may be our meat for next winter or we sell it to buy things we need. There is at least one, maybe two more behind this one. If they die, the ewe might die. We can't afford such a loss. Now do as I tell you."

Slowly, I slid my hand in. "Keep your fingers together as much as possible. Slip it around. What do you feel?"

I did. It was slimy and warm, strange, but kind of exciting, like a whole other world I'd never thought about. The whole back end of the ewe and the area around her smelled of damp wool, piss and shit. Carefully, I moved my hand around, then realized I was feeling its nose and jaw. I told Stepfather and he asked, "Do you feel its feet or legs? They should be alongside the head." I moved my hand some more, shook my head, said I couldn't feel any feet or legs. "Okay, because you're small, you'll need both hands now, get your right hand in there. Push the lamb back into the canal a way, then follow the body around on each side till you find a front leg, see if you can get both of them, next pull them forward."

I did. As soon as I got the feet and legs alongside the head, that little lamb slid out like it was greased. I couldn't believe it! I'd just helped birth a baby lamb and Stepfather said it appeared healthy. His messy hand shook mine and he smiled at me just as the next lamb, a boy, slid out. Stepfather clapped me on the shoulder. "You saved two lives. I don't think a third one is coming. This boy is good sized."

I stayed out the whole night to help him. While we waited, he told me about other positions the lambs can be in and what to feel for and how to turn them in the uterus, not the canal. I was pretty proud of myself. Later, I thought about killing the lambs after they'd grown for meat. I remembered how that might have upset me when I was younger. After several years on the little farm, I realized how life worked and felt good about helping our little family survive.

As I grew and started to fill out, I began working around the area, doing whatever I could. Mother also hired a tutor to teach me some basics in algebra and geometry. I spent the summer I was fifteen working for a survey crew to map and improve the area roads and bridges. William I, the Prussian ruler and German emperor, wanted to improve our transportation methods. I also helped build a barn. Stepfather said I could keep half of what I earned, the other half went to Mother and him to help pay my keep. Mother agreed. I saved almost all my money; there wasn't much to spend it on. Chasing girls seemed like a waste of time and money. Not that I wasn't interested in them. Mother told me to wait till I could afford my own home and support a wife and children before I even nodded to a girl.

Face Your Fears is filled with vitality as it challenges the traditional concepts of normalcy, family, disability and love. Nate is a quadriplegic with cerebral palsy raised in a family of achievers. He must be fed, dressed and toileted, yet has unique skills and abilities he gradually becomes aware of. Jude is able-bodied, one of 10 children raised on a hardscrabble Iowa farm. He can change diapers, cook, fix equipment, milk cows, and discovers his vocation as a physical therapist. Both experience tragic teen-age losses, navigate family tragedies, and come to peace with who they are individually as gay men, and eventually together.

This book shows how normal comes wrapped in different packages, yet inside each package, people are the same, whether able-bodied, disabled, black, white, brown, green or LGBTQ+.

FOR THE FULL INVENTORY
OF QUALITY BOOKS:
http://www.roguephoenixpress.com

Rogue Phoenix Press
Representing Excellence in Publishing

Quality trade paperbacks and downloads
in multiple formats,
in genres ranging from historical to contemporary romance, mystery
and science fiction.
Visit the website then bookmark it.
We add new titles each month!